The Gypsy in Me

A Contemporary Romance

ANNE CARTER

BEACON STREET BOOKS

The Gypsy in Me

by Anne Carter

Copyright © 2022 by Pamela Ripling

Edited by J.R. Turner

Cover © by Linda Boulanger, Tell Tale Covers

ISBN 978-1-7378590-0-0

February 2022

Beacon Street Books

Santa Clarita, CA 91355-2026

http://www.beaconstreetbooks.com

Printed in the United States of America

For my fans.
My patient, devoted friends.
Gypsy is for you.

A StarCrossed Prelude

Haven't read STARCROSSED HEARTS or A HERO'S PROMISE? No worries! Here's a peek at what you missed:

Jessica Taylor was one of those girls. A rising Hollywood starlet.

Like cognac and Perrier, Dane Pierce and Cory "Mac" MacKendall couldn't have been more different, but Jessica loved them both. Both divorced, both sinfully attractive, both actors at the top of their show business careers. Dane, with his sexy green eyes and lazy smile; loved his estranged kids – Alexander, Melissa and Zoe – but struggled to keep them close. He also struggled with commitment, which pushed Jessica closer to ... Mac, the true-hearted, morally sound father of daughter Megan. Mac was the solid rock Jess needed to make her life complete.

Jessica and Mac's wedding was a fairytale-come-true for everyone – everyone except Dane. The marriage was a defining moment, a knife that turned in his gut. The fact that he truly loved her beyond measure nearly leveled him, and when the knowledge of that love reached Mac, their tenuous friendship hung in the balance. Until Dane swore abstinence from his pursuit of Jessica.

Cloistered away at his ranch in Wyoming, away from Hollywood and the woman he loved, Dane managed to keep his promise and keep relatively sane. But when Mac was murdered as part of a political scheme gone wrong, leaving a bereaved Jessica and their young son Devon alone and painfully adrift, Dane set out to make things right. It wasn't easy, wooing the grief-stricken young widow back into his arms.

With Mac gone and Dane providing the safety net she desperately needed, Jessica gave herself permission to love again. Dane had always occupied a big piece of her heart, and his love for her son cinched the deal. Their marriage turned some Tinseltown heads, but the couple ignored the paparazzi and committed to their new blended family, including a daughter of their own.

Hollywood romances are not known for longevity or enduring commitment; yet Jessica and Dane managed to stay devoted to one another and to raise – or have a hand in raising – six children. Each with a personality as different as cognac and Perrier. Enjoy their stories.

ONE

The Gypsy and the Gigolo

I need a lover. Right now.

Zoe Irene Pierce was done with being a virgin. Nineteen and still unspoiled – unheard of. Trina had taught her, early on, to make sure her first time was her decision and not her potential partner's. Get it over with, she had advised, and "make sure it's with someone you care nothing about because the first time is no fun. It gets better, though, and once you get the hang of it, you can enjoy it with someone you *do* care about." Trina repeated the advice before Zoe left California last year.

So what if Trina was her father's ex-girlfriend and a stripper?

Now, Zoe squirmed on her worn sleeping bag, unable to find a comfortable spot as she stared at the tent ceiling in thought. Trina was right, of course. A virgin in the backwoods, even an overweight one, was a delicacy, and she didn't want to be some redneck's unsuspecting appetizer one dark night. Better to just get the job done and forget about it. She'd put it off too long already. That's why she'd gone to Maricela for help.

A "Pictorial Guide to Wanna-Be Modern Day Gypsies" would display Maricela's picture as a prime example. Full, brightly colored skirts and ropes of cheap, gaudy jewelry befitted the daughter of the man their band of wanderers called chief. Chimes hung from the sash about her waist, complimenting the tiny bells on her anklets and jingle bells on her backpack. She was never without a tambourine or finger cymbals and would often launch into an exotic dance at the drop of a hat. Stereotypical, but Maricela wouldn't have it any other way. "It's what people expect."

Zoe knew Maricela would know what to do. And know, she did. "I will handle this for you. I'll talk to my father," she said, "and tell him your problem. He'll see to it that you are taken care of. In fact," she'd whispered, "he can fix it so that you and your ... *lover* ... will be in total darkness. Neither of you will know the other's identity. And it will be safe."

"Are you kidding me? That sounds ... kinky." Well, fair enough, Zoe thought. It would be too awkward to stay with the troupe, having been intimate with one of the men she might know. It could even be the chief himself, Maricela suggested with a giggle. Zoe hoped not. The thought of sex with Mari's forty-nine-year-old father was wrong on so many levels.

Later, she took extra care in bathing. Maricela lugged in bucket after bucket of hot water, only partially filling the tiny bathtub they'd hauled into their tent. After all, it could be tonight.

"Smell this. Isn't it delicious?" Maricela thrust a small bottle beneath Zoe's nose before dumping half its contents into the steaming water.

"Wow. What is it?"

"Magnolia oil. I stole it from Ronnie."

"You *stole* it? Honestly ..." Zoe smiled despite her intended admonition. Maricela was, indeed, the most spoiled girl she'd met since leaving her mother and sister behind in L.A. and joining the peace-loving river gypsies of the great American South – which were nothing more than a band of glorified, nomadic hippies. Being the daughter of the group's leader had its benefits, to be sure, but Maricela seemed immature despite her twenty-three years. Zoe felt years her senior while watching her tentmate recap the perfume bottle. "Stealing is illegal."

"We're thought of as thieves and liars, why not live up to the reputation?" Maricela said with a laugh.

Zoe sank down as far as she could in the shallow water, the scent of magnolias engulfing her. Closing her eyes, she tried hard to listen to Maricela's chatter. She needed the distraction to dispel her apprehension about what lay ahead, but her friend's voice faded. Her hands crept across her round tummy, meeting in the middle, and then traveled north to cup her breasts beneath the water's surface.

Were they attractive? Sexy? Well, they were big enough, but then so was her stomach, her thighs, her neck. What if he ... her unknown knight ... what if he found her repulsive? Too fat to love? What if he was thin and gangly, what if –?

Suddenly, a muffled voice beckoned from outside the entrance to their tent and Maricela got up to answer the call. "Be right back."

Zoe thought her friend looked more distracted than usual if that was possible. She could hear indistinct conversation, and then Maricela was back, her face aglow and her eyes wide.

"Wow. A really lucky thing just happened. Well, he would say, 'auspicious.' Here's the deal. You're to go to that tent at the far edge of the camp at nine o'clock. You should wear ..." Maricela paused to dig into the trunk beside her cot. "This black veil thingy and maybe ... this cape over your gown? Speak to no one. Unless, of course, you want the whole tribe to know."

Zoe sat bolt upright and the water in the tub ebbed, leaving her exposed shoulders cold. "Tonight? It's tonight for sure?"

"Yes. You're to go into the tent and wait. Your ... man ... will be in some time later. You're not supposed to say anything to him, or he to you. That way you can stay anonymous. When you're ... *done*, he'll leave first and then you'll sneak out and make your way back here. If anyone is around, you are to go into the woods, remove the veil and cape and hide them, then circle around and get back here without drawing any attention to yourself."

"Is it ... is it going to be your father, by chance?" The thought of Martin touching her made Zoe's skin crawl.

Maricela giggled. "Uh, no. Fairly sure, not. Aren't you dying to know, though?"

Zoe sniffed and sank back into the water. "It doesn't really matter. As long as it gets done." Trina would be proud of her resolve. "It's not something to get all worked up over. After all, it's just sex. It's a process. Someday it'll be with love. But this is, frankly... a necessary evil."

"Oh boy. An evil. You've got a lot to learn, girl," her friend said with a smile.

"Most of what I need to know I've already learned from Trina," Zoe said, more to herself than to Maricela.

"Who's this 'Trina,' anyway?"

"She's a friend. She used to sleep with my dad when he was between wives. She babysat me and my sister a few times, like when my mom was in rehab."

"What does she do? Is she a gypsy too?"

"Could say. She's a stripper."

"A stripper. Your dad left you with a stripper. Perfect. No wonder you ended up here!"

"Trina helped me through some bad times. She and my stepmom. If I'd had to rely on just my mother all those years, I'd probably be dead by now." Zoe stood and stepped from the tub, wrapped a bath towel around her and reached for her clothes. "Not that Trina and Jessie ever got along. But they are both cool people."

"And Jessie's your stepmom?"

"Yup. She's cool. She and Pop duke it out like clockwork, but they are mad about each other. He can be a bit of an ass, to be sure."

"Do you ... love your dad?"

Zoe held up a thin, knee-length pink flowered nightshirt. "Will this do?"

"Don't you at least want to wear something ... sexy?"

"What does it matter?"

Maricela thought for a moment. "Well ... it could at least hurry things along a bit."

Zoe regarded the nightshirt, hesitated for a moment, and then pulled it over her head. "It's easy to take off," she concluded and then took up the black cape, swinging it around to wrap about her shoulders. "How do I look?"

"Mysterious. You didn't answer about your father."

"What about him? He's an actor. He's made something like forty-five movies. He likes fast cars, swears when he's pissed off, and throws back an occasional Jack Daniels. He was once voted 'sexiest man alive' in some magazine."

"But do you love him?"

Zoe paused, pretending to examine the black veil she'd been given. Finally, she looked up. "Of course, I do. He left us when we were little. I didn't understand then but later I realized why ... and he came and literally rescued me from my mother and evil sister when I was eight. He's not perfect. But he knows what's important."

Maricela nodded. "They say a woman often looks for a man like her father. I know I do."

Zoe stifled a spontaneous laugh. It seemed so funny to her that Maricela would be looking for a younger Martin Dupré. She thought about her own father, the legendary film hero Dane Thomas Pierce, and her smile softened. Yes. She could understand her father's appeal. And yes, she could not deny that Pop had some characteristics she would appreciate in a man.

"I guess that makes sense," she said at last. "Where's our mirror?"

She spent a few minutes brushing out her hair, pulling at the curls dampened by the steam.

"Did you ever color your hair?" Maricela wanted to know.

Zoe sighed. "No, why?"

"It's such a pretty color. Mine's just plain black. But yours..."

"Is plain brown. Big deal. Mouse brown. When I'm feeling magnanimous about myself, I call it ash brown."

"But you have those fabulous green eyes. Got those from your dad, didn't you?"

"Why all the interest in my father? Here, I'll give you ten bucks and you can go down to State Street and see his latest flick. I haven't seen it, but it's supposed to be good."

Maricela shook her head. "Did you really just say, 'flick?' Naw. I don't like movies. Look, you'd better finish getting ready. It's getting close to nine."

·♥·♥·♥·♥·♥·

What am I doing? What was I thinking? Through the black veil, she could barely see the glow of tonight's campfire and the silhouettes of those cleaning up from the dinner. But inside the tent it was dark, getting darker by the minute as the fire outside died away. Zoe shivered, feeling around on the thin bedroll for a blanket.

She'd been waiting for what seemed like an hour. It was, perhaps, only twenty or thirty minutes, she reasoned, trying hard not to chew her bottom lip to ribbons. Once or twice, she'd thought she heard footsteps, but the noises produced no visitor to the tent.

This is nuts! I must be crazy. It didn't feel at all like she was in control of her fate, and wasn't that the intention? To make her own decision about where and when she'd lose her virginity? Yet here she was, waiting on a man. Waiting for him to make the first move. At his convenience.

No. This is not right. Sighing in frustration, Zoe sat up and started to remove the veil just as the tent flap opened and a shadowy figure stepped inside. Her fingers froze, the black fabric held in her grasp. She opened her mouth to speak but remembered Maricela's words. No talking.

Despite the darkness and the veil over her face, she was almost certain the man in the tent with her had brought with him something large, a backpack or perhaps a duffel bag. He stood still, as if staring down at her for several moments. At last, he began to move about, and Zoe sensed he was removing his clothes.

She quivered. What if he was rough? What if he was crude, or worse, an abuser? Trina had shared more than enough information about heartless, cruel Neanderthals who liked to hurt women. Maybe she should just go. But before she could will herself to stand up and flee, the man lowered himself to sit beside her.

Oh, sweet lord, what do I do now?

The fire outside flickered, nearly out. The tent dropped into pitch darkness, and the man with her reached out and removed her veil, then untied the cape and carefully put them aside. His hand returned to her face, softly stroking her skin/flesh with the back of his fingers before gently grasping her chin. He leaned forward then, brushing first her cheek and then her lips with his own, and Zoe was quite certain, more than quite certain, that the man in the tent with her was not Martin Dupré.

He tasted of wine and smelled of spice. Blinded by the dark, Zoe ran her fingers along his cheekbones, up, across his forehead and into his hair, trying to conjure a mental image of the man who now lowered her back onto the bedroll. His hair was thick, and long, and was held at the nape of his neck by a thin leather string, a boot lace perhaps. His youthful face boasted lips both soft and curious as they sampled her mouth, all while his hands roamed across her back. And Zoe couldn't have been more surprised when he spoke.

"You smell like flowers," he whispered, his moist words sending a shivery shock wave down Zoe's back. An involuntary shudder followed, and he spoke again. "You really want this, right?"

I thought we weren't supposed to talk! Hesitantly, Zoe nodded her head, but stiffened as the man began tugging her nightshirt up above her hips. Her embarrassingly *generous* hips.

"Don't be afraid." His voice was soft and comforting, and Zoe wished she could relax in his arms. "Would it be easier if we talked first?"

"I thought ... I thought we weren't supposed to," Zoe said softly. She felt her companion shrug.

"As long as they can't hear us, what does it matter?"

"Are you one of ... us?"

"No. Not technically. You won't see me again if that's what you're wondering." A pause. "You're not from around here, either."

"No. I'm not. I just sort of joined one day. I was visiting in Natchez and I met Mari –" Zoe closed her mouth and swore inwardly. "I met one of the girls traveling up the river and she invited me to come along. I had nothing else to do, so I fell in."

"Pretty adventurous for one so young," he murmured, drawing his fingers through her hair and cupping the back of her head. "Why the urgency to lose your ... innocence?"

Zoe blushed and was glad for the darkness. "It's just time," she mumbled, remembering the reason they were both there in the inky darkness of the gypsy tent.

"I can't promise you'll enjoy it, but I won't hurt you ... intentionally."

Something in his voice touched her, a hint of compassion and goodness that seemed out of place. Perhaps, if she could imagine that he was a hero of some kind, and she was an equal heroine, she could fake her way through the encounter without acting the complete fool. Taking a deep breath, she thrust her arms around the stranger's neck and pressed her lips forcefully against his. She felt him smile just before he returned her kiss with more passion than she thought possible. They were, after all, strangers.

And then a bizarre thing happened. Zoe felt a warmth engulf her, something akin to what might be lust and yet ... it was an oddly familiar feeling. She no longer feared the man beside her who lifted the gown over her head and pulled her nakedness against his.

He seemed in no hurry as he stroked her body, exploring every part of her with desire and yet supreme respect, pausing only a moment to fit himself with protection. She was not quite ready to initiate touching him, but he gently guided her hesitant hands, suggesting that she participate in the foreplay he so expertly conducted.

"Oh." She couldn't help the murmur as she grasped that part of him she knew so little about. "Hmm." How would this ever ... fit? His sigh became a groan as she explored him, distracting her concern and bringing her back around. His body was a delight to touch, she decided, firm, strong, but not overly muscled; youthful, perhaps a little thin and not tall. On a whim, she reached behind his head and loosened the leather thong from his hair.

He chuckled. "And I thought this was going to be awkward." Her sigh encouraged him, and he stepped up his efforts to arouse her.

Surprised by the response within her body, Zoe stifled a giggle. *Awkward, indeed*. This was downright fun.

She had no experience with which to compare. Necking with a couple of boys in high school produced nothing like the rapture she now felt. Their rough, adolescent exploration of her breasts merely annoyed her, but her present companion's gentle nipple-play ignited her unknown erotic circuitry. This pre-arranged lover delayed his own satisfaction in favor of hers, bringing her to an exquisite high of her own before satisfying his ~~own~~ need for release.

And in those sweet, liquid moments between her peak and his, Zoe barely felt the pain or even discomfort she'd been told to anticipate.

She strained to see him in the darkness; wanted to see the face of the man in possession of such talent, the man responsible for pleasuring her so completely. Her first time. It was a fantasy, for sure. Trina would never believe it! She wanted to know his name, look into his eyes, and tell him he could *never* leave her side.

But the light within the tent was no better now than when she'd still been unspoiled. So, Zoe forced herself to lay still, her head on his shoulder while the hammering in her chest subsided. And when it had, he stirred, sat up and reached for some object in the blackness around them. Possibly the bag he'd carried in earlier.

He's done. He's getting dressed, Zoe thought with disappointment. But when the first few notes emanating from his guitar strings wafted to her ears, Zoe was charmed. His song was slow, moody, expertly picked from the strings, seducing her mind much the same way his fingers had seduced her body. It had a familiarity, but she could not recall having heard it before.

"I Belong to Us."

What?

"It's my own," he murmured. "I belong to you ... you belong to me ... we belong to us ... I'd sing it for you, but I have a terrible singing voice."

"You play beautifully. It amazes me how you can do that in the dark."

He chuckled. "It's like making love. Once you learn where all the parts are ..."

"Are you in a band?"

He didn't answer, just continued to pick out the notes, noodling a bit at the end of the song. Finally, he put the guitar down and reached for his clothes. He dressed in silence, and Zoe felt her high crashing down. So complete was her misery she could not utter a single word.

The young man knelt before her, bending close to slip his fingers behind her neck. He kissed her tenderly and whispered into her ear.

"I have to go now. Have a good life, Zoe. You are a beautiful, passionate woman. Never give it away. Be safe."

What? He knows my name? Zoe's throat constricted painfully. He wasn't supposed to know. Not only did he know her name, he knew her body. Her soul.

And she knew nothing about him but his touch. He might as well have been a ghost.

·♥·♥·♥·♥·♥·

Zoe Irene walked downstream, far enough away not be heard and sat on the riverbank to cry. She sat for two hours, waiting for the cold February moon to rise. It never did. When her tears were all spent, she returned to the campground, crept back to Maricela's tent, and crawled to her sleeping bag. The anger and fear filling her heart kept sleep away, her eyes opened wide in the darkness. She didn't realize that Maricela was gone until her friend threw back the tent opening and shown a flashlight in Zoe's face.

"You're back! Oh, thank God!!" Maricela fell to her knees and began to sob.

"What is it? What's wrong?" Zoe sat up and gently grasped Maricela's arm.

"Something terrible has happened... and I couldn't find you, I thought – maybe – something had happened to you, too."

"You knew where I was." Zoe murmured. "Who was he, Mari? I have to know."

"Zoe, you don't understand. Something happened." Maricela repeated, once her chest began to calm. "My brother was killed tonight. Someone smashed his head!"

Zoe's hand went to her mouth, her own misery temporarily abated. "Oh my God! Robert? How? Who did it? Oh, no. Mari, I'm so sorry!"

"No one knows. It happened while you were, you know, with your guy. They thought it might have been him, but I had to say, I had to tell them, Zo, don't be mad."

"Tell who, what?"

"That the man you were with couldn't have done it because he was with you."

"So, you're saying that everyone knows I had sex with a stranger tonight?"

Maricela grasped Zoe's wrist. "No. No, just my father and two others. They won't tell. In fact, my father has forbidden us to even talk about the attack."

Zoe squeezed Maricela's shoulder. "I am so, so sorry. That's horrible. Just ... wrong. When did it happen?"

"They're not exactly sure. My father went in to talk to him a little while ago, and he was dead."

"Martin needs to call the police."

"He won't. I think he knows more than he's saying."

"How can he not want justice for his own son?"

Maricela shook her head. "My dad is an odd bird. I learned a long time ago not to question his motives. I suspect there are things ... things he keeps hidden from the authorities and digging into Robbie's murder would be poking a hornet's nest."

"But surely he's concerned that the killer is at large? That we're all in danger?"

Maricela clicked off the flashlight and lay down on her cot. "Robbie was into crack. You probably knew that, right? He was lately doing Ecstasy, too. He had dealers. I can't imagine what he did to pay them. Daddy thinks maybe ..."

"Maybe his supplier killed him?"

"It's possible. And our father wants all of that swept under the rug. Oh, Zoe, I'm so glad my mom isn't here to suffer this."

Zoe nodded in the dark. Her own problems seemed so small now, so insignificant. Maricela sensed her thoughts.

"I'm sorry, I never asked about tonight. You look like you've been crying, too. He didn't hurt you, did he? Because if he did, I can tell my father."

"If I say he did, you'll find him for me? You can bring him back?"

"You wouldn't lie about it, would you?"

"We're known to be liars, right?" Zoe said sullenly. But she knew she could never lie about the greatest night of her life. "He said my name."

"He wasn't supposed to –"

"Forget it."

It was some time before Zoe figured that Maricela had dropped off to a fitful sleep. She herself would get no rest tonight. Thoughts of the charismatic stranger loomed large, and the fact that he had left the tent in plenty of time to have murdered Robert Dupré.

Two
Tramps and Thieves

"So, with that new Golden Globe gracing your mantel, are you clearing space next to it for an Oscar?"

Dane Pierce smiled and looked down briefly before answering. His history of clashes with the Academy of Motion Picture Arts and Sciences was a standing Hollywood joke. Yet he *had* garnered the prestigious award once before. "Well, my wife did move some knickknacks and baby pictures to make room." He adjusted his position on the couch. It looked a lot more comfortable on TV.

The talk show host chuckled. "We're referring, of course, to the Academy Award which will be given out to the best picture recipient in ten days. Well, we're going to go to a quick break. Dane, I hope you'll stick around, I'm sure our viewers would like to hear more about the making of *Indian Giver*."

"Glad to, Don."

"Take ten, everybody."

Dane stood and stretched, then accepted a freshly brewed cup of French roast someone handed him. Seemed odd to be drinking coffee during a late-night talk show, unless you considered it was early afternoon. The nighttime skyline view through the faux window behind the host was deceiving.

People bustled about, blotting his face and handing new cheat sheets to the host. Camera dollies rolled past and Dane smiled again, to himself. He ran a hand through his ashen hair, noting it was longer than he liked but suited his wife's taste. A young woman rushed forward with a comb.

"Enjoying this, are you?" Don Graves asked, lifting a glass of lemon water to his lips and staring up at his guest.

"Immensely. It's been some time since I've done this circuit. Wish Jess were here."

"You're lucky. Not many get to do it multiple times." Don leaned slightly forward and frowned. "They really are green. Huh."

"Green?"

"Your eyes. You're the first person I've had on the show in a long time that my wife wanted to meet. Especially when she heard *your* wife wasn't coming."

Dane huffed out a brief sigh. "I wish Jess were here."

"Too bad she couldn't make it. Hey, for what it's worth, I'd vote for you. You know, with the Academy."

"Well, we know we'd have at least three votes, then," Dane said, holding out his coffee mug in a mock toast. They took their respective seats.

Soon, the red light was back on, and Dane took a deep breath. He couldn't fathom why he was nervous; TV appearances had never bothered him before.

"During the break, we were saying that Mrs. Pierce, better known as the multi-talented actress Jessica Taylor, had a previous commitment this morning and couldn't join us. How did it feel to be working with your wife again? Didn't it all start on another movie set some years ago?"

Dane cocked his head. "Yes. Yes, it did. The film was *Lost Season,* and we got the gold for that one. And it feels positively sinful to work with her again. I'm thinking I'm probably breaking some Academy rule by having so much fun. But honestly, Jess was the best person for the part. And some say we have chemistry, hell, I don't know ..."

"Chemistry. I think your fans would agree. Now Dane, what's up with your kids? Last time you were on the show, let's see ... eight or nine years ago? And where *did* those years go? Anyway. Your oldest was in high school or something. Fill us in on the family scene."

"Alex is doing well, he's, oh –" Dane ran his fingers across his lips in an obvious attempt to muffle his words, "– years old. Let's just say he can buy booze and get into trouble with women all by himself. Melissa's great, made me a granddad a while back."

"A grandson, right?"

"Yeah. Brady. Smart kid, in first grade already. And Jillian, our little prima donna, she's already told us she'll get her own Oscar someday."

"I'm sure she will. Now, Alex and Melissa are your children from your previous marriage. You also have a third daughter from that marriage, correct?"

Dane paused, rubbing his chin while formulating his answer. *Damned nosy people!* "Yes, my daughter Zoe. She's away at school." He wondered if he could hazard a warning look without the camera noticing. He opted against it, instead choosing a change of subject. "You missed my stepson, Devon. Dev's working for our production company now. He's only fourteen, but he's a great asset."

"Ah, yes. The late Cory MacKendall's son. There was never a doubt he'd grow into the movie business, was there? Between you, Jessie and Mac, the poor kid didn't have much choice."

"On the contrary. We encourage all our various and sundry children to do whatever they choose. Devon's not sure what direction he'll take, only that he's a part of something exciting. I know his dad would agree."

"You and Mac were friends."

"Yes. We were." Dane paused, looking at a point somewhere beyond the lens before him. "I'll never get over his death."

"But you married his widow."

Dane drew in a deep breath, nodded, and lifted his hands in defeat. "Yeah. I did. That's old news, Don."

Don looked at his notes, and Dane tried to hide a sigh. Wasn't it time for another damned commercial yet?

"Now it says here that you took some flak from some local Native Americans when making this film. Can you tell us about that?"

"It wasn't in the making of the film; it was in the *titling* of the film. The term 'Indian giver' paints a negative image of Native American Indians, and we expected to meet with some resistance there. But the truth of the matter is, the term was and still is in use, it's still an American cliché and the film is about *dispelling* the myth. Once the tribal leaders understood that, they began encouraging folks to go see the film. One or two factions still sneered a bit, but only because they couldn't understand the concept."

"Great. We're going to go to a clip now. Tell us about this scene."

"Okay ... this is where Noah Barker, my character, has told the woman he met, Sarah Clive, that's Jessica, that he's intending on pushing through the ridge route despite this massive snowstorm."

The studio lights dimmed, and a screen silently rose from beside Don's desk. The clip began and Dane once again issued a long sigh. His larger-than-life image appeared, and he noted that his green eyes seemed unnaturally enhanced. Anything to sell tickets.

"So, you got sweaty palms, did you?" Jessica asked, her fingers struggling to unfasten her diamond necklace. "I thought you'd be calling all the shots on that show."

"Don started asking about Zoe. Pisses me off. The interview was supposed to be about the film, not my kids."

Jessica went to her husband and slipped her arms around his neck. "You *are* the film. *You* are what people want to know about. You, and your exquisitely imperfect family." She kissed the corner of his mouth, creating a small smile there, and then smiled herself. "Besides. There's nothing to tell, right? So what if one daughter's an unwed mother and the other has run off with gypsies. At least she didn't join the circus."

"They're hippies. Cultists. Hell, she might *have* joined the circus by now. I haven't heard anything from her for two months."

"Are you worried?"

"No. Well, yes, dammit. She's only twenty-one."

"Is this a good time to mention how old you were when you hooked up with her mother?"

"I was eighteen. Rita was seventeen. We were both more ... mature than Zoe."

Jessica chuckled. "Yeah, right."

"You'd feel differently if it was Dev who'd taken to the road and didn't call."

Jessica stepped out of her linen skirt. "Yes, I suppose I would. But somehow, I don't think he would ever do that."

It was Dane's turn to laugh. "No, Dev will still be living with us when he's thirty-nine, I'm afraid. In fact, he'll be the one to invite the circus to live with us."

The gypsies were on the move.

Zoe took her turn in the galley, stirring the great copper pot of fish stew. The warmth from the small wood stove was comforting. After her two-plus years with the vagabonds, she'd never gotten used to the chilly mornings on the riverboat. She didn't mind helping but knew her upbringing left her ill-equipped to offer much in the way of practical know-how.

There was an upside, she realized. There was no pantry filled with candy, no refrigerator keeping chocolate milk chilled. Ice cream was a once-a-month treat, and then only if they were close to a town selling it. Their meals often centered on fish, and they cooked every variety of jambalaya possible, depending upon what stock ingredients they could manage. The day-to-day chores were far more strenuous than making her bed at home or watching her mother play tennis with her latest boyfriend. She felt muscles she didn't know she had and stared in awe as her clothes became baggy. At home, she'd complained that the dryer was shrinking them.

It had all been a merry adventure for Zoe, so much so that she hadn't noticed the weight loss at first. There was no bathroom scale facing her each morning, no full-length mirror on her closet door. No fat-shaming classmates eyeing her loose-fitting fashions, whispering behind her back. Without even trying, Zoe had become lean and downright buff.

Then there was the downside. Despite the "beauty" of the simpler life, every day was the same. There was no goal, no destination, no brass ring for the rag-tag group of drifters with whom she'd partnered. Her co-travelers didn't seem to mind that there was a whole world off the river, a world passing them by as they floated along. Zoe's attention began to wane, her restlessness growing with each sunset. After her momentous encounter with the dark stranger, she'd had a couple of less-than-stellar sexual escapades, but nothing that came even close to the bliss she'd felt that night so long ago.

"Something's up," Maricela announced as they shared dish duty. "You're too quiet."

"I need to get away." Zoe's words surprised them both. She'd ignored the feelings, hiding them from even herself. "I'm not cut out for this life."

Maricela sighed and looked down at her reddened fingers. "I was wondering when you'd get around to that. How long have you been with us now?"

"Close to four years. It's not that I can't do it, I can, but I know too much about what else is out there. Don't get me wrong, I did learn a lot here."

"Okay. When do we leave?"

"We?"

"I could use a change, too. If you wouldn't mind me tagging along."

Zoe filled her lungs and drew in her upper lip. Bringing Maricela with her hadn't crossed her mind and didn't fit in with her plans. "I'm going home. Back to L.A. What would you do there?"

"Oh." Maricela turned away and began stacking the plates she just dried. "I have a relative in L.A. I could visit," she murmured. "We could fly together and part ways once we're there."

"Sure. I have a friend who will wire us some money."

"Don't tell me. Trina, right? No, I'll get my own fare."

THREE

Ashley

At 10:30 p.m. Central Time, Zoe Irene Pierce and Maricela Dupré boarded a jet at Louis Armstrong New Orleans International Airport; at just before midnight Pacific Time, Ashley Marie Pierce stepped out of the private limo and tiptoed to the guest room at her father's palatial Malibu home. After tossing her duffel bag into the closet and taking a quick shower, she returned downstairs to rummage for a bite. The red-eye flight from Louisiana had been long and foodless.

There was a note taped to the microwave oven from Jessie.

"Zoe, there's a dinner all made up ready to pop in the microwave. Sorry your flight was delayed. Sleep as long as you want, and we'll catch up mid-morning. Glad to have you home, dear. Love, Mom Two."

Ashley smiled despite her fatigue. It would take a while for her family to get used to her new name. After all, when she'd fled Los Angeles over three years before, she'd still gone by her birth name. A name she'd hated all her life. Zoe was a girl who'd battled insecurities and obesity, a girl with an alcoholic mother and a well-intentioned but often absent father. Zoe was a lost girl. Ashley was a found woman.

Carefully picking the mushrooms out of her pasta prima vera, Ashley looked around the huge, modern kitchen and thought about the years she'd spent cooking on a camp stove. Turning a spit on an open fire. Eating out of tin cans. It had been a self-imposed sentence, that living-off-the-land lifestyle she'd opted for at eighteen.

"Hmm." Thoughts swept across her mind of that time, an eternity ago, when she'd told Dane and Rita she was going. Dane had looked worried; her mother had disowned her.

Now, in the dimmed kitchen light, Ashley shook her head. No loss there. Rita Pierce had not been a good mother, and Melissa had been an even worse sister. *Society people.* Yet who'd gotten pregnant at sixteen?

Her thoughts spawned questions, and Ashley got up from the table to stare at the refrigerator door. Even wealthy celebrities were not spared fridge door magnets and snapshots, it seemed. And yes, there were photos of Melissa's young son.

My nephew. Wow.

A movement caught her eye.

"I thought I heard someone down here. Welcome home, sweet-pea."

Ashley paused to stare at her father's tall frame as he grinned at her from the kitchen doorway. Her hesitation was only momentary, however, as she hurried to slam herself into his arms. "Hey, Daddy."

His embrace was strong, and Ashley held on tightly for several moments. Presently, he forced her away and looked her up and down. "Is this really you?"

Ashley felt herself begin to tear up. "Of course, it's me."

"You are one little fox, Ash. I can hardly believe you survived your childhood to become ... so ..."

"Neurotic?" she asked, returning to her belated dinner with a smile. Thrilled that her father had not reverted to her old name, she dug into the pasta with renewed delight. "How's everyone?"

"Better than you might expect," Dane said, pulling out a chair across from his daughter. "No one's in jail, no one's pregnant and *Indian Giver* is number two at the box office."

"Yeah? Guess you've still got it, eh?"

"*We've* still got it. Jessie's in it, too."

Ashley giggled. "I knew that."

They talked until her father offered, tongue-in-cheek, to carry her up to her bedroom.

"You don't know how many times I thought about your doing that," she confessed as they climbed the stairs together. "If I'd even had a bed to be tucked into."

"Gets lonely on the road, huh?"

"It was something I needed to do."

Dane kissed his daughter's forehead and gave her shoulder a squeeze. "You get some sleep. We'll hold Jillie off as long as possible tomorrow."

"I can't wait to see her. G'night, Dad."

The bed felt just too good. Ashley lingered long past the time she would have normally risen. Stirring on the soft mattress, she sensed she was not alone in the bed and her eyes flew open in surprise, only to be met by a young girl's solemn, inquisitive expression just inches from her face.

"Are you going to wake up now?" her little sister asked, hope lifting her eyebrows.

"Jillian Leigh Pierce." Ashley sighed and pulled herself to sit up. "How *did* you get so big?"

"You were gone a long time," the girl responded, also sitting up beside Ashley. "Anyway. I'm eleven now. I'm *supposed* to be bigger. Dad says you changed your name. Can I change mine?"

"You have a perfectly fine name. I love your name. Did Mom make breakfast?"

"We're having brunch. She wanted to wait for you. Alex is here."

"He is? Mimi's not here, is she?"

"Are you kidding?" Jillian hopped down from the bed and did a little dance. "We haven't seen *Mah-lis-sa* for months. She never brings Brady over anymore."

Ashley stretched and yawned. "Bet Brady's big, too," she murmured.

"He's no fun anyway. He's a spoiled brat. Dad even says so. He acts more like six then ten."

"Figures." Ashley got out of bed and headed for her bathroom "Tell Jessie I'll be down in a bit."

Ashley surveyed the dining room from the entryway. Her father was in mid-argument with her brother Alexander. Jillian arranged forks at each place setting while Jessica poured orange juice for Devon. Ashley took pause at the sight of her stepbrother, whom, at eighteen, had matured into an astoundingly attractive young man. Dark blond hair, still tousled from bed, hung over sleepy brown eyes as he made obvious his attempt to tune out an ensuing disagreement between his stepbrother and stepfather. He smiled at Ashley when he noticed her presence.

If only he were older, she thought, smiling back and making her way to the table.

"There you are. Sleep well?" Jessica put down the pitcher and rushed Ashley with a hug. Dane stood and leaned forward to give his daughter a peck on the cheek. Alex merely nodded in her direction.

"I can't wait to hear all about your travels," Jessica said, sitting down and reaching for her coffee. "Must have been exciting."

"Not sure that's the right word," Ashley muttered, raising her eyebrows briefly. "An education, for sure."

"What are your plans? Or do you have any?" her stepmother asked.

"I want to sleep for about a month."

"I like *that*," Devon agreed, running a hand through his unkempt locks with a sigh.

Ashley cleared her throat. "I'd like to get a job."

"A job?" Alex looked up. "Why bother? I'm sure there are local hippie communes you could easily infiltrate."

Dane frowned at his son, his green eyes sharp. "Know all about that, do you? I wouldn't be so quick to judge."

"I work hard, dammit. At a job I hate. You know where my heart is. I just haven't hit the right opportunity, yet. If you'd only give me a break –"

"Boys! This is not the time!" Jessica asserted, a mock fierceness in her voice. "Save it for later."

The sexy smirk had not left Devon's lips, Ashley noticed, as he shook his head slowly in response to Alex's outburst. The sight of his dimples made her smile again. This boy was too charming for his own good.

"What's up with you, Dev?" she asked.

Devon turned his whimsical expression her way. "I'm workin' hard, too, *dammit*. I just washed my car last week." He stretched, yawned, picked up his fork. "Pop's a slave-driver. Got me workin' with the grips down at the studio."

"That should be fun," Ashley said softly.

"It's a hoot. I pretty much get to drag vid cables around, transport high-octane sodas and gas up their cars. You need a 'Mombo Bombo' stand or maybe a Roscoe fogger, I'm your man."

Alex scoffed. "Like you ever worked a day in your life."

Ashley stared at Alex. For twenty-five, he was certainly acting the younger brother rather than the older. But Alex's disdain did nothing to erase the contented look on Devon MacKendall's face. Alex was newly miffed.

"What is it with you? You smoking pot in your room or something?" he demanded. Jillian covered her ears.

"That's quite enough." Jessica's words, far calmer and quieter than her earlier admonition, brought a silence over the dining room. Alex colored and focused on his plate.

Ashley wet her lips and then cleared her throat. "Is there any coffee left?"

The next few minutes passed in silence. Jessica finally spoke, her voice now pleasant with interest. "What are your plans for today?"

"I'd really like to get my bearings. I need a few things; maybe I can get a ride to a mall."

"Feel free to take my car," Jessica offered. "I'd go with you, but I have a fitting this afternoon."

"No, that's okay. My driving's a bit ... rusty. I can grab a cab. Or, rather, it's Uber now, right?"

Dane looked up, but before he could comment, Devon responded. "I'll take you anywhere you want to go."

"That's cool. Thanks."

Ashley helped Jessica clear the table as the others went their separate ways. As she watched her stepmother rinse dishes, Ashley marveled at Jessica's calming presence.

"Something up?" Jessica asked, noticing Ashley's pensive expression.

"No. I was just thinking about how glad I am to be back. To be home."

"We're glad to have you back. Your dad's been more worried than he let on."

"I know. I'm sorry, truly, about that. I don't know what made me go, but –"

"You don't have to explain to me, babe. By the way, I'd like to have a little party for your birthday. We didn't get to celebrate the last three, obviously."

"I wouldn't miss it," Ashley said. "As long as you don't go to a big fuss. It'll be nice to see everyone again."

"We have lots to celebrate."

FOUR

Devon

H e had an hour to kill before Ashley would be ready to go.
   His father was, by all accounts, a good man. Cory "Mac" MacKendall's greatest fault was a fiery but mostly dormant temper that surfaced only out of an intense jealousy over his wife's relationship with his best friend. Devon knew little about those days before his father's murder, when his mother had believed she'd married her one true love and soul mate. Who could have known Mac's plane would be shot out of the sky, leaving her and four-year-old Devon so crushingly, desperately alone? At least that's what he'd gleaned.

There were still people around who'd known Mac. "People must tell you all the time," and they do, Devon thought with a sigh, "you look just like your dad. Your real dad, that is."

My real dad. Devon's memories of Mac MacKendall were a combination of scrapbook snapshots and hazy, movie-like images; strong hands, intense, looming brown eyes and a soft, soothing voice in a dark bedroom. Closer to the memory of a well-liked book read many years ago, years before he could read more than LOOK, SEE DEVON RUN. His feelings for Mac amounted to a fondness for a distant, benevolent uncle he only barely knew.

Devon turned the page of his mother's photo album. Why today? He hadn't looked at these photos in ages. Perhaps it was Zoe's arrival, *Ashley's* return home that had stirred up the familial fires. The final item was a memoriam from Mac's funeral. The rest of the album was filled with blank pages. She'd started a new book upon her marriage to Dane Pierce.

He closed the album and slid it back onto the shelf, then pulled out the next in line. A few wedding photos of Jessica and Dane on a foggy-bright Wyoming morning. A smile twitched on Devon's mouth. Here was a likeness of himself, tugging on the groom's tuxedo jacket with upturned face.

My real dad. Dane had embraced him like a precious jewel found on a lonely beach. No, more like an abandoned puppy huddled on that beach. Never a hint of the discord that had existed between him and his dead rival. Discord? Devon chewed his bottom lip thoughtfully. To hear his sister tell it, it was more like a world war. A complicated relationship, to say the least. Mac MacKendall and Dane Pierce; friends, business partners, opponents in love with the same woman. *His mother.*

"We called him *Uncle* Dane back then," Megan told him. "She was with him before Dad, you know."

Devon turned another page. He'd never asked what "with him" meant to his sister.

There were no pictures of Meggie at the wedding. She'd stayed away, home with her mother, Mac's first wife.

"I was mad. I didn't want her to remarry, especially not to *him*. It was an insult to Dad. He'd only been dead a year." As if in apology, she reminded, "I was only eleven."

Devon shook his head slowly, his smile now wistful. Megan had been screwed up ever since. The six years between them were years he couldn't possibly fathom. They shared a father she adored, and he'd never really known; their mothers were opposites. Megan was deep, he knew, and still troubled by their father's premature death. She had a good heart, he was certain. She just couldn't open it more than a hairline crack.

Luckily, she opened it to her little half-brother when necessary. There were times, times when his parents were at odds, times when his mother was unavailable. She hadn't meant to abandon him; at eighteen, he now understood the drive, the constant pull of the cameras. His mother and father were entertainers in the first degree. But in those scary days and nights when Dad practically lived at the studios, when Mom would come home from a Hollywood party and Dane became surly and vindictive, it was Megan's voice on the phone that had calmed his childish heart.

She'd never asked for help in return, and Devon couldn't begin to offer it. His sister's trauma was too deep, too personal, and too old. The hurt was so obvious, yet he was powerless to do anything about it.

Turning his eyes upward, focusing on nothing physical, Devon wondered if Megan would come to Ashley's birthday party. It would thrill his mother, he knew. There was a mostly unseen "family" rift there that pained Jessica, an eternal loose end in a life of many. Devon closed the album and reached for his phone.

FIVE

Megan

Leaning close to her computer monitor, Megan MacKendall squinted at the photograph on the screen, her right hand carefully moving the mouse pixel by pixel. *Click*. The pimple on the bride's forehead magically dissolved, and Megan exhaled. *There. Perfect*. Under her desk, her toes sought the warmth of her slippers. She'd turned her bedroom heater off a little too soon as utilities were expensive.

Sitting back now, she saved the photo and reached for the neat stack of folders on her desk, searching for the correct contract.

Weinberg-Rubin wedding. She opened the folder and re-read the order form.

"Always the photographer, never the bride," she muttered, now giving her photo printer a quick check for paper and ink levels. The ringing of the phone gave her a start. She stared at the device for a moment, considered letting it ring through to her voicemail. But the caller I.D. changed her mind.

"Dev, what's up?"

"I need some pictures of my abs for *Buff Brute* magazine."

Megan smiled. She could almost hear Devon's lazy, sweet smile. "Do you even have abs, little brother?"

"Somewhere. Hey, listen, I want to ask you something. Now, don't get all clammy on me."

Megan did stiffen. The last time he'd started off that way, he'd asked her to take him to Mac's grave. But she forced a breath and rolled her shoulders, looking back at the deliriously happy, acne-free bride on her screen. "Okay, ask."

"Mom's throwing a big splash for Ashley's birthday. We want you to come."

A sigh escaped. "Whose birthday?"

"Zoe's beamed herself back from the cosmos. Only now she's forty pounds thinner and goes by *Ashley*. That's a headline, eh?"

"Forty pounds?" Megan could feel her own eyes open wide. *"Forty?"*

"Yup. Looks seriously good, too."

Megan clicked her "calendar" icon. Uncomfortable, but not awful. "I'll check my calendar. Her birthday's around the fifteenth, right? When's the party?"

"March seventeenth. Our house. You can bring a date if you can scare one up."

A guest. *A date.* Moving the cursor to March 17th, Megan clicked and typed in: *Zoe's Party.* "What time?"

"Anytime you want, sweet sis. You know Mom and Dad; they'll party-hearty all night."

A date. Megan raked her fingers through her long, dark brown locks. "Forty pounds. Honestly?"

"Dad called her a stone fox, whatever that means. But she is *hot*. I'm taking her out for lunch later. Possibly dinner, too."

"Devon. She's your sister. Knock it off."

"Half-sister. By marriage."

"She's like, five years older than you."

"Four. But it doesn't matter. Anyway, I wouldn't talk about *my* love life. At least I have one."

Megan licked her lips. *Damned cocky kid!* "Just ... just watch yourself, Dev. Zoe's a big girl now ..." *Bad choice of words.* "I mean to say, she's not the same girl we played with back then."

"I never played with her back then. She was fat and compulsive and always off in some dream world. She left when I was fourteen. I was glad."

Watch your heart, little brother. There was nothing more to say. "What can I bring?"

"Like you have to bring anything."

"I mean, like a gift for Z – *Ashley*. What would be good?"

"I'll email you some ideas. So, what else is up?"

Megan stood from her desk and left her office, heading toward the living room where a half dozen easels displayed black and white photographs. "Oh, a wedding next Saturday, and I've got that show tonight. Or did you forget?"

"Uh, sure, no, I didn't forget. You weren't counting on me coming, were you?"

"Nope. You've seen all these photos anyway. I promised Eric I'd do the show; nothing will sell. It's just a time filler. A space filler."

Her brother grunted. "You freak. Your pictures are awesome. If they don't sell it's because you stand around looking suicidal. Maybe I should come, just to drum up some excitement."

"Don't you dare. You'd embarrass the hell out of me."

"What are you bringing? Not the cemetery shots."

"No. These are pictures of people. The old people in the park, the guy who plays sax on the freeway off ramp, that girl jump roping, and a few others. Like I said, they're boring."

"Only because you make them so. I gotta run. Love ya."

Megan ended the call and placed the phone on the coffee table, then stretched. So, Zoe was back.

She went to the kitchen and fired up her single-cup coffee maker, unable to stop the onslaught of memories that she knew would come flooding back. Zoe was Dane's youngest daughter, Alex's little sister.

They had, indeed, played together a few times. But while custody of Alexander was awarded to Dane, his ex had mostly raised the girls and Megan had only rarely seen Melissa and Zoe, much less shared dolls or crayons with them.

She checked the date on her single quart of milk. Still okay. Splashing a bit into her coffee, Megan stared out the kitchen window of her third-floor condominium at the freeway in the distance. *Can't think about those days right now. Too much to do.*

She'd gotten rather good at sweeping the memories aside, but one thought was inevitable, because it still mattered.

Alex. Would he be at the party? Would he be with someone?

Alexander Pierce. Dane's son and her childhood playmate. Playmate until, of course, her father had been cruelly, thoughtlessly murdered, and Uncle Dane had ridden in on his steed and carried off her stepmother. Jessica, the love of her father's short life. He clearly had no regard for Mac's memory.

And Jessica had been easily taken.

Megan's adult mind never tired of reminding her that Jessica could and should be forgiven. The aching, shattered child inside refused.

Only Alex remained faultless. He couldn't help being Dane's son, and now, by fate and by marriage, he and his sisters were her own brother's step-siblings. Megan sniffed in disdain. She had no use for Melissa, a snob by anyone's account, who'd abandoned her brother and sister for her mother's warped lifestyle. A girl who, as shocking as it seemed, became pregnant at sixteen and refused to marry the father. Who was now raising a bratty son under her mother's obsessive eye.

Zoe was a different story. Zoe, she knew, had taken Megan's place in Jessica's life after Mac's death. Zoe, unwanted by her biological mother, hardly known by her father, overweight and under loved; passed back and forth between parents like so much community property changing hands.

How can I dislike a woman I don't even know? Megan mused. *By association.* How often had Alex complained, as a child, that Zoe got all his father's love? Truth or not, it colored Megan's world of heroes and villains.

Megan sighed and sipped. The question about Alex remained, and she couldn't bring herself to ask. She had to assume he'd be at his sister's party and had to expect the successful young screenwriter wouldn't be alone.

Whom would she invite? There was no one special, *had been* no one special. No one, of course, except Daddy.

But it didn't really matter, did it?

Wandering back to the make-shift gallery, she lifted the jump rope photo and peered at it. Was Devon right, did she kill her own sales with her negativity? With a sigh, she replaced the picture and went to her room to pick her clothing for the event. Maybe tonight she would pretend to be the girl she would have been.

Six

Alexander

Even though wearing a carpet thin will not make a phone ring, Alex walked across the living room again, this time with a cold Bud Light in his hand. They weren't going to call, and he'd known it all along. The script was good, it was dynamite. But because his own father had passed on producing it, Alex was a pariah in Hollywood. No one would touch it.

"Not what we're looking for, but thanks."

"No room in our production schedule for two or three years. Sorry."

"What else have you got?"

"It's good, really good, but ..."

"We did a story like that three years ago."

"We'll call you."

And the worst: *"So why isn't StarCrossed Productions picking this up?"*

Why *wasn't* Dane Pierce interested in his son's screenplay about the police cover up of a high-profile murder?

"He's jealous. Damn jealous!" Alex shouted out loud, kicking at a soccer ball in fury. The ball slammed against the wall above the couch then rocketed into the glass coffee table below. The results were to be expected. Blood near boiling, Alex pitched his beer bottle into the heap of broken glass and roared out a primal growl.

A blonde woman wearing a miniskirt and a faded "Free Britney" t-shirt entered the room from the hallway. Calm and clearly unshaken by the melee, she carried a small, zippered sports bag. With one hand on the front doorknob, she turned toward Alex, her face expressionless.

"I hope things straighten out for you. Call me if you ever get a handle on this anger thing you got going."

When Alex only stared, she opened the door and stepped outside, looking back once. "Good luck, Al."

Alex looked around as she closed the door. There was nothing handy, nothing he could hurl with any purpose. Tilting his head down, he ran his hands through his no-nonsense haircut and shuddered. "Don't-call-me-Al," he muttered through clenched teeth.

Closing his eyes, Alex sat down where he stood on the carpet. *Breathe*, he ordered himself. *Breathe, dammit.*

When the phone did ring an hour later, he didn't hurry to pick it up. The glass was cleaned up and the metal coffee table frame deposited into the dumpster behind his apartment. He didn't guess nor did he care who was calling, but his stepmother's voice was the last he'd expected to hear. Her invitation to his little sister's party was not particularly welcome.

"I don't know if I can make it," Alex said, struggling to sound sincerely remorseful. "I need to check the schedule at work."

"Don't worry about it. She'll be disappointed, of course, but if you're already booked ..." Jessica said with just a touch of guilt-provoking tenderness. Damn, she was good at that.

"I'll try. Maybe I can shift things around."

Truth was, with Angie gone – and he was sure she was gone for good this time – he had few commitments. Not that he'd been committed, in any way, to the girl. He wasn't ready for any ties. After all, he was an up-and-coming screenwriter with no time for obligations, aside from his day job. He'd liked Angie. But being honest with himself, she deserved better. He hoped she got it.

When his phone rang again a half hour later, he was staring into the bottom of a near-empty Chinese food carton.

"This is Alex," he answered, cradling the phone at his neck while he opened his second carton of pork fried rice.

"It's Mel," a woman's voice informed him, a voice so devoid of warmth he thought he could feel the chill at his shoulder. His older sister had never been the warm and fuzzy type.

"Okay," he answered, bracing himself for unpleasantness, a feeling that normally accompanied her rare phone calls.

"What's this about a party? Were you invited?"

"Yup. You weren't?"

"I'm sure it was an oversight. I haven't been home, I –"

"Your voicemail is turned off; your mailman was kidnapped with all your mail and your ISP has been down for a week."

"Shut your pie hole, freak."

"Always the lady. How's Brady? In jail yet?"

Melissa was angry. Alex could hear her all but sputtering on the other end of the line, and he smiled to himself. What was that grinding sound?

"Braden is spectacular, thank you. Top of his class. And you? Sold that fabulous screenplay yet?"

"There's interest. Look, I'm busy, did you just call to whine about not being invited to Zoe's deal or do you have something of value to share? And how did you even hear about it if they didn't invite you?"

"You're a piece of work, Alex, you know that? I saw it on Facebook, nimrod. Jillian's been rattling on about it. Who is this Ashley chick, anyway?"

Alex pulled the phone away from his ear while his sister continued to rail. He almost hung it up but remembered something. Bringing the phone back, he muttered two words sure to shut Melissa's mouth.

"It's Zoe. She's back."

The quiet on the line told him he'd hit his mark.

"When?"

"Week ago."

"She still flipped out?"

"Some. No more than any of us."

"Speak for yourself," Melissa challenged. "You two are the ones that went with *him*."

"Correction: it was only me until Zoe ran screaming from Mom's house. Speaking of which, how's Mom? Still sober, I hope?"

"I won't dignify that with an answer." A pause. "She does miss you, although I can't fathom why."

"I miss her, too. I have since I was born."

He thought about his sisters as he prepared for bed that night. Mel was wrong; they were all screwed up in one way or another. And although Zoe had lost weight and changed her name, there was still a neurosis he could feel in her presence. Something was amiss with his little sister. It didn't scream at you like it did with Melissa, but it was there, nonetheless.

Was it their upbringing? He thought about his childhood. Movie-like frames ran through his mind. Rita, his mother, shouting at Dane to get out of the house. Dane grabbing nothing but his coat and stalking out, not even saying good-bye to his young children. Melissa crying at the window, Mom sending her to her room. Mom making friends with a bottle of vodka, Dad making friends with a stripper.

Alex chuckled. Crap, his dad wasn't all bad. The days in the courtroom came to mind, when a serious and confident Dane Pierce had petitioned to keep Alexander away from his less-than-stellar mother. The nights when his father would stare out the huge picture window in the dark, worrying, contemplating, or perhaps musing. His obvious suffering when Jessica married MacKendall, and his devastation when Uncle Mac died.

He wanted a drink. He was already standing at the well-stocked wet bar, searching for the right tonic, the right formula to ease the pain in his gut. He thought about his missing coffee table and Angie's face as she left. He poured.

"Cheers," he told himself in the mirror behind the bar, clinking his glass against it in salute. "Here's to Melissa's nasty temper, Zoe's paranoia, and Mom's fondness for booze. Here's to Dad, too, and his penchant for wandering away." He smiled before taking a gulp. "Here's to ... *me*."

SEVEN

Melissa

Melissa threw her cell phone into the cat's litter box.

"What the hell are you doing?" Rita asked, her hands on her hips.

Her daughter sulked. "They're having a big party for Zoe – correction, *Ashley* – and they didn't invite me."

"Well, la-di-dah. They didn't invite the prodigal daughter to the grand house on the hill. Are you surprised? Troubled by this newest twist to the knife in your back?"

"Alex is going. Can you believe Zoe's back? She's living with Dad and Jessica."

"And? You want sympathy from me?"

"I wouldn't mind," Melissa flung hotly at her mother. "Just once you could show a little concern."

"Ha. I'm shocked that you'd even want to go." Rita turned to leave her standing in the laundry room when the cell phone rang, and Melissa froze. Her eyes darted towards the cat box, and she lunged for the phone. Holding the device close to but not quiet touching her ear, Melissa managed to answer the call with two fingers. Rita shuddered and dampened a rag with disinfectant.

"Hello? Hello? I'm here, who's calling?"

"Melissa, it's Jessica. I wanted to let you know we're having a little party for your sister."

"A party? When?" Melissa's face burned and her mother grinned.

"March seventeenth, here in Malibu. I hope you and Brady can make it."

"Brady? Oh, yeah. Sure. Everyone wants to see Brady."

"And you," Jessica repeated. "No gifts; just come prepared to have fun. Dancing, buffet, the usual routine."

"Sure. Thanks. Uh ..." Melissa pressed a hand to her forehead, pushing back her bleached-blonde bangs. "I heard she came back."

"Yes, she's here. I'm sure she'll be calling you." Jessica said in a voice obviously meant to console. "She's still getting settled. I hope you'll make the party, Mimi."

Mimi. Ack! "I'll be there," she said quickly, glancing nervously at her still smirking mother. "Not sure if I'll bring Braden. He's been a little hellion lately." Jessica's silence was unnerving, so Melissa hurried on. "But we'll see. Bye."

She handed the phone to her mother, who took it from her with the readied rag.

"I'll be upstairs," she told Rita, then dashed from the room before she broke down.

Her pillow had absorbed more tears in the last ten years than most would in a lifetime, Melissa thought from time to heartbreaking time. Shambles did not begin to describe her life, a life that should be filled with happiness and joy. She wanted for nothing, financially. Her father had seen to a generous trust fund for both herself and her son when he could have just as easily turned his back. Her mother could have tossed her out, when, at sixteen, she'd walked in boasting that she was pregnant and hooked on Valium.

But Rita Pierce knew all too well the consequences of addiction. She'd alienated two of her three children due to hers, and she would fight to save her daughter from a similar fate. "The apple doesn't fall very far from the tree," Dane had loudly accused, reminding Rita that she, too, had conceived Melissa out of wedlock, and had turned to the bottle for solace when things had gotten dicey between them.

The difference, Melissa realized, was that her mother had *married* the father of her baby. Brady's father knew nothing of the child, nor did he need another wife.

Tears came readily. She didn't know what prompted this fresh onslaught, nor what, if anything, could soothe her tortured heart. Tossing herself onto her bed, Melissa grasped that often wet pillow and began to sob. She did have a knife twisting in her back, a knife she couldn't quite reach. And everyone around her had a turn at it, an endless procession of merciless attacks that left her staggering. It was Alexander's heartless betrayal. It was Zoe's indifference. Her mother's self-righteousness. Brady's insufferable behavior.

It was even Jessica's sympathetic tone. *Don't be nice to me, Jess. I don't deserve it. I can't live up to your good graces.*

On the nightstand was the letter from Braden, received in yesterday's mail. Through swollen eyes, she reread the words that added so much heartache to her already ruined life.

"Dear Mom,

"Please, please, please come and get me! These people are so mean to me. I can't watch TV and no computer. They make me eat awful food. I HATE IT HEAR. I so much promiss to be really good from now on, only just let me come home!

"I know you hate me or elss you woundnt sent me hear.

"HELP I AM LOCKKED IN!

"I AM DIEING!

"Love,

Your son Braden"

She folded the letter and sniffed, tucking the missive into her nightstand drawer. The boarding school staff, Melissa was certain, was only doing its job. Brady had become so unmanageable, she'd had little choice but to send him away. Her mother had refused to deal with him. "I'm done raising kids," she'd said, "except for you."

When Jessica had gotten wind of the situation, she'd offered to take Brady in and work with him. Pride had slammed the door on that option. Melissa, refusing to concede failure, had since had second thoughts. What was best for herself was not necessarily what was best for Brady. Still, things could turn out okay. Brady could get better and come home a model child. She could meet a wonderful man who'd adopt Brady when they married, and she could leave her mother's house for good.

Her father could love her again. *Might as well wish for everything while I'm at it.* Dabbing at her eyes, Melissa straightened. She would go to the stupid party and she would be a queen among paupers. She would be the best and brightest and most lovable daughter in the universe. She had to try.

EIGHT

Jockeying For Position

A shley was in no hurry as she strolled the upper level of the mall with Devon. The lights, the decor, the sheer decadence of it all overwhelmed the senses. Even before her swipe at freedom, she'd not been much of a shopper.

"Hungry?" Devon asked as they approached the food court.

"A little. You?"

"Yeah. Only let's go to a sit-down. I feel like being served."

Don Rodrigo's Mexican Restaurant was dark and cool, with Spanish guitar music and abundant salsa for the tortilla chips.

"I shouldn't," Ashley complained with a grin. "Next thing you know, I'll be blimp-girl again."

"You were never 'blimp-girl'. You were just ... healthy, right?"

"Yeah, right. Healthy. Is that what they call childhood obesity these days?"

The dimples appeared as Devon looked down at his napkin. He had no answer, Ashley knew, because she *had* been fat. "I'll have a *tostada pollo*," she told the waiter. "Hold the sour cream."

"Give me the macho-macho burrito with carne asada and extra-hot salsa."

"And to drink? A margarita for the lady?"

Ashley looked across the booth at Devon, who colored.

"No, a Sprite. A Diet Sprite."

"A Coke," Devon said and smiled in apparent relief, saved from the humiliation of being carded. "I'm trying to cut down my alcohol consumption."

Ashley laughed. "Me too."

"So, uh, how did you do it? Get skinny, I mean."

"It was involuntary. I starved." Ashley took a judicious second chip. "We ate a lot of fish, rice, vegetables ... "

"Sounds healthy to me. I mostly eat at Burger King myself."

"Does Jess, um, *Mom* cook?"

"Sure. Sometimes. She's been working a lot the last couple of years. I say, more power to her. She's ... she's sensational."

"You really love her, don't you?"

"She's a good mom. Of course, I do. Dad's not half-bad, either."

Ashley nodded. It was all good. "Dad's mellowed some. He seems more settled than before."

Devon shrugged. "I guess. Hard to say. He's different, for sure. I dunno." He took a long sip from the drink the waiter set before him. "I want to hear about the gypsies, what you did, where you went ... did you make friends?"

"Well, yeah, I guess you could call them friends. One girl in particular, Mari, she and I shared a tent, and then a room. I miss her already."

"Any guys?" Devon's expression was serious now as he licked cola from his lips and stared into her eyes. It made Ashley wince a little, and she also took a draught from her soft drink.

"A couple. Here and there."

"Anyone special?"

"Depends on what you mean by special," she said, pushing a smile. "No one I'd bring home to Dad, if that's where you're going."

Devon shrugged. "Well, I just meant, did you ... did you get like physical out there on the road?"

"Physical? If you mean what I think you mean, it's none of your business, little brother."

Devon set his jaw and his cheeks again flushed. "I'm not really your brother, you know."

Ashley felt her own cheeks begin to heat up. Lifting her chin, she drew in a breath. "Not by blood, no, you're right. Still, it's personal, Dev. What does it matter if I slept with anyone? It's nobody's business but mine."

"Okay, fair enough. Did you steal? Did you dance for coinage?" Now Devon smiled, a playful, whimsical expression on his lips.

"Oh, sure, with a tambourine and everything."

By the afternoon they were each lugging two shopping bags to Devon's sport SUV. Each purchase was difficult; Ashley was not used to having cash to spend. "You gonna wear that bikini to your party?" Devon asked, opening the hatch on his truck.

"Maybe," Ashley teased, lifting her eyebrows. "Depends on who's there."

"He won't like it."

"He, who? Daddy?"

"He can be stodgy as hell when it comes to his own kids."

Ashley waived him off. "Too bad. In that case, I'll wear it for sure."

"Good. I can't wait."

She'd done well on the drive to the Mall, busying herself with small talk about Devon's car, the weather, anything to distract her. But on the way home, Devon was quiet. Ashley tried not to tense up as they crossed crowded intersections and turned corners. Near-terror gripped her with every lane change, every horn honk, and everywhere she looked people seemed to be talking on cell phones. She didn't know how to explain that she'd grown fearful of drivers. She'd had her license for barely a year when she'd left and hadn't driven since. Worse, there was a part of her that still thought of Devon as an adolescent.

"I wish they wouldn't do that," she murmured.

"Do what?"

"Talk on the phone while driving. It makes me nervous."

"Me too. I mean, hello? It's illegal! I refuse to carry one in the car. Too many people have bought it because of some idiot talking on the phone instead of paying attention to driving."

Ashley nodded, finally laying her head back against the headrest and closing her eyes. She'd get over it, eventually. She'd not only get over her fear, she'd drive again. Someday.

"What do you want for your birthday?" Jillian took two steps to Ashley's one as they crossed the backyard.

"Nothing I can think of." Ashley squatted next to the pool and reached as far as she could for the floating lounge chair. "You have any ideas to help me out?"

"I got you something cool. Well, Mom paid for it, but I picked it out. It's something you could wear in Wyoming. Did you go to the ranch when you were little?"

Ashley gave up trying to reach the lounge and went for the pool skimmer. She felt a smile tug at her lips. "Yup."

"Did you like it? Where did you sleep? Did you ride the horses?"

"I loved it, I slept in the middle room on the left, and I once got to ride Whiskey all by myself."

"Whiskey! No lie?"

"No lie. Dad walked him with me on his back. He is one big horse." Ashley finally gained her floating chair and eased herself into it. "Eee! Cold."

"It's heated. Don't know why you wanna swim in March anyway. Are you excited for the party?"

"Absolutely. Who all is coming?"

Jillian strolled along the perimeter of the pool watching her sister drift. "Um, Alex, Uncle Teddy, um, Megan, Aunt Roxie and Uncle Tom ..."

Ashley's eyes opened. "Megan? Megan MacKendall?"

"Yeah, she's Devon's other sister."

"I know who she is. I haven't seen her in ages." *Wonder what she's like now.*

As if reading her sister's mind, Jillian went on. "She's really pretty but she never smiles."

"No?"

"She always looks sad to me. Her dad died when she was little. Mom's first husband was her daddy. He was Dev's dad too."

Ashley started to explain that she knew the entire family tree already but decided to let the girl go on.

"My teacher says we are the most complicated family she's ever heard of."

"They call it a 'yours, mine, and ours' type family," Ashley said, closing her eyes and thinking about her siblings.

"So, Megan and Devon had the same father but different mothers. Me and Dev have the same mother, but different fathers. You and me have the same father, but different mothers. But you and Dev have no same parents."

When Ashley did not respond, Jillian raised her voice. "Did you see your mom yet?"

"Nope. Don't plan to."

"Melissa might come to the party, too."

Once again Ashley's eyes fluttered open. "You're joking."

"Well, she might. I heard Mom on the phone with her."

"I hope not," Ashley muttered. "We don't get along."

"I'm glad *we* get along," Jillian pronounced, turning away and then prancing toward the back patio doors. "And I'm glad you came home!"

Me too. But something had changed in the last thirty seconds. The prospect of seeing her step-sister, and worse, *much* worse, her "real" sister Melissa, had put a kink in her day. With a sigh, she surrendered to the fact that she could not avoid either Megan or Melissa. They were both part of her life, her family, and brooding would not alter her course.

Black shimmering material hung from her shoulders to just above her knee. It wasn't in mourning, Megan insisted to herself; she merely liked "little black dresses." This one had a modest smattering of glittery black beads around the neckline but was otherwise simple. Unremarkable. Boring.

Like me, Megan thought again. Eric Wold touched her elbow, causing her to nearly drop her Perrier.

"Smile, girl. *Smile.*"

Wasn't I smiling? "Right."

"The guy with the black silk shirt was asking about your Maserati photo. I told him $200.00."

"What? You told him *what*?"

"Chillax, Meggers. It's worth more than that. He'll buy, just watch." Eric walked away, ready to descend on a new patron. Megan felt her color rise; the guy in question was coming her way.

She couldn't help but stare. Like herself, he was dressed all in black, his near-ebony hair almost brushing his shoulders in a casual, boyish cut. He sported a spare, trim mustache and a fair, youthful face. All he needed was a black eye mask.

"Are you Ms. MacKendall?"

"Yeah. Yes, I – I am. Can I ... help you?" Her tongue seemed to forget how to work.

"I was wondering ... the picture of the car. Where did you take that?"

Megan cleared her throat and considered. "Um ... let's see. It was parked at ... at the Marina, I believe. Do you like it?"

The man smiled. A smile, Megan noticed, that involved his dark brown eyes as well as his lips. "The car, or the print?" he asked with a tilt to his head.

"The print, I guess ... I mean, the car, the car is, well, anyone would like the car, right? If you like cars, I mean. So, the print. It's a little off-center, I kinda took it in a hurry, the driver was getting ready to leave and ... oh." *Shut up, Megan.* The man's smile deepened, a testament to her lunacy. "I'm sorry. I think Mr. Wold already quoted you a price, but if you want it, I'd –"

"I already bought it. I might not have had it not been ... off centered. Have a good evening, Ms. MacKendall." The man turned and walked toward the door, calling over his shoulder, "*Bon chance.*"

Megan's pasted-on smile faded as he disappeared into the night. "*Merci,*" she whispered. "I need all the luck I can get."

I also need a better mattress. Megan turned again, now impossibly tangled in her bed sheets. Instead of lining up to hop over a white picket fence, her mental sheep were gossiping about Zoe and Dane and the Maserati guy. Devon had a crush on Dane's daughter; Zoe had returned from the past; and the hottest guy she'd met in years had bought one of her photos. And here, nothing had happened in weeks. Months, probably.

Zoe's party loomed. Alexander would be there.

Megan shifted onto her back, her eyes wide open and staring into the darkness.

What will I wear? No way will I get into a swimsuit. Sighing, she raised her arm and rested it across her forehead. *Maybe I won't go.* Another sigh as she decided staying away was not an option. She owed Jessica, at least.

Jessica. Pictures began to flash, snapshots of her father and Jessica on their wedding day. It was, what, eighteen years ago? It was a foggy picture, one that needed no editing; Daddy was smiling, Jessie was radiant. She remembered that despite being only six, she knew of their great love and devotion to one another. Mac MacKendall adored his bride; Jessica idolized her groom. For a little girl still recovering from her parents' painful divorce, it was heaven.

Her mother had remarried not long after, and all seemed as good as it could be, despite the shuffling between two families. She'd loved Uncle Dane, too, back then. He was her father's best friend, and the occasional family get-togethers were a hoot. Alexander Pierce was her pseudo cousin and confidante, Zoe a moody and distant, sometimes playmate.

And then Daddy was murdered. For a moment in time, Uncle Dane had been a suspect. But even when the true assassin had been tried and convicted, the taint remained. For despite his grief and eventual vindication, Dane Pierce had wasted no time in resuming his courtship of Jessica, a courtship that had begun even before either of them had met Mac MacKendall.

It was only natural, Megan had told herself repeatedly. There was no reason for Jessica to live her life alone and miserable. Dane was good to her.

This is nuts. Maybe some warm moo.

In the kitchen, Megan heated milk in the microwave and then went to the bathroom medicine cabinet for eye drops. Her contacts were due to be replaced. Opening the mirrored door, she peered at all the prescription bottles lining the glass shelves. *Prozac. Zoloft. Celexa. Luvox.*

Megan's hand hovered over the *Trazodone.*

Just one?

The beeping of the microwave brought her around. Scowling, she snapped up the eye drops and closed the cabinet door with a bang. *I must get rid of all that crap. I don't need it anymore.*

I don't!

Sipping the milk, she padded to the studio and turned on her computer. She sat, the colors of Microsoft Windows lighting her face in the darkness. She opened a file labeled "Old Photos" and began clicking.

Jessica had generously lent her the old family photo albums to scan. Here was Daddy, youthful and happy, Devon riding on his shoulders at the zoo. A funny shot of Mac holding a touring bicycle over his head in the garage. Megan and her dad at Ventura harbor, a dripping ice cream cone in her five-year-old hand.

Click. Uncle Dane and Daddy cutting it up with light sabers around the pool.

Click. Megan and Alexander, aged nine, in midair over a fifteen-foot trampoline.

Click. Jessica and Megan during a private moment in the kitchen, just before Mac's death.

Megan drew in a slow, deep breath. Warm milk or not, she knew she wouldn't sleep this night.

Tiring of the melancholy, she opened another folder. Here were some of her favorites. A sunset in Santa Barbara. A sleeping cat on the lap of a sleeping grandmother. A smiling waiter taking an order at a sidewalk café in Paris. His smile made Megan smile. Paris had been great. Maybe someday she'd go again, only next time with someone she cared to go with.

The thought tickled her brain, and she clicked on "maserati.jpg." Here was the sleek black car with the privacy glass windows, not a speck of dust on its glossy paint, chrome exhaust pipes peeking out the back; and the suggestion of an outline, a man getting ready to drive away. She'd nearly fumbled the camera; afraid he'd seen her focusing from across the street.

Her thoughts invariably turned to the photo's purchaser. The man in black. What an intriguing piece of humankind, that one. *I should have talked longer. Maybe there are other prints he'd like. Maybe* – Megan slowly shook her head, the photo becoming blurry before her eyes. There were already too many "maybes" and "what-if's" in her life. No room for more.

Still ... Eric would have gotten his name and address. It was customary. A follow up might be in order. In the living room, her electronic mantel clock chimed 5:30 am. No reason to even bother going back to bed. Standing to roll her shoulders, she noted the deserted street below. A good time for a run.

"Where did you and Devon go yesterday?" Jillian took two steps to Ashley's one as they crossed the backyard.

"The mall. I needed a bunch of new things."

"What do you want for your birthday?"

"Nothing I can think of." Ashley squatted next to the pool and reached as far as she could for the floating lounge chair. "You have any ideas to help me out?"

"I got you something cool. Well, Mom paid for it, but I picked it out. It's something you could wear in Wyoming. Did you go to the ranch when you were little?"

Ashley gave up trying to reach the lounge and went for the pool skimmer. She felt a smile tug at her lips. "Yup."

"Did you like it? Where did you sleep? Did you ride the horses?"

"I loved it, I slept in the middle room on the left, and I once got to ride Whiskey all by myself."

"Whiskey! No lie?"

"No lie. Dad walked him with me on his back. He is one big horse." Ashley finally gained her floating chair and eased herself into it. "Eee! Cold."

"It's heated. Don't know why you wanna swim in March anyway. Are you excited for the party?"

"Absolutely. Who all is coming?"

Jillian strolled along the perimeter of the pool watching her sister drift. "Um, Alex, Uncle Teddy, um, Megan, Aunt Roxie and Uncle Tom ..."

Ashley's eyes opened. "Megan? Megan MacKendall?"

"Yeah, she's Devon's other sister." Jillian sat down at the pool's edge, took off her sandals and dipped her feet into the water.

"I know who she is. I haven't seen her in ages." *Wonder what she's like now.*

As if reading her sister's mind, Jillian went on. "She's really pretty but she never smiles."

"No?"

"She always looks sad to me. Her dad died when she was little. Mom's first husband was her daddy. He was Dev's dad too."

Ashley paddled herself closer and started to explain that she knew the entire family tree already but decided to let the girl go on.

"My teacher says we are the most complicated family she's ever heard of."

"They call it a 'yours, mine, and ours' type family," Ashley said, closing her eyes and thinking about her siblings.

"So, Megan and Devon had the same father but different mothers. Me and Dev have the same mother, but different fathers. You and me have the same father, but different mothers. But you and Dev have no same parents."

When Ashley did not respond, Jillian raised her voice. "Did you see your mom yet?"

"Nope. Don't plan to."

"Melissa might come to the party, too."

Once again Ashley's eyes fluttered open. "You're joking."

"Well, she might. I heard Mom on the phone with her." Jillian raised here eyebrows and kicked her feet, splashing her sister.

"I hope not," Ashley muttered. "We don't get along. And stop splashing me."

"I'm glad *we* get along," Jillian pronounced, standing and then prancing toward the back patio doors. "And I'm glad you came home!"

Me too. But something had changed in the last thirty seconds. The prospect of seeing her step-sister, and worse, *much* worse, her "real" sister Melissa, had put a kink in her day. With a sigh, she surrendered to the fact that she could not avoid either Megan or Melissa. They were both part of her life, her family, and brooding would not alter her course.

Waterlogged and hungry, Ashley slogged up the pool steps and went for her towel. Jillian had left to work on homework, and all the good sun was gone. She debated on whether to change clothes but opted to grab a snack before going upstairs.

Jessica was on the phone in the kitchen. She beckoned to Ashley. "She's coming in now. Here she is." Jessica held out the phone to Ashley. "It's Meggie. She wants to say hi."

Ashley took a deep breath before taking the phone. "Hey, half-step-sister-in-law. How's everything?"

·♥ · ♥ · ♥ · ♥ · ♥·

Megan found it hard to exhale. "Great. Just grand. I was ... I'm glad to hear you're back. Shocked, actually. Didn't imagine you would, that is."

The sound on the line made her wonder if Ashley was exasperated or amused.

"You thought I was gone for good, did you?"

"No, no, that's not, not what I meant. I just didn't think you'd pick now to come back. I imagined, I guess, that you'd get settled somewhere, maybe get married or at least committed to some other locale." Megan ran fingers across her forehead and sank onto her couch. She could never talk to Zoe before, why should she be any better with the new and improved Ashley?

"Nope. Back. In the flesh. And glad to be."

"So ... I'll see you at the party."

"Great. It'll be fun."

Megan nodded to herself. "Of course. It'll be a hoot to see everyone." She paused, weighing her chances of sounding as aloof as she didn't feel. "Is ... Will Alex be there?"

"You got me on that one. If he can climb down from that wooden horse long enough to enjoy life a little, I imagine he'll be there."

Megan tried to hide her sigh. Might as well go all the way. "You bringing a date?"

Now Ashley laughed outright. "What's that? A date? Not unless I happen to stumble over one before then." She paused, then more seriously, "I'm not looking to see anyone right now. I just need to ... well, as cliché as it sounds, I need to find out what I am now. I'm ... I'm sort of walking around in a fog, you know what I mean? The last thing I want is a guy hanging on me."

"Yeah, right. I guess I can understand that. You've been gone a long time, things change, people change ..."

"I barely even recognized my own sibs. Well, I gotta fly. I'm going to dinner with our dear little brother. He wants to watch planes land at Van Nuys. Hey, that's like a pun, isn't it? Fly ... airport ... ha!"

Megan swallowed hard. She didn't like what Devon was doing, didn't like him going to the airport where Mac had kept the plane in which he was killed. Why did he insist on keeping all the pain in the front seat?

"Well, have a good time. See you at the party."

NINE

Party On

Megan didn't frequent the card shop next door to the gallery, but today it provided a welcome convenience. She was dragging by the time she loaded her unsold photos into the back of her little hybrid wagon, but she locked the car and headed into the shop in search of a birthday greeting.

It was always a struggle, picking out cards and sentiments for her extended family. Normally, she would have sent an e-card, but Ashley was not a girl who spent much time in front of a computer monitor these days. And anyway, she was going to the party with a gift.

Idly, she perused the funny cards, the serious ones, the vague and proper messages, passing on every one.

"What do I care," she murmured, plucking still another one from the rack. Finally, she opted for a blank card with a photo of the ocean on the front and dug in her handbag for some cash.

"That's a beautiful picture," the clerk said.

I have hundreds better than that at home. But she never made cards for people who were not ... her people. And Ashley was certainly not one of hers.

Yet this time, she had made an exception. The exquisitely wrapped gift in the backseat of her car was, indeed, a photograph she'd printed and matted herself. A vintage print, one that was sure to evoke emotion. Especially for the birthday girl's father.

Pocketing her change, she snatched the bag from the counter and left the store, glancing at her watch as she walked. The party was only two hours away, and she still had to shower and dress. The gallery had closed at one o'clock today, and Eric had asked her to lock up. As she bent to unlock her car, she noticed a man standing in front of the shop peering at the photos displayed behind the tinted front window. She watched for a moment, then caught her breath as the man turned around and she got a look at his face. It was the man who'd bought her Maserati.

"Can I help you?" she called.

"I hope so," he said, walking up to her car with his hands stuffed into the pockets of a well-worn pair of jeans. "I was wondering if you do work-for-hire."

"Me?" Megan closed her car door and stepped out of the street. "What kind of work?"

The man smiled, looked away. He looked different in the daylight, out of his black silk and into a white collared shirt and brown leather jacket. Younger. She hadn't noticed the slight British inflection before.

He turned back to address her. "Photography. That's what you do, isn't it? Take pictures? Of cars and such?"

"Oh, sure. Yeah. That's what I do all right."

"I was wondering if you could take some pictures of my other cars."

"Your ... other cars?"

He turned again and Megan followed his gaze to the black Maserati parked across the street. She could feel the heat as the blush flooded her face.

Unconsciously brushing the wispy dark bangs from her forehead, Megan avoided his eyes. "I see. So. Your car. Right."

He chuckled then, shaking his head. "I'm sorry. I should have mentioned it that night. I was just so struck by the sight of the photo; it was so cool. And I have a couple of others, I thought it would make a nice montage in my office."

Megan ventured a look into his eyes. "That's why you bought it. It's your car."

"No, I bought it because I like the picture. I love the photo. That's why I bought it. And why I'm standing here on the sidewalk begging you to do more."

"Begging doesn't look good on you," she said at last, finally smiling herself. "I wish I could put you in touch with my agent, but as I don't have one, I guess you'll just have to negotiate with me."

"Might we discuss this inside? Or over coffee?"

"The gallery is closed and I'm late for a party."

His eyes twinkled. "I'm good at parties."

Taken aback but not put off, Megan lifted her chin. "I'll bet you are. But this party is ... well let's just say there will be a variety of characters there worthy of daytime TV. I would be remiss in exposing a total stranger to the potential lunacy that may prevail."

"Christian Collins. There. Now we are not strangers, Miss MacKendall. And I specialize in families of lunatics. How do you do?" He held out his hand, and Megan paused. He was squinting slightly, dissecting her body language. Finally accepting his handshake, she sighed.

"How many cars do you have?"

"Including the limos ... I'd say ... seven. Only five that run, however. Only three that are worth photographing. Where's the party?"

"Malibu. But –"

"Okay, it's crazy." He paused, his face losing some of its frivolity. "You look like a nice girl. You impress me as an artist. I'm pushing. I'm sorry."

"No, it's ... it's okay."

Thoughts pogo-sticked around Megan's brain. He was cute, witty, apparently wasn't a bum. But he was a stranger. Was this even safe?

He spoke before she could voice her regrets, slapping himself on the forehead. "Of course. You already have a date for this ... this party thing. I'm such a clod. I'll call you about the job. Or better still, you call me when you decide if you want to do it. I won't bother you. Here's my card."

The card had a tiny sports car as a logo. The business name read, "Destiny Drives." The address was in Malibu.

"What do you do, exactly?"

"I drive," Christian answered, squaring his stance with a grin. "I deliver cars, provide limo services, and arrange trades. I handle international trades as well."

Maybe he is for real. Ashley said something about stumbling over a date. Maybe I have.

"I live in Calabasas. Not far from here. The party's at 4 p.m. Can you pick me up?"

Whose voice was that? Surely not mine.

"How am I dressed?"

"Unless you want to swim, you are perfect."

"I have my gym stuff in the car. Give me your address; I'll pick you up at 3:30."

Megan's heart missed a beat, and her knees began to quiver as she dragged her own business card from her bag and hastily wrote her address on the back.

Christian examined both sides of the card.

"Cool. *Megan*. What can I bring?"

"Well, if my entire family shows up, a baseball bat and a can of mace would be good."

"A nice bottle of wine, perhaps? Does your family imbibe?"

"Only on days of the week that end in 'Y'," she responded, now getting into her car.

She never raced her car, rarely broke the speed limit by even a mile-per-hour. This day was different. Traffic was nasty, and it seemed to take hours to get back to her condo. She tore up the stairs and could barely get her key into the lock before slamming her body inside and against the door. She was panting.

"No time," she whispered, bounding to the bedroom on her way to the shower.

Her hair would take too long to dry, so she French braided it. Expertly applied her make-up, being sure to use the waterproof liner and mascara. Her swimsuit wasn't that old, having been purchased at an end-of-summer sale in August. She tried it on before the full-length mirror in her bedroom.

"Okay. Okay. Okay. This is ... okay. No. Shit. I don't know. What have I done?" She turned to the side, the back, peering over her shoulder. "It's okay. I probably won't even swim."

She dropped a slender Hawaiian print dress over the suit, frowning at her reflection. It was too bright, too cheery for her usual somber demeanor.

But maybe not for today. Maybe today was okay for shedding that grim self.

Earrings. Necklace. Rings. Perfume.

Sandals. One was missing. *Damn!*

Gotta calm down. He'll be here any minute. I have to do something before I freak out.

In the kitchen, in the pantry beside the refrigerator, was a quarter bottle of Pinot. Grasping it by the neck, she rushed to her china cabinet for a glass and filled it, stared hard at it before drinking it down.

Megan MacKendall could not have known it, but at the exact moment the red wine hit her stomach, Alexander Pierce was swallowing his tenth mouthful of Cabernet Sauvignon. Parked poolside in his beige Dockers and white polo shirt, he stared at the churning pool water as his father swam laps.

"You ought to try it. Good for stress. Better than booze," Dane called between breaths, now climbing out the pool and reaching for a towel.

"Yup. Sure."

Dad looked damn good, Alex thought. *For an old guy.*

Mopping his face and neck, Dane approached him. "Not that a drink now and then is a bad thing," he said, grinning, as he reached for his own glass on the table where Alex sat. "Can you believe this weather? It's why we live here in March and not in Wyoming."

"It's why I live here 24/7. Can't take Wyoming."

"I hope your disposition wasn't this sour when you bought your sister's birthday gift."

"What gift?"

"I'll remember that when your birthday rolls around. Too bad your little gal couldn't make it."

"She's not a little gal. She's a grown woman. A dancer. And she's not here because she split."

"Dancer. Hmm. I knew a dancer once." Dane smiled briefly, the distraction of a memory on his face. "Seems like another lifetime ago. Well. I'm going to shower and dress. See ya later."

"Yup. Sure."

Ashley helped Jessica arrange hors d'oeuvres on the patio tables. "Any surprises I should know about?" she asked, noting Jessica's preoccupation.

"No one's jumping out of the cake if that's what you mean. No, the only surprises might come from the various attendees. Some are not known for their ... tolerance of others, shall we say?"

"You do have a way with words."

"I'm well-read," Jessica answered, and both women laughed. "And still reading."

It was a family joke, the stacks of unread scripts occupying space on Jessica's desk. There was always the possibility that her next film, her huge, chart-busting epic Oscar winner was in one of those stacks. If she only knew which one it was, she could toss the others.

"I love your dress," Ashley said, smoothing out a tablecloth over the table.

"You look really good yourself. I can't believe how trim you are. Did you starve yourself?"

"I was hungry at first, for a while. But there was so much to do, and the food was drab, to me. I simply lost interest in eating."

"I just wondered if there was some new diet out there. I might have to lose five pounds for a role I'm considering."

"No kidding. You? You are skinny!"

"No, not skinny. But the role is for a very thin woman, she's poverty-stricken, not well, struggling, but gets her big chance, etc. A rags-to-riches story but with a few twists."

"Sounds good. When do you start?"

"If I take it, a couple of months. I haven't told your dad yet, exactly. He gets a little crazy when I start a new film."

"Didn't he just wrap one?"

"Yes, but ... you know how he is. And this picture shoots in Portugal. Dad's going to be hung up here on post-production work and wouldn't be able to go with me."

"Oh. Well, perhaps I can distract him some."

"Good. And I'll be coming back and forth, too. I can't leave Jillie that long."

"Back and forth to where?" Dane asked, coming from behind Jessica to embrace her around the middle.

· ♥ · ♥ · ♥ · ♥ · ♥ ·

Melissa took a quick drag off her Virginia Slims Light, then snuffed it out with her new, high-heeled sandal on the asphalt. With fumbling fingers, she unwrapped a peppermint cough drop and tossed it into her mouth. From the trunk she lifted a large, brightly wrapped gift, slamming the lid and nearly dropping the gift in the process.

Muttered curses escaped her lips as she angrily chastised herself for even coming. It was stupid, would be a stupid party with droves of stupid imbeciles who pranced around trying to look better than everyone else.

But she would show them. She would drop the gift and leave early. No reason to give them someone else to kick around.

As the steep roadway challenged her untrained ankles, Melissa wobbled her way toward the Pierces' private driveway, hefting the over-sized package in her arms. She needed, badly, another pull on the cigarette, and began crunching the cough drop with her teeth. The music and laughter, the waterfall flowing into the pool, were all sounds she recognized but were not a part of her life. Pausing on the driveway, she considered going back home.

Her thoughts were belated, however, as a gleaming, black Maserati turned into the drive behind her. Still grinding her teeth, she noted that whoever the hell it was must be seriously bold to park in front of her father's garage.

·♥·♥·♥·♥·♥·

Christian was out of the car and opening the door for Megan before she could even gather her purse from the floor. Hand extended, he offered her welcome assistance; the car's low profile made climbing out in a short dress awkward. She thanked him then stared at the woman on the driveway.

"Melissa? Is that you?"

Melissa pasted on a broad smile. "Megan. Megan MacKendall. It's been years."

After brief introductions, they walked in together. Megan had given Christian a bare-bones family tree description on the way to the house, hoping to keep her nerves at bay and give him a heads-up to what he was walking into. Christian seemed unaffected by her warning and laughed his way into the backyard with a bottle of pricey Chardonnay in his hand. They found Dane holding court near the fire pit that overlooked the ocean view.

Dane spied her approach and locked his eyes onto hers. "Excuse me, gentlemen. I need to greet someone." He turned just as she reached him.

"Megan. What a wonderful surprise."

"Dane," she murmured, lifting herself to exchange the obligatory Hollywood cheek kiss. "How nice to see you."

"Thank you. I'm so glad you're here." He turned to Christian. "I'm sorry, have we met? Dane Pierce."

"No, *I'm* sorry," Megan quickly asserted. "Dane, this is Christian Collins. Chris, Dane. Dane was ... my father's best friend."

A brief shadow crossed Dane's face, but he took Christian's hand for a hearty handshake. "Pleased."

"Honored, sir," Christian replied. "I'm quite the fan. Your films are, well, awesome. And this is ... wow. What can I say? The view is stunning."

"From across the pond, are you?" Dane asked.

"No. From here, actually. Lived in England for a few years, though. It tends to stick a bit, yeah."

"I see. Well. Enjoy the party." Dane turned back to Megan. "You look wonderful, my dear."

"Thanks. I'm looking forward to seeing Zoe and ... Alex."

"Only if you're looking for abuse. He's over there getting plowed."

Megan's eyes perused the partiers on the far side of the pool, finally pausing on the young man slouched in a patio chair at one of the tables. She filled her lungs, and then turned back to Christian. "Come. I'll introduce you to the others."

"Come *on*. Let's go in," Devon insisted, then took a long draught of beer.

"Dev. No. No one else is swimming." Ashley whirled on Devon, her arms akimbo. "And go easy on that stuff."

"Aw, c'mon Ash. We can be the first ones in. We heated it up to 80 degrees. Come on!"

"No. I'm not ready to swim right –"

Before she could get the words out, Devon had tossed his beer bottle into the planter and swept Ashley off her feet, carrying her screaming and kicking to the pool and dropping her in. Then, quickly stripping off his Hawaiian shirt, he dived in after her.

The splash caused laughter and commotion around the pool, and Dane turned to his wife with a mock frown. "I wish you'd control that son of yours," he admonished.

"Your daughter," Jessica began, gently swirling her wine glass before lifting it toward her lips, "is baiting him."

Dane's frown softened into a more serious expression. "You don't mean that, do you? Because she would never do that."

Jessica's response was interrupted as Ashley pulled herself out of the pool, her new flowered wrap dress soaked and sticking to her skin, leaving little to the imagination.

"You little sonuvabitch! I'll get you for that."

"Oh, I hope so," Devon responded as he climbed the poolside ladder. Ashley was waiting for him, using a well-placed kick to the chest to send him back into the deep end.

"Drunken little prick," she muttered, storming toward the house.

Dane cringed visibly and Jessica raised her eyebrows.

"No doubt whose daughter *she* is," Jessica said quietly, turning to lend a hand to her son, who was again trying to exit the pool.

"I don' feel so good," Devon croaked, leaning against his mother heavily.

"You might have tangled with the wrong girl, babe," Jessica told him, helping him toward a chaise lounge. "Why don't you sit here a bit? I'll get you a soda."

· ♥ · ♥ · ♥ · ♥ · ♥ ·

Christian poured Megan a second glass of Chardonnay. "Interesting couple, there."

Megan shook her head. "That's my little brother. Lusting after his older stepsister. Hey, can you spell dysfunctional?"

"I coined the word. And who's that somber-looking gentleman? The one looking as if he might slide right out of that chair at any moment?"

Megan licked her lips. "Alex," she murmured.

"Excuse me?"

"Alexander Pierce. Dane's son. Looks a bit down on his luck, wouldn't you say?"

"How about we go spread some cheer, eh?"

Do I really want to do this? She let Christian lead her to Alex, who looked up with the most insincere smile she'd seen yet. "Why, Megan MacKendall. How the hell are ya? Surprised to see you here," Alex slurred.

"Alex, this is Chris. Chris, Alex and I practically grew up together."

"A lucky man, then," Christian said, holding out his hand, which Alex did not take.

"No, you are the lucky man, my friend. Meggie here is one fine lady. Deserves the best." His eyes moved over to Megan. "I'm surprised you came. I know Pop is not on your A-list."

"That's not true, I ... of course I have nothing against Dane."

"You should know, I don't blame you. He's a real jerk most of the time. And yeah, he went after Jess when Mac –"

"Alex, please. Not now."

"No, not now. You're right. Always right."

Megan turned to Christian. "Don't say I didn't warn you."

"Indeed. But no worries! A pleasure to meet you, Alex."

Alex nodded, and Megan decided he resembled a dashboard bobblehead. She pulled Christian away.

As they walked, Christian leaned close and added his remarks. "Families are messy. My own included. It took me a month to get rid of a lovely but cloying houseguest, whom, I might add, just left this morning. So, is this all you've got? That's the worst of it?"

Megan had to smile. "Yes, you've met them all."

"I didn't meet the wet girl."

"Ashley? Oh, yeah. Might be smart to let her cool down at bit before we go there."

"Must say, I admire her spirit."

"Dev deserved it."

"He's probably a nice kid. Just has some hormonal imbalances, right?"

"But she's his sister!"

"Last I heard, stepsisters were not blood related. And she's an incredibly attractive stepsister, nothing like those found in fairytale lore."

Megan chose a seat at an empty table and Christian sat also. "Still, it's just wrong." She took a moment to reflect, and then looked to her guest. "So, what's your family like? Are they in England?"

"No. My family travels a lot. I don't see my relatives much at all. I went to England to study medicine, of all things. Wasn't for me, though. I was gifted some money, used it to buy my first limo, then things grew from there."

"Do you cater to celebrities?"

"All kinds of people. I'm so busy, I can't see straight most of the time. I need another driver, so that I can have time to enjoy my wealth and play a little."

"Why don't you hire one?"

"Too busy." He took a sip of wine. "What about you? Is photography your whole deal?"

"Yes, but not like you'd think. I do weddings, babies, retirement, and family portraits. Not particularly fun, but it pays the bills. And I work in the gallery the rest of the time."

A waiter came by to light the outdoor gas heater above them, and another paused with a tray of canapés. Near the house, a band was setting up.

"Your ... late father's friend ... knows how to throw a party."

"Yeah, he's good at that."

"I like him."

"Good. It's only just starting."

Ashley combed out her wet tresses and then scrunched them into long curls. She pulled on a pair of white jeans and a sleeveless shirt that tied at the midriff, then slipped into her white sandals.

"Damned kid," she muttered, still fuming over her unexpected dip in the pool. Inside, she felt a dull remorse. She should have seen it coming. Devon had a major crush, and she had led him on without knowing it. Now, she had to tell him. Break his young heart. And still live with him.

"I'm such an idiot." She'd seen Megan and her apparent date just before her dunk. *They must think me such a fool.*

She put on a smile and returned to the backyard, stopping beside the table where Megan sat. "Megan. I've been trying to get to you all evening!"

"Zoe. I'm sorry, *Ashley*! Oh my God. I'm sorry. I was going to be so careful." Megan shook her head.

"No problem. It's okay. I'm glad you came. It's been so long since we've talked."

"Oh, this is Christian. Chris, *ASHley*. My – well, we're really not anything, are we?"

Christian stood and took Ashley's hand. "Ashley. The birthday girl." He tilted his head and narrowed his eyes slightly, then smiled. "It's a pleasure."

"Christian. Nice to meet you, too."

"Won't you join us?" Megan put no real muscle behind the invitation.

"I would love to, but I have some business with our mutual brother. If you'll excuse me?"

"Don't be too hard on him, he's still young," Megan blurted.

"Don't worry. I actually owe him an apology."

Christian watched with interest as Ashley walked away. His eyes still on her retreating back, he spoke with distraction. "You called her what? Zoe?"

"It was her old name, before she changed it. She left for several years. Dane doesn't want people to know it, but she ran off with gypsies. When she came back last month, she'd lost a lot of weight and changed her name. That's why everyone is taking such an interest in her. Including our brother."

"Gypsies, you say? That *is* interesting."

"Well, not to me. They were just a bunch of romanticizing hippies. She and I were never good friends. She was, is, younger than me; I remember her as being rather whiny and always eating. After my father died, I stopped seeing Dane's kids. Jessica invited me, but I didn't want to see anyone from here. It was difficult."

Christian covered her hand with his. "It's hard to lose your parent. Even harder to go on. I think you've done remarkably well considering that devastating loss."

Megan could feel her eyes misting over. Could he even begin to understand what she'd gone through? Her own mother didn't get it, and Devon had been so young when Mac died, he barely remembered the warmth, the love and caring that was Mac MacKendall.

Ashley found Devon propped up on the chaise lounge. She sat down on the adjacent lounge.

"I'm sorry I kicked you," she began, fidgeting with her fingernails. "You got to me. I don't take well to people forcing me to do things."

Devon smiled.

"And it's more than that, Dev. You and I, we're, like related. I'm like ... your sister. You do get that, right?"

Devon continued to smile, a sweet, blameless smile that threatened to short-circuit her plan.

"Stop it. Listen to me. That's what there is between us. Family. That's it. No more. Please understand."

The smile wavered. "Ash, it doesn't have to be that way. If my mom had never married your dad, we could have met on the street. We don't have to be brother and sister."

Ashley sighed. "No. You're not getting it. Dev, I don't need –"

"You don't even know what you need. You're lost. I can help you. I'm good for you, Ash. When we're together, you laugh, you have a good time. You need that."

"No. You don't know what I need. You don't know me, Devon. Not really. Now, please. Let's just go back to being family. I can't let this go on any longer."

Devon looked surprised and wet his lips. Without another word, he got off the chaise and started for the house.

Ashley dropped her gaze and shivered. She was not near one of the heaters, and the temperature grew colder by the minute. Several guests were now in the pool, relishing the warm water against the chill of the evening. Ashley felt suddenly very tired.

·♥·♥·♥·♥·♥·

Christian stood just as Devon reached the table. Megan had gone inside. "Hello, mate. I'm Christian Collins. You must be Megan's brother?"

"Yep. That would be I."

"Sit for a spell, will you? I'm rather like a fish out of school here amid all these high rollers, know what I mean?"

Despite his melancholy, Devon smiled and sat. "You're dating my sister? She never mentioned you."

"Not exactly dating, we just met. She invited me along at my insistence."

"Oh, cool."

"She's a very nice girl."

"The best."

"So I hear."

"If you just met her, how did you hear that?"

Christian smiled. "That rather liquid gentleman over there mentioned it."

"Oh, you mean Alex. My stepbrother. We don't exactly get along."

"He likes your sister."

"Yeah, he does. It's a long-term thing, those two. She's had the hots for him, off and on, he's a knucklehead and doesn't know it. She's too cool to tell him. Oops, I shouldn't have said that."

"No, it's quite alright. I won't say a word."

Devon looked miserable. "She'd kill me for telling you all that. Meg's got a thing for misery, too. Ever since our dad was murdered."

"Murdered? How? If you don't mind my asking."

"Hell, I don't mind. About now, I don't care about much. Some dude shot at his plane, and it crashed. He was a good pilot. It was a small plane. It about killed my mom."

"But she recovered enough to marry Pierce."

"Yup. Meggie hates that, too." Devon pondered the sky for a moment. "Dane's a good guy, though. A real good guy."

"Of course."

Zoe had never been one to enjoy opening gifts. Probably because as a child, if it wasn't sweet or colorful, she was hard-pressed to show enthusiasm. Aside from being boring, clothing almost never fit her. Tonight would be different. Ashley pasted on a smile and gracefully accepted the elaborately wrapped presents arranged around her patio chair. "Nice! This is so awesome. Thanks so much," she said, the words rearranged and repeated with each opened gift. The last, a large, flat item with some weight, was handed to her by Devon.

"Not from me," he murmured, and Ashley perused the faces of the others around her.

"Let's see." She pulled off a taped-on envelope and opened it. "Oh! Megan." Glancing up briefly, Ashley began to carefully peel the taped edges of the gift.

"Oh, go on, dammit. Just rip it," Melissa called out.

Ashley gave her sister a withering look but took her advice. Revealed behind the dark blue patterned paper was a large, framed photograph. She held it away to take in the entire picture.

"Oh, my," she whispered. "It's wonderful."

Someone yelled for her to turn it around, and after a moment of reflection, Ashley stood and turned to display the stunning, black and white photograph of a smiling Dane Pierce with his arm around an also grinning Mac MacKendall. Her eyes went directly to her father's, and then to Jessica's. She wasn't sure which of them was more shaken.

"A picture!" Devon rushed forward and took Ashley's hand. "Meggie, get up here. We need a matching picture."

Megan backed away, but Christian gently grasped her wrist. "Do it; it's a good idea," he said into her ear and walked her toward where her brother
stood beckoning.

"Ash, put your arm around Meg, like this..." Devon arranged the girls into the same pose as their fathers in the portrait, then lifted his iPhone.

·♥·♥·♥·♥·♥·

True to her nature, Megan began to worry as soon as she got into Christian's car. The agony of the party behind her, she could now obsess over how to say goodnight. At the door? Invite him in? And if so, what then? Would he try to kiss her? Should she offer him a drink?

"Do you think she liked it?"

Megan snapped back to the present; Christian had asked her something.

"The portrait. Did Ashley like it?"

"Sure, she did. How could she not?"

"But her father ... Pierce looked a little dazed."

"Oh, yeah. Well, it was a gamble, wasn't it? It was, perhaps, a little unfair."

Christian glanced her way. "Why is that? It was a beautiful, sentimental piece of art. Your dad was a handsome man. They were both young and vital."

"Jessica took the photo of them. Dane had recently returned from his second trip to the Far East, and she had him over to dinner. I was there that night. Daddy was showing him our new car, and they were standing there in front of the house. Jess snapped the shot. I scanned it recently and I was taken by how ... happy they looked. Like best friends."

"Hmm. Clearly so."

He walked her to the door of her townhouse, and she dug through her handbag for her key.

"I'm sorry. It's here somewhere."

"No worries. You'll find it when you're ready to go inside."

Megan paused, looked him in the eyes. "You must think I'm a lunatic."

"You're the nicest, smartest, most beautiful lunatic I've met in ages. Would you like to meet some of the other lunatics in my life? I've a gathering to go to on Wednesday night. I would be so grateful for your company."

"Seriously?"

"I'd be honored."

"Well, sure, yeah. I'd like that." Megan looked back down; her keys were in plain sight, in the side pocket of her purse where she always kept them. She unlocked the door and turned to Christian, but before she could ask, he leaned close and kissed her cheek.

"I'll call you with details. Thanks again for letting me tag along tonight."

"No, thank you. For putting up with the crazies."

Christian grinned and took his leave.

TEN

Christian

It wasn't possible, was it?

Christian propped his feet on the balcony railing outside his bedroom and sipped on a glass of port.

Zoe. An overweight girl, who ran off with gypsies. How many could there be?

Unbidden, a soft chuckle escaped as he remembered the night in the campground. He'd been slightly drunk and royally pissed off at his father, who clearly had pneumonia and refused to seek help. Christian couldn't, *wouldn't* stand by again and watch stubbornness claim another of his parents. Worse, they'd argued about Robbie. Christian's smiled faded as he recalled the fateful night his brother had died.

"I can take care of this," his father said between coughs.

"Like you took care of Mom? I don't think so. You talk a big story and then stand by and watch. You open the door to death. Robbie needs help. He needs medical attention and protection from those thugs. You think you can keep him safe? Think again."

"You don't know what you're talking about. You show up here after a long time away, a time when you didn't bother to get in touch –"

"And how was I supposed to do that? Pony Express? It's not like you have a cell phone or email, Dad."

"The post office box in Natchez. You could have written."

"And what good would that have done when you leave that mail for months unopened?"

Martin Dupré looked away. "Don't worry about Robert. I will handle this. You just ... go about your business. I assume you aren't here for long."

"I'm leaving tonight. I just stopped in to make sure you were all still alive. I have one favor to do for someone and then I'm out of here. You do know how to reach me, however, so if you want my help, I hope you'll get in touch."

Martin waved his hand, dismissing his son's admonitions. "You're much too important to be bothered by us. Living in England, traveling to Paris ... our little world here is of no concern." Martin's words dissolved into a fresh coughing fit, and he again waved Christian away. "Go. Do your favor or whatever. I'll see you in another three or five years."

"If you're still alive."

Christian stormed from the tent and strode briskly to his brother's quarters. Robbie was stoned, as usual. "Get up. You can't do this, bro. This has to stop."

Robbie stared up, bleary-eyed. "Chris. Don't worry about me. Please."

"The guys told me you're in hock to a bunch of dealers. That they might be gunning for you. Is that true? How much do you owe?"

"More than you want to know. More than will ever be possible to raise. I'm cool with it. What happens will happen."

"No! You can't do this. I won't let you. Come with me tonight. I'll get you to another place, a safer place."

"Yeah? And will you take Dad, and Mari, and the others? Because they are on my references list, dude. They are my collateral. These guys don't play

games."

"Oh, for fuck's sake. I can't believe you did this, Robbie. For what? For a stupid high?"

"Not much else to do around here. You know that. You were lucky, you and Joey escaped. Me, I'm a lifer here. No schooling, no money, no job, no point. No place to go but down."

"That's not true. You could have gotten out. I tried to get you to go with me, but you refused."

"Someone had to stay for them."

Christian's gut twisted. The fact that his mother had died and left him in charge broke his heart. But now, he had a chance to save his brother. "Look, I can raise some cash. Maybe enough to hold them off until we can get the rest. How much?"

"Fifty K."

Christian's hand went to his forehead, and he closed his eyes. He'd expected less than ten thousand. "I can get my hands on about seven."

His brother shook his head. "Won't be enough. I've put them off too many times already. Listen, it's okay. I'm good with it. And if you interfere, they'll take Mari. They've made that clear."

Christian's anger flared. "How could you do that? Endanger your sister like that? You asinine fool!"

Robbie struggled to his feet. "I'm sorry. I didn't mean to –"

"You're sorry! I should kill you myself. You weak, disgusting crackhead!" Christian rushed forward and smacked his brother hard across the cheek. Robbie fell back against the cot with a cry. "You don't deserve to live."

Christian exploded from Robbie's cabana and went to sit beside the campfire, where some of his friends were passing around a bottle of cheap wine. He took a big gulp.

"What's up with you Dupré? You look pissed."

"It's Collins. I left Dupré back on the Bayou. And yeah, I'm more than pissed off." He took another swig and swirled the wine in his mouth before

swallowing, as if he could wash his own caustic words away. "I just did something terrible that I probably can't fix."

"Robbie?" a friend asked.

Christian nodded. "I didn't want to hurt him. Fecking idiot." He let the wine mellow him. He'd figure out a way to fix this. To get Robbie away from the mob and still protect his family. Hell, he'd move the entire tribe if he had to. It would all be okay. By tomorrow, he'd have the solution. For now, he'd made a promise to his sister. A homely girl was suffering and needed a little attention. An easy task. Christian prided himself on his romantic prowess, learned mostly on the streets of Paris. It was a simple task, helping someone to feel loved and valued. That, at least, he could handle tonight.

Christian took another swallow of wine, shook his head.

"Zoe, Zoe, Zoe." Despite his reservations, he'd discovered that Mari was correct. She was a sweet girl, one who was both beautiful and sensual, and he'd been able to ignore the extra pounds. Granted, he'd not seen her in the light, but he sensed her qualities, nonetheless. Could he reconcile that girl with the trim, hot babe he'd seen tonight at the Pierce estate?

At work, he fielded calls. An exec in Irvine needed a Porsche 911 brought to the John Wayne Airport on Thursday. A Sweet Sixteen party wanted a limo to take girls to City Walk in two weeks. Most important was the eminent delivery of two new limos, and a message from one of his drivers that he'd quit.

Christian blew out a breath. *It never ends.* Now he needed two new drivers if he wanted to keep his business growing, which he definitely did. He picked up the phone.

"Gustov? I've got an extra for you. Wednesday night. You'll be driving Lincoln 33 to a party in Brentwood. Who? Me. And my date. Thanks."

Christian perused the top of his desk and eventually plucked a business card from a stack on his desk calendar. Spinning around to face his computer, he typed in Megan's email address.

"Looking forward to Wednesday night. This deal is black tie, so –" His fingers paused, hovering over the keys while he thought. *How do I word this?* He hadn't dated in a long time. "– dress accordingly. Pick you up at seven."

Christian spent the rest of the day placing help wanted ads and organizing the company calendar. He made service appointments for two of the vehicles, ordered groceries and called about his missing dry-cleaning delivery. After reading through the latest communication from his health care organization, he was toast. Christian turned off the lights in his office and went to his bedroom to change. Working from his Brentwood condo was the best part of being self-employed, but it also demanded the discipline to get going and to stop going when it was time. Part of that regimen included dressing for business every day, whether he left home or not. Now, as the hands on the clock approached five, he pulled on a pair of trunks and grabbed a beer from the bar before heading out to the hot tub on the balcony.

Once settled into the steaming, jetted waters, Christian closed his eyes. He thought about the girls he'd recently met – and how strange did that sound, anyway? Meeting any girl these days was a peculiarity, but two? One with such a ... colorful past. A past that bisected his own.

He took a long, slow sip of the Heineken. Megan MacKendall might be a puzzle to some guys, but Christian already had her sussed. Her small heart was encased in a chilled Plexiglas case, and she wasn't ready to crack open that protective shell. Depressed and trapped in a spider web of sorrow, she couldn't break free of the ties to her painful past. Instead of letting her late father's love guide her, she allowed it to keep her captive. He'd seen it before – in himself.

Zoe – or Ashley, he reminded himself with a smile – was a different story. She was a true enigma. He'd thought it odd to begin with that any girl would ask to be, well, deflowered as they say. Yet this one had known what she wanted, asked for it, and had made it one hell of a night for them both. Fat? He hadn't noticed past the first few minutes; body shape was more of a visual thing anyway. In bed, what mattered was passion. Desire. Willingness to abandon inhibitions and fears. This girl had learned, shared, and reciprocated.

But what, now? Sleek, tough, sexy, and possibly available. He could see Devon's attraction to his stepsister, despite their familial ties and age difference. But there didn't seem to be any love-lost between the other siblings; older sister Melissa was a hard case, seething with jealousy and envy. Megan herself couldn't see over the stony walls she'd built. The besotted, self-absorbed Alex harbored anger and a surprising lack of confidence. Perhaps he was more likable when sober.

Devon, Christian liked. What he lacked in maturity he made up for with youthful charm and whimsy. Spoiled, yes; but Devon had potential. He needed direction and a good role model. Like himself. Christian chuckled, wondering if Devon would make a good limo driver. He made a mental note to pursue the idea.

A long night followed. Plagued by uncharacteristic nightmares, Christian tossed in his bed, alternately nesting down and throwing back the covers. Too cold, too hot. Restless legs. When sleep did come, he found himself wandering in a dark place, searching for someone he knew he'd never find.

"Robbie? Where are you? I've gotta go, dude, I want to say goodbye."

Robbie appeared in the shadows, in the corner of his vision. "Why did you do it, Chris? They're saying you did this to me. Do you see my head?"

Christian reached out but could not quite grasp his brother. "No, I didn't do it! It was someone else. Surely you saw who hit you?" He looked down, suddenly aware of the warm, sticky wetness covering his hands. And now, his shirt, dripping with blood. Robbie's blood. "I would never hurt you! I love you, Robbie. I love you. I love you ... "

But Robbie had stepped back, into the shadows, and now Christian could hear a woman sobbing, her heart broken beyond repair. While he couldn't see her, Christian knew it was his mother that held Robbie in her arms.

"I didn't kill Robbie, Mom! It wasn't me! It was those mob guys!"

Christian fell to his knees, his head bowed as he began to cry.

Daylight fueled his late-morning headache. He'd forgotten to draw the draperies the night before, and his east-facing windows provided a clear, hot spotlight on his bed. Christian fumbled for his iPhone and squinted at its screen: 9:35 a.m.! Tumbling out of bed with a curse, he headed for the bathroom and hit the shower. He never slept in. Never missed an appointment, which he now almost had – with his insurance agent. He'd have to forego his morning walk and café misto.

"Damn!" The dry cleaning was still MIA. Slamming hangers, he selected a sky-blue dress shirt and a blue and red patterned tie. His less-favorite suit was clean, at least, and he made it to the kitchen with three minutes to spare.

He hated instant coffee. "I've become quite the snob," he murmured, while stirring some non-fat milk into his cup. He'd come from less. So much less. Those campgrounds and stew pots and bonfires seemed like they belonged in someone else's lifetime, not his own neighborhood playground. They drank lukewarm tea and homemade lemonade when they could get it. The tea was always bitter and the lemonade weak. Kool-Aid was a treat; they'd once found a box of the sweet stuff that had fallen off a delivery truck. It was cherry.

Why now? Why dredge up those dark, difficult years spent with his poverty-ridden family on the road? Christian stared into his coffee cup, then put it down on the counter. It was the dream.

Turning quickly, he paused before the entryway mirror, straightened his tie and his shoulders. That past was ... just that. The past. Something he couldn't change, couldn't go back for a do-over. Robbie, his mother – regrets could not bring them back. He'd failed them, and in some twisted, inexplicable way, he'd failed his father, too. Christian huffed out a sigh and tried to make it all go away.

In his car on the way to Century City, Christian fought to keep his thoughts on the day – what was left of it to salvage – ahead. Still, the dream lay lurking in the back of his mind, ready to pounce at the first sign of his weakening resolve. So much blood ... and yet, he'd never had blood on his hands in his life. No, Robbie was alive when Christian left him in the tent. Yet the question still lingered, choking him at every turn. Had Robbie moved after Christian had struck him? When he hit the cot, did his head slam against the sharp metal corner of the trunk on which rested Robbie's wallet, few coins and framed photo of Mom? Christian hadn't hung around to notice.

Far more likely, the mobsters to whom his brother owed money were behind Robbie's death. No one had seen anything, but plenty had heard the brothers' loud argument through the thin canvas walls.

Christian turned onto Avenue of the Stars and looked for the parking structure sign. He steered his car into a slot and sat, staring at the voucher in his hand. The thoughts came because of the dream, but the dream came because of the girl. Zoe would have been his best alibi, but he'd refused to betray her trust. When rumors began to spread that Christian Dupré had killed his fraternal twin brother Robert, Christian kissed Maricela goodbye and left at morning light.

ELEVEN

Who Is Alex Pierce?

Alex drove to work on autopilot. He regretted the comment he'd made about hating his job; it wasn't all that bad. He'd graduated the Academy with honors and passed his physicals barely breaking a sweat. Only two years into it, he'd moved up to Level II and now, after three years on the force, he achieved Level III. The captain was talking about an opening in the Missing Person Unit as an investigator. There'd be a transition from his current role as a Patrol Officer, but Alex was reluctantly excited about the new position. The reluctance, he knew, came from the fact that he'd never intended to stay on at the L.A.P.D. this long.

He sat in the car after he'd parked and turned off the radio. His shift didn't begin for twenty-five more minutes. Twisting around, he reached for a folder from the backseat floor and dragged it onto his lap. The screenplay. Pages were disheveled, threatening to escape the folder, and he tried to neaten the mess. The title page was particularly dogeared. A red circle marked the position of last night's glass of wine. Pencil scratchings exposed the indecision around the title -- crossed out, erased, rewritten and erased again. Alex knew in his heart the script wasn't ready. With a heavy, painful sigh, he tossed the folder back onto the floor, and the pages of the story he'd sweated over for five years again flew about.

In the locker room, Akex nodded at the other guys dressing as he tore the plastic sheeting from his fresh uniform. Acquaintances, not friends. Good guys, of course. But working in law enforcement had never been his dream. It was a means to an end. A good paycheck that would keep him afloat until he sold his script. He'd only meant to be here a year, two at most. He hadn't planned on being exemplary, or valued, or lauded in any way.

"Pierce?"

"Good morning, Cap'n. How's it going?"

"Can't complain. You give any thought to our little discussion yesterday?"

"Uh, yes Sir, I have. It sounds good. When do I need to commit?"

Captain Stu Loserelli tilted his head. "As soon as possible. Take the weekend. Talk to your girl. Give me an answer on Monday."

"Sounds good, Sir. Anything special going on today?"

"Nah. Just the usual. See you later."

The usual meant driving the streets of the South Valley with Officer Lawrence Roerden in tow. Larry was a good kid. He'd go far – all the way to the top, someday. Alex didn't feel worthy of mentoring him.

As Alex cruised down Owensmouth Avenue, Larry's eyes scanned the businesses and parking lots along the way. "How was your family party?"

"Okay, I guess. What I remember of it."

"Get powdered?"

"Didn't mean to. I couldn't deal with all the drama. All the sibs were there. You know how it is."

Larry gave him a sideways look. Even with his eyes on the road ahead, Alex could feel his gaze. "Yeah, I guess. I mean, I like my brothers and sisters. I miss them."

"They all in Nebraska or something?"

"Ohio. Yeah. Haven't seen them in a couple of years."

"Oh. That's, uh, rough. My little sister just came home from being gone, like almost four years." Alex chuckled to himself, thinking about the girl with the new name and new body. "I hardly recognized her."

"Four years! That must have been hard. Where was she?"

"Don't know. Traveling around in the South."

"Man."

"Yeah."

Alex turned onto Ventura Boulevard and peered up the crowded street. "I hate this town sometimes," he muttered. "I just can't get why –" His words were clipped by the radio coming to life.

"... *10-67, corner of Ventura and Woodlake Avenue* ... "

"Didn't we go there Friday?"

"Yeah, that one also came over as a *person calling for help*," Larry agreed. "Probably another domestic squabble. Let's see if it's the same one."

"10-4. Rolling now. ETA ten minutes."

Alex's memory proved correct. Angry words emanated from the front screen door as he and Larry approached from the driveway.

"What seems to be the problem, folks?" Larry asked, his voice calmer than Alex could have managed.

"She broke my controller. Again. I swear, she must think I'm made of money. I been waitin' three days to play my game, and she goes and runs over it with the damned vacuum!" The thirty-something complainant was walking in circles with the broken video game device in his hands.

Alex couldn't help a smirk, but Larry remained ever responsible. "Did you make the call, sir? The 911 call?"

"What 911 call? Look, I only wanted to play Fortnite. I gotta be a work in two hours. And that bitch—" The man gestured toward a back room in the dark house. Larry turned to Alex and raised his eyebrows.

Alex stepped forward. "Look, pal, I get it. She's probably pissed that you play games when she wants you to pay attention to her. We've all been through it. Right Lar?"

"Sure." Larry shrugged, his hands on his hips.

"But I gotta tell you, man, you can't be calling us for every little gripe. Mr. Salazar, is it?"

"It's the second time. The second time!" Salazar became more manic and his circles became tighter. "I just can't let her get away with it."

Alex watched as the man paced, and then noticed something that turned his blood cold. "Manny? It's Manny, right? Manny, I need you to drop the controller and get down on the floor. Down, Manny, now. Officer Roerden, we have a possible 240 in the bedroom."

Larry sprang into action and went to investigate while Alex talked Salazar into at least getting to his knees. "How'd you get that blood on your hand, Manny?"

"She makes me so angry sometimes!"

"She was pretty banged up," Larry commented when they were back in the patrol car.

"She broke his controller," Alex muttered. "What did she expect?"

Larry looked over at him. "I know you don't mean that."

"Of course, not. Just being an ass. Truth is, the husband's been out of work for a few months, he's finally working but it's a part-time shit job. The wife is pissed because he made her give up her job before he lost his. She wants a baby. He wants a baby, but he knows they won't make it. And worst of all, her mother moved in with them."

"How do you know so much about them?"

"Believe it or not, I listen. I listen because I'm interested in stories."

"Ah, I get it. You're gonna put them in one of your movies. Someday."

Alex smiled. "Maybe. Maybe I will."

He thought about the Salazar family on his way home. How would that be? To have no money, your ego in the toilet? Your wife bitching at you, and her mother's disapproving eye on you while she is eating your food and sleeping in the room you planned for your kid. A kid that you shouldn't have but will come along anyway and your wife will be buying clothes for him at the dollar store.

Alex blew out a discouraged sigh. Thankfully, he'd never had to worry about money. He'd never had to labor away in a gas station or a taco joint or had to decide between groceries or rent. Even the girls he'd dated were mostly already cashed up.

It wasn't like he didn't work hard. Being a cop wasn't a walk in the park. Sure, there were good days, almost lazy days when nothing much happened; but they barely balanced out the tough days, when a cop in another city shot a person of color and riots formed nationwide, some of them within his own precinct. Those were days he'd gladly trade if he could.

While sitting at a light, he envisioned a future where he wouldn't carry a baton, a gun or a badge, and the only big gatherings of people he had to deal with were the crowds outside Grauman's Chinese Theatre on the night his big film debuted.

TWELVE

Millennials Can Work

Melissa refolded the letter and tucked it back into the crumpled envelope with the barely legible address. She stared out her front bedroom window at her mother, who struggled to drag the heavy rolling trash receptacle back from the curb. Rita paused to swipe at her cheek; Melissa couldn't tell if it was to relocate a wisp of hair or to smear away a tear. Regardless of the reason, the action enhanced Melissa's own overt sadness, a result of the message from Brady. He wanted, badly, to come home. Somehow, the image of her mother laboring with the waste-wheeler underlined exactly why he couldn't. Not yet.

Her sister's party had pulled out all the stitches from a wound not yet healed. The realization that the family existed, possibly thrived, without her, opened her eyes to some truths she'd purposely ignored. Dane had embraced her warmly. Jessica had taken her arm, introduced her to friends as "our daughter." Zoe herself had – albeit with effort – asked after their mother and Brady and had admired her shoes. The fold expanded right before her, with Aunt Rox asking if Melissa had any time to do a little marketing work for her. *Me? Work?*

She'd never held a job. Never even tried, so certain that she had no talent, no skill, no experience. No one wants to hire an unwed teenage mother, a high school dropout besides, right? Dane provided her a stipend. No huge amount, but enough to stay healthy and in good clothes. Her mother worked, part-time, for an interior designer, but it was more for something to do. A reason to get away from the problems at home that would never go away. Yet her mother had not abandoned her. Ever. When the Pierce household had imploded, when Daddy had hit the bigtime and Mommy had hit the bottle, when the man in the black robe had slammed his gavel and said the children should stay with Rita – her mother took them out for pizza. She had, of course, also downed a bottle of vodka.

Love, hate, love, hate. Melissa and Rita had formed more of a sisterhood than a mother-daughter relationship. They were, after all, only eighteen years apart. They shared clothes, politics, diets, and a mutual distrust of men. They also shared secrets: her mother was the only person who knew about Ricardo, Brady's married father; Melissa was the sole listener to Rita's heartbreak when first Alex, then Zoe, had left them to live with Dane.

Rita sobered up and held her hand during Melissa's monstrous labor and delivery, and even stayed dry for the first few months of Brady's life. When Brady had nearly drowned at age three in the bathtub while under Rita's care, she gave up drinking for good. Now, she continued to devote her life to her daughter and grandson, rarely dating or even meeting eligible men.

This is my fault. Mom has sacrificed everything for me, and all I do is sit around and bitch. My family is still out there, and yet I stay behind these walls, wrapped in my own problems and anger. I can't even deal with my own son, my baby.

"Mom?" Melissa called down the stairs. "Do you need any help?"

Rita appeared at the bottom and stared up at her daughter. "What kind of help? Like you want to deal with the gardener when he comes? Tell him about that tree? Or maybe you want to call the insurance company and follow up on that claim? Your car looks like hell."

"I –"

"Your father called this morning, while you were still asleep."

Melissa felt her cheeks color. "What did he want?"

"He just wanted to say thanks for coming to their party. He asked if you were okay."

"Okay?" Melissa murmured.

"Apparently he's having a memory lapse. How could you be okay? Asshole."

Melissa sat down on the top step and her mother looked away. "He was really nice to me, Mom. All of them were."

"They must want something. Although what it could possibly be escapes me. Unless he's running for office or something."

"No," Melissa said softly. "It felt real." She stood up, filled her lungs. "I'm going out. Do you need anything?"

"A fifth of Jack would be nice."

"Ha ha. As if."

Rita finally broke a weak smile. "Thanks for asking, love. No, I guess there's nothing. I'm going out myself in a little while. Bridget needs me to work with her on some designs. Will you be home for dinner?"

"Don't count on it."

Later that afternoon, Melissa was surprised she still remembered the way to Roxanne Jarrick's house. Although "Aunt Rox" was not a biological relative, she'd acted as one during those tough years. A paradox, since she was Jessica's best friend. Jessica, the woman Rita held responsible for the family's demise. Still Rox was a solid, down-to-earth woman who didn't pull punches, and Melissa had always admired her.

"Do you have any experience at all, babe?" she was asking, handing Melissa a cup of coffee.

"Depends on in what." Melissa squirmed a little. "I've never worked at a real job. I've helped Mom with some bookkeeping, and I took a night class once in Microsoft Word. Other than that, and changing diapers, not much."

Roxanne smiled warmly. "It's okay. I'll be honest. I know your history. Better than you can imagine. I had a front row seat back when things went sideways. You might not know this, but I have my own nasty history with your dad. And I think if we're going to work together, there shouldn't be any skeletons lurking." She took a sip of coffee and put her cup down on the table. "I had a rough patch back then, after Mac died." Roxanne looked down and pressed her hand against her chest. "Sorry. I still get choked up when I talk about him. Hang on." She took a deep breath and looked back at Melissa. "Okay. I'm okay. Anyway, I was having some physical and emotional issues. I couldn't get pregnant, then I did, then I miscarried. Jess had Devon – God what a beautiful boy! – and she was trying to get custody of Mac's baby nephew. There were rumors circulating that Dane – your dad – was somehow responsible for Mac's death. It was a load of malarky, of course, but I glommed onto it and made life miserable for him and Jess."

"You don't have to –"

"No, I do. Everything's fine now. I got treatment. I came out of that dark time with a new love for my friends and my life. I had my own child. Tom and I are rock-solid. But I want you to know that I understand that no one is impervious to bad luck and pain and suffering. As I sit here and look at you, I see a woman who's taking steps to make her life better, rather than wasting away waiting for life to come knocking. I applaud that."

Melissa's hands began to tremble so badly she had to put her cup down. Tears welled and spilled down her cheeks.

Roxanne handed her a napkin. "Now, let's talk about what I want you to do, and the pay and all that. There are a few things you'll need to remember. First, please, never be late. I mean, obviously, there are problems with kids, and illnesses, etc. I only ask you call and let me know. Second, you ask questions. Never, ever, ever harbor anything. You don't understand something? Ask. You don't agree? Speak up. Get angry? Tell me. Got it?"

Melissa smiled through her tears. "Yes. I got it." *I got it. Someone values me. Someone cares. I'm allowed to be a real person, and I don't have to be my mother.*

The work wasn't difficult. Melissa made phone calls to Roxanne's clients, mostly small boutiques in the best parts of town. Beverly Hills, Brentwood, Newport Beach. One shop in New York City had an East Coast exclusive on Roxanne's designs. Gowns for the wealthy, the well-connected, the elite. After Angelina Jolie had worn one to a recent premiere, Roxanne had to turn away business. Now, she'd hired a second seamstress and Melissa. Shy on the phone at first, Melissa soon absorbed Roxanne's talent for getting cooperation and satisfaction. She next took on calling suppliers, shippers, manufacturers. She took copious notes and transcribed them at night into something legible for Roxanne. It worked. Her confidence, once non-existent, bloomed.

"Can you call these ladies and tell them their gowns are ready?" Roxanne asked one morning. "These are custom dresses for special clients. I only have a few I work directly with."

"Sure. No problem." Melissa took the short stack of order forms back to her desk, located in the rear of Roxanne's massive home addition. After the first two clients scheduled, Melissa turned over the next page. "Jessica MacKendall." Her lips parted, and she started to ask Roxanne if it was a mistake. Surely, she would want to call Jess herself. Roxanne was on the telephone, arguing with a sewing machine company about a defective bobbin case.

Melissa looked back at the form, cleared her throat, and picked up the phone. Jessica answered immediately and was graciously happy to acknowledge Melissa's new role. "I had no idea! What a wonderful job for you, dear. So ... Jillie has her Brownie scout troop coming over this afternoon. Could I get it tomorrow? Or maybe Dev can swing by after –"

"I'll drop it off," Melissa blurted, before she could change her mind. "I have to come right by your house on my way to pick up some supplies for Rox."

"That would be just wonderful."

When Roxanne heard about Melissa's impromptu offer, she tilted her head and smiled. "I am so proud of you. You go, girl. Tell Messy Jessie I said hi."

I hope Zoe doesn't answer the door, Melissa thought as she parked her car. Taking a deep breath, she got the gown out of the back seat and approached the house, smiling a little as she passed her freshly repaired front fender. Jessica let her in, and the two moved to the living room where Melissa showed her the dress. "Do you want to try it on?"

"No need. Rox has been dressing me for so many years, she's got it down to a science. I can't thank you enough for coming by. The girls are in the backyard. Can I get you anything?"

"No. I can't stay. I ... just ... wanted to do this."

Jessica nodded, then turned her head to the sound of a small beep coming from the hall. "Someone's home."

Melissa tensed. Jessica was one thing, but she wasn't quite ready to face the others. Relief washed over her when Devon strode in.

"Hey," he said with a nod.

"Hey." Melissa stood and picked up her purse. "I was just leaving. I hope I didn't block you from parking."

"Naw. No sweat."

"Melissa is working for Aunt Rox now. Isn't that great?"

Devon smiled and nodded. "That's cool. Good peeps, Rox and Tom. Congrats."

"Where have you been? Dad said you didn't show up at the studio," Jessica asked.

"Um, well, I have some news, too. I got a job. A real job. I'm gonna work for Chris. As a driver. Can you believe it? My own limo?"

Jessica's smile faded. "You already have a real job. Have you discussed this with Dane?"

"Uh ... well, here's the thing. I –"

"I'd better go," Melissa interrupted. "Congrats to you, too. And, um, good luck. With Dad."

Devon's dimples appeared, and he leaned forward to give Melissa a brief hug. "Thanks, Sis."

Melissa smiled as she backed down the Pierce driveway. A simple, nothing hug. She remembered that Devon had always been an affectionate kid. But the hug filled her with joy. She was making her way back into the family.

"You did what?" Dane got quickly to his feet from where he sat behind his desk. "Aside from just ditching me, do you know how worried I was about you?"

Devon didn't remember ever seeing his dad so mad. What was the big deal, anyway? Shouldn't Dane have been happy that his notoriously lazy son had gotten a job, on his own?

"I'm sorry. Really. I didn't believe anyone would even notice. Everyone else is happy." Even Ashley looked at him with new respect when he'd announced that Christian Collins was training him to be a professional chauffeur. Jessica had quietly agreed that Devon had shown initiative but reprimanded him for walking out on his father's production gig.

Dane huffed. "Not everyone is happy, I can assure you. And of course, we noticed. I'll have your final check prepared."

"Yes, sir. I'm sorry, again."

Dane sat down and began writing on a scratch pad, so Devon took his leave.

"You hurt his feelings," Jessica later admonished. "You should have told him first. You don't just go MIA and then show up working for someone else."

"I get it. I didn't think. I didn't think because I always felt it was just a fake job for the boss's kid. I never did anything important down there, Mom. Making Slurpee runs and dragging cords around? What a joke." Devon paused, and then found more fuel. "It's a high school kid's job. I'm out of school. I want to start doing something. A career."

"You should be in school. Any school you want. We could –"

"I know. And I appreciate that. Maybe someday I'll go to college. But right now, this is what I want to do. Chris is such a cool guy. And he's practically family."

Jessica let out a sarcastic breath. "He's taken your sister out once. I wouldn't call that exactly family, or even dating. Just ... apologize to your dad and be careful, okay?"

"I love you, Mom."

Ashley sat in the driveway behind the steering wheel of her new Acura and sighed. Closing her eyes, she envisioned her fifteen-year-old self on a Sunday morning sitting in a massively empty factory parking lot, the comforting voice of her father beside her in the passenger seat.

"Foot on the brake, then put it into drive. Good. Ease off on the brake 'til you get a feel for how the car's going to move. Now put your foot on the gas pedal, and slowly, SLOWLY! Good God, Zo, back off! Okay, better ..." The car lurched and stopped, jumped, and slowed as she tried to get the hang of it.

"I'll never get this," she huffed, slamming the gear shift back into park. *"It's too hard."*

"Nonsense. You'll be a great driver. You'll see."

Yep. I saw. But that was over five years ago. Now, she opened her eyes, and tried to concentrate. *I hope I can do this. I can't go on hiding my terror.*

Grasping the steering wheel, Ashley repeated the steps she already knew. Foot on brake. Put in reverse. Ease off brake. Let car roll back, down the driveway. Press on brake! Too much.

The rapping of knuckles on her window gave her a major shock. She whipped her head around to see Christian Collins grinning at her. She quickly put the window down.

"Nice wheels, eh? Bet she's a smooth ride."

"She is, thank you. Are you looking for Devon?"

"Yeah. Supposed to pick him up. Is he here?"

"No. He's on his way home from the studio. Would you like to go inside to wait?"

Christian shook his head. "You were obviously just leaving. I'll wait out here."

"No, I'm just getting home." Ashley got out of the car and locked it. "I was playing with all the gadgets. This thing is like sitting in a jet cockpit."

Once inside, Ashley poured them both some iced tea. "My brother got into a bit of a row with Dad."

Christian grimaced. "I heard. I'm so sorry about that. I assumed he'd tell Dane first. He has a little bit of maturity ahead of him."

Ashley smiled. An understatement. And Christian seemed genuinely regretful. She watched with interest as he ran a hand through his black locks. There was something about him she couldn't quite define. "You look a little familiar to me. Like we've met before."

"Shouldn't that be my line?" Christian responded, taking a sip of tea.

"Line or not ... you resemble a man I used to know. His name was Robbie."

Christian swallowed, frowned. "Where did you meet this ... Robbie?"

Ashley chuckled softly. "In another lifetime. He's gone now, sadly. A nice boy. Anyway, you look like him. A little."

"Well, if I have or had a double somewhere – and they say, we all have at least one – I'm glad he was a nice guy." He cleared his throat. "Anyone ever tell you, you look like Keira Knightley?"

"She's an actress, right?"

"A beautiful one, yes."

Ashley took a quick sip of tea to hide her immediate fluster. *Did he just call me beautiful?* "My father may have tried to cast her once. So, how's Megan? Still seeing her?" *God, I hope I'm not as red as I feel.*

Christian scratched at his eyebrow, then grinned. "I hope so. I've been so swamped I've barely had time to call her. But we do have some plans to get out next weekend. Perhaps you and ... someone ... would like to join us?"

"Would love to, if ... someone ... would come with me. If I meet him before then, I'll let you know."

"Good deal."

THIRTEEN

He's Not Preoccupied With Sex

I'm not preoccupied with sex. Am I? Christian had to admit that he'd been thinking about having sex with Megan since, well, since he saw her standing in front of the gallery weeks before. She'd looked so woebegone, forlorn perhaps, and he'd always been a sucker for the "lost fawn" types. Now that he knew her better, recognized that darkness within and felt her deep disappointment with life, he wondered if getting physically intimate with her was a good idea. Wounded chicks were often confused, and a night of casual sex could quickly become an iron-clad contract.

Still, Christian liked Megan. She was attractive, intelligent, and talented. She knew the difference between the bulls and the bears, the left and the right, the haves and have-nots. She had opinions and was ready to back them up. She didn't play games, either, as evidenced by the question she'd just asked.

"So? What will it be? My place or yours?" she reiterated as the limo came to a red light stop. "Or if you'd rather not –"

"Um, no, yeah, sure. Let's hang at my place for a while. We can let Gustov go, and I'll give you lift home later if you want."

Megan flashed a brief, tight smile, and Christian again had a pang of discomfort.

She tucked her legs beneath her on his couch, drinking down the last of her second glass of port. "You ever get tired of the view?"

"Nope. It's why I chose this place. It's ... inspiring. I think about all those people out there. All the lives, the stories, their loves, their needs. Right now, I just get them from place to place. Someday, I'll do more to get them where they want to go. In life." Christian smiled and felt his face warm a little. "Presumptuous, right?"

"Not if you don't think so. I wish I were that ambitious. I don't know what the hell I'm doing. I have no purpose in life. Maybe I did, once."

Christian joined Megan on the couch and took her hand. "Of course, you have purpose. Everyone does. You just haven't –"

"Found myself yet? Yeah, that's it. I'm waiting for the big message. The angel to come into my room at night, and –"

Christian cut off her words with his lips, quickly leaning over and pulling her body against his. Probing her mouth with his tongue, he was remotely aware of her tensing posture, her hands on his shoulders, neither pushing nor pulling him. *She'll relax. She wants this. She needs this.* He kissed her again, and transitioned into a hot assault on her neck, her throat, her chest. Megan sighed, encouraging his foreplay. Still, she felt stiff in his arms. "You okay with this?" he murmured against her ear.

Megan nodded quickly and began to unbutton his shirt. Her fingers worked feverishly and yet they fumbled. Christian pulled away. "Let's go in there. Take this easy, okay?"

She nodded again, letting him help her to a stand and direct her to his bedroom.

He thought perhaps she'd loosen up, once in bed, with the lights low, the soft music playing, the wine mellowing in her stomach. Yet Megan seemed to move into autopilot, performing what she perceived to be her sexual responsibilities. Christian felt driven to break through her rigid, manic routine; something was missing. Hovering above her, he paused and stared down at her closed eyes, long enough that she sensed his appraisal and opened them.

"What?"

"Shh. Just relax, okay? Take this slow. Enjoy it a little?"

Megan closed her eyes and turned her head to the side. Christian stifled a sigh and sat up, straddling her. He placed his hands on her shoulders and slowly drew them down her body, detouring to catch up her small, firm breasts and engage in a little foreplay. Megan caught her breath but lay still. Christian slid down to lie beside her, continuing to caress her body with long, sensual strokes, making his way down to the neatly trimmed triangle below her belly. His fingers edged closer, slipping silkily into her most private depths. Again, Megan issued a restrained gasp, and clutched his wrist.

"Is this ... not okay?" Christian asked.

A frown creased Megan's brow. "No, I mean, sure, I just ... it's just been ... a while, you know. Maybe I'm not, oh, Hell's bells, I'm sorry."

"It's okay. I get it." As smoothly as he'd slipped them in, Christian withdrew his fingers and turned onto his back beside Megan. "Just need ... a minute."

"God, I feel stupid," Megan whispered. "It's not you, truthfully. It's me."

Christian chuckled under his breath. "You do realize how that sounds."

"Yes, I know ... so cliché. But it is. Me. I'm such a prude."

"So, this has happened before?"

She nodded. "I'm embarrassed to admit it, but I guess now, what's there left to be embarrassed about? You – You're the first guy to even look my way in ... a long time, and here I go blowing it. I thought I could do it. You're so hot and so nice and everything, and you really do turn me on and all. It's just that I can't seem to let go."

Christian moistened his lips and nodded. "You're very brave to admit all that to me. You're a beautiful woman, Megs. Talented, smart, witty, and yes, sexy. I can't figure why your confidence is in the can. Has someone hurt you in the past if you don't mind my asking?"

"No. No because I've never let anyone that close. Honestly. I mean, I've dated. I've had sex. Lots of times. But it's never been special. Never been anyone special."

"But did you ever just have fun? I mean, yeah, sex with someone special is the best. It's what we all want at some point. But sometimes, sex can be simply for fun."

Megan shrugged. "I guess I make it out to be too serious."

Christian touched her throat, dragged his fingers down between her breasts and onto her tummy, where he flattened his hand and swept it gently across her skin. "That could be. You, uh, wanna try again? Nothing serious, nothing life-changing, just a little mutual admiration?"

She giggled a little, then reached tentatively for his cheek. "You're a cool guy, you know that?"

"Been told that, don't really believe it." He felt a little sorry for her now. She'd been honest and forthcoming about her feelings, and he didn't want her to go home so empty. He curled his fingers around the far side of her slender waist and pulled her close for a kiss. When she tried to return to her programmed mode, he stopped her. "Let me take this lead." When at last she gave in to him, she came with such force that she cried out, clamping on to his shoulders and rocking her hips against his with fury. Christian was later to wonder if, perhaps, the duration of Megan's climax had set some sort of world record.

He lay awake long after she'd drifted off into a smiling sleep. He contemplated their future. Words and truths had been exchanged tonight that would likely head off any kind of serious attachment. Still, he'd enjoyed seducing her, appreciated her honesty and delighted in her ultimate, orgasmic joy. Their immediate relationship might be perfect for them both, for a while.

·♥·♥·♥·♥·♥·

Melissa stacked her folders neatly and dropped them into her desk drawer. Roxanne had already gone out with Tom, so Melissa used her newly acquired key to lock up. She didn't feel like cooking dinner, and her mother hadn't entered the kitchen in days, choosing instead to let her daughter throw together meals on the fly. What had changed? Was it the new career? Was it because Brady was home for the summer? Rita was behaving suspiciously, not unlike the days long ago when Melissa had to fight for any shred of attention.

A spontaneous decision compelled her to seek out her favorite Chinese restaurant, where she parked and pulled out her phone. A brief smile passed over her face at the sight of the latest Apple device, purchased for her by the Jarricks, "in case" they needed her. Such nice people. Nine rings went unanswered before her mother's sleep-heavy voice came on the line.

"What time is it?" she murmured.

Melissa glanced at the clock on her instrument panel. "6:45. I'm getting us Chinese. Is that okay?"

"Sure. Whatever."

Had her mother just slurred her words?

"Mom, where is Brady?"

"Little shit's around here somewhere. I just ... dozed off. Where'd you say you are?"

"At Chen's. Look. Go find Brady and tell him I'm on my way, okay?"

"He's around here somewhere," Rita repeated, and this time Melissa knew. Her mother had been drinking.

She tossed the phone down into her bag and got out of the car. The knot forming in her stomach was a familiar one not felt in a long while. After pacing for fifteen minutes, she grabbed the bagged order from the counter and hurried home. Even after 7 p.m., traffic from the West Side to the Valley crept along. Patience had never been her strong suit, and she drummed her fingernails on the edge of the steering wheel, willing the cars and the traffic lights to move. Tapping the Bluetooth icon on her nav screen, she tried to call home again, only to listen to her own voice telling callers she was away from the phone. The knot grew.

Dane had purchased the four-bedroom tract home for Rita and "the kids" years ago, after his ex's rich boyfriend had left town and left the Brentwood mansion in default. Built at the center-end of the cul-de-sac, the Valley house was roomy and comfortable, with a small kidney-shaped pool in the back. Melissa had just finished redecorating Brady's bedroom with planets, stars, and spaceships. She reminisced as she drove, recalling the bedroom as a nursery, a toddler's room and briefly, a haven for dinosaurs a la Jurassic Park. When Brady returned from the school he hated so much, he'd stepped into a sci-fi buff's paradise. It made his mother smile as she remembered the huge embrace he'd shared.

The warm feeling didn't last long, as the sense that something was very wrong returned.

·❤·❤·❤·❤·❤·

Jessica thumbed through the bradded pages of a script with a pink cover. The storyline appealed to her, but the package didn't feel right. Theo Parkington was attached, and she knew they'd never gel on the screen. She tossed the screenplay onto a growing heap on her desk with a groan, then brightened as her husband appeared in the doorway.

"Anything?" he asked, lazily leaning into the door frame. Jessie shrugged and stood up, stretched, and went to Dane.

"Nothing. I mean, some of it's good, well, reasonably good. But ... I'm getting too picky in my old age. Maybe I should have taken the deal in Portugal."

"You've earned the right to be picky. And you're not old," Dane cooed, taking her into his arms. "You'll find something you want to do. No rush, right?"

"I might be doing this because I want a reason to turn down that TV show."

Dane nuzzled her ear with his lips. "You don't need a reason. For anything. And if you happen to find the right script, we can produce it ourselves, however we want to. You know that." He pulled her hair away from her cheek and pressed his mouth against hers, stirring the embers of a love that had stayed hot forever. "And what's wrong with being a female space cop, anyway?"

Jessica giggled. "Mmm. As long as you're the handsome alien I have to collar."

"Could happen," Dane said, drawing in a deep breath. Jessica reached to stroke his face and noticed the fine layer of perspiration on his brow as he took another breath.

"Are you okay?" she asked, stepping back a little in appraisal.

"Just got a little winded coming up the driveway. I went down to check out that broken sprinkler so I could tell Raul about it. It's damned hot out."

"You look flushed. You should lie down."

"I just might do that. If you lay down with me."

"The idea is to rest," Jessica teased, tapping his lips with her finger. "Let's go out for a nice dinner after. It'll cool off by 7:30."

Jessica left Dane lounging on their bed with a magazine and went to the kitchen for something to drink. Her husband's apparent fatigue worried her, but her concerns were soon set aside as Alexander strode into the room.

"Hey Mom Two. What's up?"

"Alex. What a nice surprise. I was getting some iced tea, want some?"

"Sure. Great. Dad around?"

"Upstairs, resting. I'm sure he'd be glad to see you."

"Actually, I'd like to talk with you if you have a minute," Alexander said. "Here, let me get that." He lifted a hefty camera bag off the table for Jessica and then sat down. Jessica poured their tea and then sat as well.

"I'm all ears."

"Not sure if I told you but I recently moved over to Missing Persons. It's different. I mean, I like it, I do. It sure beats tooling around the West Valley all day and cuffing dopers and cons. But it's no secret it's not what I want to do."

Jessica folded her hands. "I know that. You want to be a screenwriter. Alex, you've wanted that since you were in middle school. I was so surprised when you applied at L.A.P.D."

"Well, that's the thing. I had to do something. Can't get by on my good looks." Alex ran a self-conscious hand through his ash blonde hair. "I might as well just ask. Do you think Dad will ever help me make my film?"

His stepmother looked down at her glass, ran her finger down its side to collect the moisture forming there. "You must realize I can't answer that. Your father is his own man. He makes his own choices. That said, I don't quite understand it myself. Your script is good. Better than good. Could use a little tweaking, but they all do. It's high-profile, the right length, reasonable to produce."

"He hates it."

"No, he doesn't. It likely has more to do with you, your being his son, and getting the way paved for you. He thinks no one in Hollywood will respect you if he bankrolls your project."

"Then you do understand it. You just said it. But Hollywood wouldn't have to know. He could put up the cash under one of his sub companies."

"Hollywood knows everything, Alex. Everything. You'd be shocked at what goes around."

"So bottom line is, he'll never help me. Not unless someone else is willing to take a chance on me. And if that happens, I won't need him to help me."

Jessica covered Alexander's hand with her own. "I'm sorry. I don't know if he's right or wrong. If it was up to me ..."

"If it was up to you, what? You'd do it? I know you've done some producing, right? With Uncle Mac?"

A wistful smile drifted across Jessica's face. "Not really. I did try, once, after Mac died, to do a movie. I failed. I wasn't ready – not by any stretch of the imagination. It's a tremendously tough business, kiddo."

Alex got to his feet, picked up his tea and drank it down. "I get it. I do. Thank you for talking with me." Jessica stood also, and Alex surprised her with a hug. "I know I haven't been the best son, Mom. I know it upsets you when I get after Dev. You know I don't mean it, right? He's a pretty decent kid."

Jessica didn't know what to say. The embrace, the kind words – so uncharacteristic of Alexander. "Thanks, babe. I wish I could offer something more."

Alex broke away, embarrassed, and headed for the door. "Tell Dad I said hi."

·♥·♥·♥·♥·♥·

Melissa tore into her driveway and rushed into the house, white bags of dinner in hand. The sight of Brady playing video games on the family room floor relieved her. "Where's Gramma?" she called, quickly unloading the Chinese food cartons onto the kitchen table.

"I dunno. Maybe upstairs. She said she's having a sick day." A sick day. The same thing she used to say when we were little, Melissa thought with despair. She went to the bottom of the stairs and stared up.

"Mom? Dinner's here," she called. When Rita didn't answer, Melissa climbed the stairs and went to her mother's room. Her mother was sprawled across the bed, snoring loudly. Melissa debated; let her sleep it off, or wake her up and confront her? She considered Brady, and the effect an argument might have on him. She decided to let her mother sleep it off. She'd talk to Rita in the morning.

Fourteen

Wheels, Weddings and Whiskey

D evon slid his hands around the steering wheel, an involuntary grin gracing his youthful face. He took a quick glance over his right shoulder. The limousine extended back into the next county. Black leather seats with air-cooling slits outfitted the passenger cabin, wrapping around plush flooring and high-tech entertainment, a well-stocked bar in the center.

Growing up amid the affluence of Hollywood's golden couple, Devon was no stranger to riding in luxury as his parents brought him along to movie premieres and high-profile parties. But sitting behind the wheel of this beauty gave a whole new dimension to his life. That Chris trusted him with the pricey vehicle raised his self-esteem several notches. Sure beat gophering for snob-nosed studio pimps.

Christian was a patient teacher. His calm, easy demeanor while training Devon to navigate the posh ride gave the younger man a sense of pride and connection. Tonight, his first gig would take him into Brentwood for the pickup and out to Palos Verdes for the drop. He'd come back after around three hours to grab the bucks-up couple and return them to their West L.A. digs. Should be a piece of a cake, and the boss had given him free reign with the car during the lag time. He planned to make good use of it.

He left the limo at the curb and hiked up the steep driveway. Inside, he passed by his little sister, who sat before the TV with a bowl of popcorn in her lap. "Where is everyone?"

"Mom and Dad went out. Ashley is in the back. Did you bring any food?"

"Nope." Devon tousled Jillian's hair as he swept past her toward the patio doors. "You hungry?"

"I'll live. Unless you're going to Chipotle."

"We'll see." Devon headed outside and perused the back yard. Ashley sat at a patio table reading a book. She looked up and smiled.

"Hey, what's up? How's the new job?"

"Very cool. I thought you might like to see the wheels. It's out front."

"Sure." Slipping a bookmark into her novel, Ashley followed her stepbrother back through the house and out the front door. "Wowsers. That is very cool."

"Here, get in," Devon directed, holding the driver's side door open for her. "You've gotta feel the seat. The wheel. Nothing like it." Without waiting for her, he went around the car and got into the front passenger seat.

Ashley slipped into the car and grinned, shaking her head. "You're right. How does it drive? I mean, it's so long and all."

"It's no different. Smooth. Lane changes are a little more challenging on the freeway. Wanna take it around the block?"

"Uh, no. I don't think so." Ashley started to get out of the car, but Devon reached over and grasped her arm.

"It's okay. I understand. We can just sit."

"What do you mean, you understand?"

Devon pulled his hand away and looked to the floor. "I know you're afraid. It's okay. I'm afraid of stuff, too."

"I'm not sure what you think I'm afraid of," Ashley said softly, keeping her own eyes averted.

"Driving. Don't worry, I won't say anything. But I can help you. I'm a good teacher. I can show you. I guess you never learned before you went away?"

Ashley smiled. "I have a driver's license. I got it the day I turned seventeen. It's just that ... it's been so long, and I wasn't too good at it when I did drive. I was in an accident within weeks of getting my first car. It was awful. No one was seriously hurt, but it was kind of my fault."

Devon slowly reached over and slipped his fingers between her hand and the steering wheel she still gripped. "It's okay. I can so relate to that. I once got super sick with the flu after I'd just eaten some strawberry ice cream, and I haven't been able to eat it ever since. So, I get it. But you'll get past it. Driving is ... can be ... fun. And necessary. But crap, I'm so sorry that happened to you. That really blows. I'm sure it wasn't your fault."

"Thanks. I've thought about it six ways to Sunday. Was I not paying enough attention? If I'd been driving a little faster, a little slower? If it hadn't been raining so hard?"

"It doesn't matter, now, does it? Why beat yourself up over something you can't ever figure out?"

Ashley smiled and squeezed Devon's hand. "Are you eternally up?"

Devon blushed and pulled his hand away. "It's smoke and mirrors, as Dad would say. Um, Dane, that is. Sometimes I feel like I have to qualify that."

"I don't remember too much about Uncle Mac. But what I do remember was his smile. He was always nice to us kids. A little hard on Megan but caring. You got that from him."

"Now you're gonna make *me* cry. Because that's how I remember him, too. It's vague. Just glimpses, snips of scenes, like when you're looking at someone, but the sun is right behind their head and you can't see their face."

Ashley cleared her throat. "We're a couple of sad sacks today, aren't we? But hey. Maybe on Saturday or Sunday, if you don't have a job, we can use my car and you can go with me. To a parking lot or something. Let me try."

"You're on, sis." Devon hurried out of the car and around to open the door for Ashley. When she got out, he stood in front of her. "Um, I wanna say something else. Thanks for not hating on me for being such a douche last week. If you knew, if you could see how totally beautiful you are, you wouldn't blame me."

Now it was Ashley's turn to color. Against what would have been her better judgment the week before, she slid her arms around his waist and gave him a hug. Devon was quick to return her embrace, but Ashley sensed a brotherly affection. "You're not so bad yourself, little brother. You're gonna make some girl deliriously happy someday."

Megan kicked off her shoes and stepped up onto a chair, leaned over and took an overhead shot of the round, elegantly decorated dinner table, set for eight guests and lit with tiny LED seed lights attached to the delicate tree-like centerpiece. The bride's family had spared no expense. *Would I want a reception like this?* Seemed over-the-top, possibly garish ... but in her heart-of-hearts she longed for the romance of it all. The full, white lace gown sewn with small pearls, the satin pumps, the sheer veil. A big church with both a guitarist and the traditional organ music. *"Are you with the bride or the groom?"* the ushers would ask.

She zoomed in on the centerpiece and the elaborately written table place cards. The bride and groom's first initials, printed in a fancy font, graced the top of the folded tent cards. She imagined her own: "M and ... "and what? C? Stepping down off the chair, Megan scoffed at her own silly thoughts. Christian wasn't husband material, not for her, not by any stretch of the imagination. She liked him, and the sex was good. Relaxing. Eased her days and nights. But marriage? Not in the tea leaves.

On a whim, she leaned down and straightened one of the name cards. "Mr. Peyton Worthington." Again, she looked at the engraved initials and squinted. "M and ... A." A. Quickly, she buried the thought of "A" because no one could know about her obsession. "A" barely knew she still existed.

Across the room, the bridal party had finally congregated for the group shots. Megan pulled her bigger camera out of the bag and attached it to the tripod already set up. "Where is the groom?" she asked, noting the bride's uncertain expression.

"He'll be here in a minute."

"Let's go with a nice Bride with Father shot," Megan suggested. "Mr. Kellogg? If I could have you stand right here ... "

His eyes were red-rimmed. At first Megan wondered if dear old Dad had spent some time at the country club bar, but she soon realized that tears of joy and melancholy had the older man's eyes irritated. "I'm sorry," he croaked, dabbing at the corner of his eye with a pinkie. "She was just a little girl, only yesterday."

"Aw, Daddy," the bride comforted, her missing groom forgotten. "I'm still a little girl. Right?"

It was stupid thing to say, a blonde thing, Megan thought, but the father's response cost her. The warmth and deep-felt love that shown from those pre-Photoshopped eyes sucker-punched her as she remembered, again, that her own father would not be at any wedding with his only daughter. Swallowing hard, Megan turned her back and pretended to fiddle with the zipper on her empty camera bag. She sucked in a deep breath and lifted her chin before spinning back around. "It's okay, Mr. Kellogg. Everyone will be looking at Kristin anyway."

· ♥ · ♥ · ♥ · ♥ · ♥ ·

"Why are you drinking?" Melissa blurted, arms akimbo, as Rita poured out two fingers of Maker's Mark into a glass.

"What. I'm not allowed to have a little drink once in a while? I beg your pardon, but this is my house, and I'll do as I damn well please." Rita picked up the bottle and sighed. "Forgotten just how good Kentucky whiskey is."

"Damn it, Mom. You know what I mean. Don't you remember how hard it was to quit? *Why* you quit? Do you really want to go down that path again?"

"Pish. It's not like that. It's just one little drink."

"Third time in a week. Even when you're supposed to be watching Brady!"

"You don't think I'm good enough to watch my grandson, get yourself another damned babysitter. And good luck with that because he's not an easy kid. Surely that's clear."

Frustration turned to anger, and Melissa shook her head. "He's a kid. He needs some attention now and then. Needs you to play with him. Bake cookies with him. Watch a movie or go to the park. You can't do that if you're drunk on your ass, Mom." Melissa paced the room, her pain building. "Ask me how I know that, Mom. Ask me!!"

Rita drank down her cocktail and placed the glass on the table before Melissa. "A little late to start blaming me, don't you think? Or has dear Daddy seduced you over to his side? Have you forgotten how he walked out of me, on us? Don't you have a sympathetic bone in that body of yours? If I've had some problems, God knows where they came from. You got a lotta nerve, chickie."

"Mom, all I'm saying is that something must have triggered this ... this drinking spree. Have I done something wrong? Is it my job that's bothering you? Because I can quit ... although I'd rather not. This is the first time in my life I've felt valued. The first time."

"Yeah, you're right. You're that girl, the one who needs rich bitches like Jessica MacKendall and Roxanne Boudreau to make you feel worthy. Huh? Am I right?"

Melissa's mouth opened and her eyes widened. Rita had not mentioned Jessica or Roxanne in years. That the pain was still so fresh, so biting, it surprised her. But instead of allowing her mother to let the air out of her bright balloon, Melissa tilted her head and leaned toward Rita. "I'm so sorry you feel that way. I feel worthy because I am. I'm doing something useful, and I'm being paid for my work. My son is getting better, thanks in part to you for caring for him while I do that work. And for the record, I'm extremely grateful to Rox and Jess for giving me a leg up."

Her mother seemed taken aback, and Melissa detected a slight quiver as Rita poured herself another drink. In two swallows, the whiskey was gone. "They're just using you. You're too blind. You don't know them, their conniving ways. Jessica is a thief of hearts and souls. She stole your father away from me without so much as a second thought for his wife, his children ... me, the one who worked so hard all those years while he dabbled. While he sat on casting couches and lunched with self-important studio execs and took directors to fancy dinners on my paycheck. Did I complain? Never. It was his life's dream to be a star. And as soon as he made it, I was history."

Melissa let out a breath she'd been holding. She'd heard it all before. Listened to it all before. Sympathized. But no more. Like every coin having two sides, so did the story of her family's demise. They each had their own versions, their own paths derived from the dissolution. Realizing that no words could change her mother's course – at least not tonight – Melissa turned and went upstairs to get Brady ready for bed.

As she laid out his favorite Captain America pajamas and listened while he brushed his teeth, scenes from her own childhood flashed across her mind's eye. Happy times, stressful times, family times ... a visit to the zoo. Alex running ahead, shouting excitedly about the bears or giraffes. Herself holding Dane's hand, happy just to be with him on a rare weekend he was home. Rita pushing a stroller while Zoe rode with a bag of cotton candy in her lap, her fingers stained blue. A normal American family. But ... not.

Was it all Dane's fault, as she been led – spoon fed – to believe? Was he a philanderer, a user, a man lacking in morals and ethical behavior? Were his children merely the result of an insatiable sexual appetite and a lack of responsibility? Or, had her mother entrapped a man who never wanted to be married at all? Melissa was only sixteen when she'd happened upon a marriage license, filed away with three certificates of birth. She'd needed her own for a passport she'd never used. Being her inquisitive self, she'd looked over each document and discovered what she'd naively thought was simply a typo: her parents hadn't been married until she was ten months old.

"I'm done!" Brady bounded from the bathroom and dived onto the bed, clearly expecting her to help him dress. Of course, at almost ten, her son was totally capable of dressing himself. It was because of the turmoil. The roller coaster ride between his mother and grandmother. The lack of a father. Even his teacher had commented on his neediness. She had to do a better job of building his confidence.

"You put on your own jammies, big boy. Captain America dresses himself. And his jammies have pictures of you all over them."

Brady giggled and began dressing. Melissa's thoughts returned to her father and their most recent meeting. Had he changed, or had he ever been different? Probably both, she decided. So much had happened that would surely change a man. And the fact that she'd only now discovered his loving, caring, fatherly side was likely behind her mother's renewed angst.

Fifteen

Awards Night

The kid was all right. Devon had been driving for two, no, three weeks now and Christian was impressed. A perfect record. No complaints, no mishaps, no tickets. If only he could clone him. As he wrote out Devon's paycheck, Christian chuckled, recalling Devon's insistence on wearing full chauffeur livery. He had to admit, the cap did look pretty fly. He put the check into an envelope and reached for his phone, startled when it rang before he could dial.

"Hey. It's me. I got a job for you."

"Sy Raffianello. Thought you'd taken your business elsewhere. How ya doin'?"

The gruff voice on the phone softened a little. "Chris, Chris, Chris. Why would I go anywhere else? You got the cleanest ride in town, and I like that your guys don't have eyes in the back of their heads. You know what mean? Listen, I got a special request. I got a friend comin' into town from the Bronx. An important friend. I need you to pick him up from LAX and stick with him all day. He's got a lotta stops to make around town. Of course, I'll make it well worth your while."

"Sounds good. I'll personally escort your ... friend. What day is it? I'll ink you in." Christian grinned and pulled up his calendar on the screen. This would be easy, big money. After agreeing to an eight-hour window the following Friday, Christian hung up the phone.

It took him a few moments to remember what he was about to do. Sy had been a long-time client. Christian had taken him on after a bad incident had sullied the "businessman's" reputation in L.A. and no other limo service would touch him. Christian was hungry and desperate to grow his business. Raffianello had saved him from bankruptcy and the two of them had remained loyal since. It was true that Christian and the occasional other driver paid little attention to whatever "business" was transacted in the back of the limo. He didn't like to think about what the probable con might be involved in, but he could never forget that the "incident" had involved the death of a local city councilmember. Nothing was ever proven.

Christian blew out a breath and picked up his phone to resume his call to Megan. She answered right away, and the two chatted about upcoming plans. She had a new gallery showing coming up next month in Santa Barbara, and they talked about getting a room at the beach. "I haven't been up there in ages," Christian recalled.

"How's my bratty brother doing?"

"He's the best. He treats the job with respect. What more can I ask?"

"Good. I've noticed he's very devoted. He told me he didn't know if he could come to the awards ceremony next Friday because he needed to be available in case you gave him a job. Doesn't matter that this is most important night of my whole career, right? But I get it. I'm glad he's so dedicated."

"Uh, next Friday?"

"We talked about it. Remember? The Phoenix Focus Awards? You said we could take the white limo. Downtown, at the Bonaventure."

"Oh, right. Of course. It's right here ..." he lied, staring at his calendar in chagrin at the words "Raffianello" in all caps ... on Friday. In ink. "Well, it turns out I do have a job for him. So, it's all good."

"Great. I can't wait. I haven't been this excited about anything in a long while."

"Not even ... last Saturday night?" Christian ventured, a smile tugging at his mouth.

"Well, now that you mention it, there have been a few ... stimulating experiences lately."

Christian hung up and rubbed his eyes. Damn it! How could he be so stupid! He'd been the one to submit her portfolio and was shocked when she'd been named a finalist. Megan had been talking about the upcoming awards for weeks, and he'd never put it on his calendar. Now, he'd committed himself to drive around some New

York Mafioso on the same day. No way he could do both. How would he get out of this? His gaze fell upon the paycheck in the envelope. Devon. He'd be perfect to escort the East Coast Don. *I'll coach him. Don't ask questions, keep your eyes on the road, be friendly but don't engage. Keep your thoughts elsewhere and drive smooth.* It would be fine.

Melissa turned in front of the mirror. The dress was pretty but years out of style. While she'd purchase some new clothing for work, her evening apparel was sadly lacking. The fact that "the family" had invited her to Megan's award presentation floored her, and after a brief, unwelcome knee-jerk thought about not going, she humbly accepted. Her father had even offered to pick her up!

Sadly, this dress needed to go away. She longed to try on one of the lavish gowns that hung all around the room where she worked but would never suggest anything of the kind. Roxanne was already too good to be true, and she didn't want to take advantage of her good graces. Instead, she'd stop in at a little dress shop near her house that sometimes had good deals.

The clerk was young and knew nothing about style or fashion, but Melissa knew what she wanted and found a gown that would do. It needed a little alteration, yet her mother had taught her how to sew at an early age and she was satisfied with her purchase. Melissa took the gown home and hung it on the wall so that she could stare at it from her bed.

Alexander stared at the invitation in his hand. Slightly curled from lying alongside the bills in his wallet, the ornate message didn't reveal the winners' names but clearly enticed. He understood that Megan, along with three others, would receive coveted trophies for their work in philanthropic photography. He'd known for some time that Megan was good but had never attended any of her showings. While he cited time commitments and work conflicts, he suspected he had deeper reasons for avoiding the woman. Megan was no longer a childhood playmate. Alexander feared he would let on that he'd always wanted more. She'd been cute, smart, and lovable as a kid, but as years passed, she'd grown right before his adoring eyes into a woman of substance. Wise, talented, beautiful. Accomplished. That she'd even look twice at him now remained in the land of make believe. Besides, she'd hooked up with that Collins guy.

Christian Collins. Brooding, dark good looks. Well-muscled. Smacked of success and confidence. Owner of a thriving business and well connected. Alex looked in the mirror and imagined Christian standing beside him. His own ashen hair could have been cut from his father's head, and his green eyes matched as well. Tall, lean build. He had good shoulders, however, and worked out regularly at the gym. A peace officer had to stay in shape. Did Collins pump iron? Did he run the streets of Century City?

Jealousy is dangerous, Alex. Don't go there. You clash with him and you risk pushing her further away. Maybe you shouldn't be going to this thing.

He'd already swapped shifts with another guy, and it was too late to mess with the schedule. The awards were tomorrow night. Would be easier if he had a date. Jess had mentioned that Melissa was coming, so if he wanted to ride along, they could all crowd into Dane's big SUV.

Ugh. Not a fun ride, stuck in the tiny rear seat with Jillian or Mimi, because Dane would surely pick Zoe to ride in the roomier second row. After ruminating for several minutes, he dialed his sister's number.

"I, uh, thought, since you're going tomorrow night, and I don't particularly want to walk in alone, maybe you'd like to ride together?"

The line went silent. Alex thought they'd lost connection when she finally spoke. "I think that would be great. Yeah. Dad said he'd pick me up, but it would be nice to see you. Mom will be asleep, so if you want to come in for a bit and say hi to Brady ..."

Alex cleared his throat, pushed back his hair. "Sure. I, uh, yeah. I haven't seen the rug rat in a while. Not too keen on running into Mom, though."

"She won't be around. We can talk about it on the way downtown."

"Okay. Cool. Um, look forward to it. Same house, right?"

"Yep. Same house. See you around 5:30."

·♥·♥·♥·♥·♥·

Christian moved at the speed of blur. Multi-tasking didn't begin to describe his day as he went about getting flowers, a haircut and after-show dinner reservations. He rushed through his flat, tying his tie and giving Devon last minute instructions on the phone.

"I'm glad everything went well at LAX. Where are you now?"

"South L.A. The don went into the back door of a nightclub. Wild stuff going on. You should see the guys he's with. They look like they're from *Breaking Bad.*"

"Dev, man, I told you not to even go there. Don't talk about it, don't think about it. Don't look at it. You are deaf, dumb, and blind unless he tells you something he wants. You got it? Don't even tell me. Not tonight anyway. Please."

"Okay, okay. I got it. I'm good with this. And tell ... tell my sister I love her and I'm sorry to miss it."

"Don't worry. There'll be seventeen vids on YouTube by tomorrow morning. You're doing great. Text me when you dump him off tonight, will you?"

"Sure, man. No sweat."

Christian ended the call and turned his thoughts elsewhere. The white limo was out front with Anton behind the wheel.

Megan looked stunning in a form fitting, sequined teal dress. In awe, Christian shook his head slowly and took her hand to his lips. "You look ... exquisite. Wow."

She smiled. "You clean up well, yourself."

He helped her into the limo and then climbed in beside her. "Tonight will be special regardless of the outcome."

"You don't think I'll win."

"I do think you'll win. But whether you do or not, this is your night. You finalled out of thirty-nine entrants."

"Thank you."

Christian stared at her as they rode downtown. Something was different about her. He couldn't quite pin it down. Her hair was loose and curly, not pulled back into the severe bun she often wore. Her makeup was artfully soft, accenting her brown eyes with only a subtle smokiness. It wasn't until they pulled up in front of the Bonaventure Hotel and he offered her his hand that he realized: she wasn't wearing a black dress.

Why then, wasn't he enthralled? She'd come a long way, this lost, broken girl. Tonight, she exuded happiness and something akin to stability. She walked with poise and grace. He knew she had all the right parts under the satin dress. With a painful stab in his chest, he realized that he would never love her. He'd known all along dating her was a long shot, but seeing her like this, in her absolute best splendor, and not feeling it, not feeling the rush, the blood pumping head rush that one feels with the onset of love ... made him sad.

Alex swallowed hard and tapped on the front door of his childhood home. It looked smaller, drabber than he remembered. Melissa opened the door immediately and he stepped inside. Brady approached him warily. "Hello, Uncle Alex," he murmured. Alex squatted and held out his hand.

"Hello, Brady. How's it going?"

"Fine, thank you. Can I go now, Mommy?"

Melissa smiled. "You did good, kiddo. Now remember, Danielle is coming over to watch TV with you later for a while so Gramma can sleep. But don't let anyone else in, you understand?"

Brady nodded, and Melissa kissed his cheek. "I love you. Be good."

On route to L.A., Alex questioned his sister about the babysitter.

"I hate to tell you this, but Mom's swimming in it again. Just started up a few weeks back. I don't know what to do."

"Why do you have to do anything? She's an adult, right? You don't have to take care of her."

"No, but she's the one taking care of my son. I can't trust her. I can't let her be like she was to us."

Alex chewed his lip while he drove. Melissa was different, too, than he remembered. "You're right. Can you kick her out?"

"Seriously? It's her house. And the part you don't know is, she was ... profoundly good to us for a long time. When I got pregnant and wanted to die, she stopped me. She cleaned up and helped with the baby. We became something like friends. But now, with me getting the job with Rox, and reconnecting with you all ... she's falling back into that old abyss. I can't fix what happened between her and Dad, and you, and Zoe and me. I'm learning to move on; I'm forgiving and looking ahead instead of back. I can't tell you how much I hated you, Alex. And Zoe, and Jess ... but guess what? It isn't worth it. It's made me sick, all that anger. And Dad was so nice to me. I couldn't believe he even remembered me as his daughter. He was downright kind."

Alex drove in silence as he digested his sister's surprising confession. Dad, kind? Was she talking about the same guy? But the fact that his mother had seesawed back into the booze made his gut ache. He didn't think it was possible to care anymore, but he clearly did.

"What about some kind of rehab? Intervention?"

"She's so stubborn, and so deeply angry inside. Nothing could fix that. And you know as well as I do that she has to want to change."

"Have you thought about moving out?"

"Me abandon her, too?"

"Mimi, you have to think about yourself. Your own life. And Brady's. Don't let her issues hurt him or you'll never forgive yourself. You don't want him to turn out like me."

"You've done okay. Look, you're a cop. A good cop, I hear. You don't do drugs, or booze, you don't smoke, you have a good family, people like you ... "

"I do drink. More than I should. I don't let it affect my job, but I hate myself when I do it. All I can think about is Mom, sleeping it off on the floor."

"Alex. You're not an alcoholic."

Alex clenched his teeth. He wasn't so sure. Maybe it was genetic. "Look. If you ever need a place to go, a place you can bring Brady, I have room. I mean, it's just a townhouse, but I have two bedrooms and a den. If things get too dicey with Mom."

Melissa stared at him for several moments. "Wow, that's ... that's so generous of you to offer. No roommates, girlfriends?"

"Nope. I make enough to live comfortably there. It's an older building, but safe and clean."

"I don't make enough to live on my own, but I will remember your offer if I need a brief place to land."

"Good. I mean it. So, we're almost there. You okay with seeing everyone? Ash?"

"Zoe and I need to have a heart-to-heart one of these days. But for tonight, yeah, I'm good. I liked talking with you. I almost feel like I have a brother again."

"Almost?" Alex smiled for the first time in a week. He left the keys in the ignition and took a receipt from the valet while joining his sister at the hotel's lavish entrance. "No almost about it. I have to tell you, I had my reservations about riding with you. Scared. I didn't know what to expect. You've been quite the shrew in the past."

"I have. I've been living on another planet. A planet like Hell. I'm still fighting my way back."

Alex took her hand and gestured with his other. "I see the rest of our eclectic brood in the lobby. Let's fight our way back together."

Sixteen

Win Some, Lose Some

The awards presentation started on time, with the second row of the theater filled with the Pierce clan. Megan's mother and her husband sat at one end of the row; Megan and Christian were seated on the aisle, with Ashley, Dane, Jessica, Jillian, Melissa, and Alex filling out the remaining seats.

Ashley's leaf-green chiffon dress, understated but a testament to spring gowns, hung well on her slender frame. She crossed her legs and in doing so, accidentally bumped Christian's knee. "Sorry," she murmured, adjusting her position.

"No worries," he whispered back.

The action was not lost on Megan, but her ramped up anxiety pulled her attention away from scene. As the honorable mentions and also-rans were celebrated, Megan sat stock-still as those around her faded away. Second and third place nominees were read off, and the tension turned palpable. Megan closed her eyes while the presenters talked about what a difficult decision it was, how close the various contestants came to winning. She was startled from her focus when Ashley reached across Christian and gently squeezed her arm.

Megan looked back in surprise as the envelope was opened. The crowd became silent. Dane reached for Ashley's and Jessica's hands and gestured to those round him to do the same. Soon, everyone in their row had formed a human chain, collectively hoping for a win. Megan had never given credence to such attempts but felt it couldn't hurt. She pondered the question as the name was read, a name that was not hers.

Okay. At least it's over. I knew I wouldn't win anyway. Megan exhaled but lifted her chin and applauded loudly. Christian muttered something about it being a mistake. After the winner was soundly congratulated and vacated the stage, a new presenter came to the podium. The audience again quieted.

"Our last award remains. I want to tell you, ladies and gentlemen, that we had one portfolio that stood out. Unfortunately, the entry was short one photo, and the rules are quite clear that twelve photos must be submitted to win. However, we could not allow this entry to be denied acknowledgment. The President's Trophy for outstanding achievement of philanthropic photography effort is hereby award to an individual whom, by all accounts, has put unmatched heart and soul into her work. In addition to this trophy, Megan MacKendall's work will be published in our annual *Eyes of the World* publication. Ms. MacKendall, please come up and get your award."

Megan's lips parted, and she turned to Christian with a frown. Had she heard right? Did they read her name, after all? His response was to pull her into a joyous kiss and then help her to her feet.

The reception ensued in the adjoining ballroom. Dane commandeered a table for eight and ordered celebratory drinks all around. Hot and cold hors d'oeuvres came out. Music commenced. Dane stood and lifted his drink. "To Megan. Meg, I can't tell you how much it warms my heart that you're sharing your shining moment with us. I hope you realize that ... you are just as much family to us as any of these other young whelps. Congratulations!"

·♥ · ♥ · ♥ · ♥ · ♥·

The evening progressed with other guests stopping by the table to offer congratulatory remarks. Jillian delighted everyone by taking photos with her iPhone, promising to follow in Megan's footsteps. Melissa, while quiet, enjoyed the familial banter and camaraderie.

"I should have brought Brady," she thought aloud.

"You could have," Ashley responded, sitting down beside her. "Dad would have loved that."

"I know. I didn't want ... it was a lot just getting myself here."

"Didn't Alex pick you up?"

"He did. I didn't mean ... physically. I haven't been the most pleasant member of this family. Wasn't sure I should come at all."

"Oh. Okay." Ashley nodded. "I get it. I almost didn't come, either."

"Why? You're like, central. Like you're a star. No offense."

"None taken. No, I'm not close to Megan, and Dev and I have a couple of issues we're working on, and Alex thinks I'm a spoiled hippie."

"Alex thinks what?" Their brother sat down on Melissa's other side.

"Don't deny it, bro. You were rude to me when I came home, and you've barely spoken to me since."

Melissa rolled her eyes. "Give me a break. *I'm* the exile in this little trio. You can't hold a candle to my shortcomings."

Ashley chuckled. "I don't know about that. I'm the one who ran off with gypsies."

"I thought that was just hearsay."

"No, she really did," Alex interjected. "And they starved her."

"Clearly. Shortage of candy bars?" Melissa grinned, and Ashley stuck her tongue out. Alex poured himself a second glass of wine, his eyes focused on Megan dancing with Christian. Eventually, he turned back to his sisters.

"Did you tell Ash about Mom?"

"What about Mom?" Ashley asked, picking up her own glass of wine.

Melissa sighed. "She fell off the wagon."

"Didn't realize she'd ever gotten on it. How bad?"

"Bad enough to pass out on her bed at four in the afternoon."

Ashley shrugged. "Shame."

Alex nodded. "Shame, indeed."

"Is she watching Brady tonight?"

"Not entirely. I got a sitter. I told her if we're not back by 11:30 and Brady is asleep, she can go on home. She only lives a couple of blocks away."

"Then I'd say she's gone. It's almost midnight. And I'm toast. You want a ride home?" Alex said to Melissa.

"That would be great."

Ashley stifled a yawn. "Could you give me a lift also? I don't know when Dad will be ready to go, and I'm wiped too."

"Sure. If I can stay. Malibu's not exactly in my neck of the woods."

The three rode in silence for a while, and then Melissa began to giggle. Her giggle grew into a laugh before the others finally asked what amused her so.

"Us! Look at us, after all these years apart. Just riding along like normal siblings. We've all changed and yet, something is still the same."

"Something? You mean, like, psychosis? It's a flamin' wonder we're not all locked up somewhere," Alex said.

"You're being awfully negative. We all experienced the breakup differently. We didn't make our own decisions, and we can't be responsible for what our parents did. Yeah, we're all damaged but we're survivors." Melissa folded her arms and nodded to punctuate her thoughts.

Ashley yawned again. "And we're all alone. We're probably all petrified to get into a relationship."

"I've been in relationships," Alex muttered.

"We all have. I just meant, nothing lasting."

"Yet. I plan to settle down with a nice girl someday. Raise a bunch of kids and make sure they never have to watch their folks tear each other apart."

Melissa and Ashley exchanged a glance. "Well said, bro," Ashley responded.

Melissa fell quiet as she thought about her own son, a boy with no father at all. Maybe someday she'd find ...

Her thoughts were interrupted as Alex turned into her neighborhood and brought the car to a stop. Orange cones blocked his way, and he pulled the car to the curb. A uniformed man approached.

"What's going on?" Alex fished for his badge and flipped it open. "Can we get through?"

"Sorry, Detective Pierce. There's been a fire, around the corner on the cul-de-sac. We're in mop up. You have a reason to turn down there?"

"Oh my God!" Melissa covered her mouth.

"My sister lives at the end of the street," Alex said while quickly getting out of the car. He walked with the fireman to the front of the car.

"It's the house at the center. There is at least one fatality.'

"Fuck," Alex muttered, turning to intercept Melissa who'd already exited the car and was hurrying toward the corner. Ashley joined them.

"We can't go down there yet. A house fire."

"Brady! Brady! Oh my God, Brady!" Melissa pushed past her brother and started running down the street with Alex and Ashley close behind. Embers still glowed bright red in the darkness and smoke drifted upward from the ruined structure. An ambulance sat idle, and behind it, a vehicle marked "Coroner."

Two firemen rushed forward to stop Melissa, and Alex took her from them, wrapping his arms around her as she sobbed. Ashley went directly to those standing beside the ambulance. She dialed her father as she walked.

Once she reached Dane, she quickly told him what she knew and promised to call back.

"Please tell me what happened. Are there any ... survivors?" she asked one man who seemed to be in charge.

"And you are?"

"Ashley Pierce. Melissa Pierce is my sister. She lives ... lived in this house with her son and our mother." Ashley quickly produced her wallet and showed her I.D.

"I'm sorry, Miss Pierce. We've removed the remains of one person who succumbed to burns and smoke inhalation."

"An ... adult ... or a child?"

"We believe the victim to be an adult woman."

Ashley drew in a ragged breath. "Are you sure there is no one else in the house? There was a teenage babysitter and a ten-year-old boy."

The official shook his head. "So far, no, and we got here within minutes of the call. It looks like the fire started in an upstairs bedroom, where the deceased was found." He gestured to the upper right of the home. "The burn was mostly limited to that half of the building. But these rooms over on this side were all empty."

Ashley thanked the man and went back to her brother and sister. Melissa grabbed her by the sleeve of her evening jacket. "What did he say? What did he say?"

Ashley swallowed hard and then grasped Alex's hand.

"It's Mom. She's ... gone. No one else was inside the house."

Melissa let out a cry of relief mixed with anguish. After a few moments, she dug into her purse for her cell phone. "I'm not even used to this thing yet. Oh! Oh! Look! A message! Zo can you read it to me?"

"Um, it says ... 'cable went out so am taking Brady to my house for the night. Sleep late and call when you get up. Kristin.'"

Upon hearing the message, Melissa's legs gave way and she slumped against Alex. The three stood together on the wet sidewalk, the smell of burning wood filling their noses and grief and gratitude filling their hearts.

"I can't believe Mom's dead." Melissa accepted a cup of decaf from Jessica and sank into the living room couch.

Dane shook his head and wiped at his eyes. "Did I hear right? Did they say she was smoking?"

Alex shook his head. "They can't say for sure, yet. She probably was."

Ashley sat down beside Melissa and wrapped her arm around her while her sister wept.

"How am I going to tell Brady?"

"Don't worry about that right now, dear. Give yourself a little time to ... to absorb all that's happened. For now, it's enough to know he's safe and miraculously survived," Jessica soothed. "Did you call the babysitter?"

"We texted her," Alex said. "Just to make sure. She responded. She'll keep Brady until later in the day."

"I used to be afraid something like this would happen when you all were still little," Dane said.

"I once had to turn off the stove. Mom had left the kitchen and Zo was reaching up with her little fingers ..." Melissa broke into another quiet sob as her sister held her.

"It's okay, Mel. It's okay."

Alex paced, unable to sit with the others. "Did anyone tell Meg? I hope not."

Dane and Jessica looked to one another. "We did not. No reason to ruin her beautiful night," Jessica finally said.

"I agree. I, uh, think I'll go home."

"No, stay here, Alex. We have plenty of room," Dane offered. "It's nearing 4 a.m. You could just go out and crash in the pool house if you want."

Alex shrugged and Dane stood up. "I'll get you some clothes and toiletries. I'd rather we were all together." As he started to leave the room, Dane detoured and went to his son. "I know we both have mixed feelings about your mom. But somewhere inside, she had a good heart. I'm so sorry."

Alex looked Dane in the eyes for several moments, then slowly reached out and embraced his father.

SEVENTEEN

Devon and the Reseda House Incident

Devon popped a piece of gum into his mouth and looked around. He'd parked the limo under a shady tree while waiting for Sy to conduct his business. Smiling, he rejoiced in the knowledge that the important client had taken a liking to him. This was his third gig, and Raffianello had again requested Devon for the day. Chris seemed surprised, but happy that Devon had made a good impression. After all, hadn't he forfeited his sister's big event the week before? And what a piece of cake! All he had to do was drive around L.A. and laugh when *the boss* made a joke or two.

Not that he was happy about missing Megan's award. Or the fact that his step-sibs had lost their mother so tragically that same night. He'd only met Rita Pierce a few times, and she'd been cordial. But Devon had sensed that the Pierce kids' relationship with their mom was sadly lacking. Maybe it was better that way. Maybe they wouldn't grieve as much. He only knew that if he ever lost his mother, it would flat out kill him.

Devon shook off the thought. So far today he'd driven down to Venice Beach, then downtown, and now he bided his time in Reseda, in a rundown residential neighborhood where the limo looked out of place. It was after sunset, and Devon's stomach growled. The lights went on in the house being visited by the don. He hoped there'd be time for a quick drive-through visit soon.

"Siri. Find closest Del Taco." Devon stared at the screen on his cell phone. A map appeared with a myriad of familiar fast-food logos within a five-mile radius from where he sat. He mentally chose the one between his location and the freeway on-ramp, then realized that with Sy Raffianello in the car, a triple-pack of soft tacos was probably out.

Loud voices coming from the small house caught his attention. Men argued, and Devon looked away, remembering Christian's instructions. The shouts grew louder; he couldn't help but glance toward the open front window and the men on the other side. A few words rose above the others: "money" and "ransom," and then "or else." Unable to look away, Devon stared in awe as the men moved around in what appeared to be a kitchen. One of them paused and looked out the window, then quickly pulled the blinds closed.

Devon's lips parted and he finally tore his gaze away. What was Christian doing in the house, and was the mobster one of the angry men? The argument continued, but Devon kept his eyes focused on the cellphone in his lap. Chris obviously didn't want him to know about his dealings with the Italian businessman. Devon wrangled with feelings of betrayal and curiosity. He felt both foolish and anxious. Something crappy was going down in that shabby little tract house, and he suddenly wanted to be far away from it. Far away and –

The gunshot shocked Devon to the core. A second shot reverberated from within the house. Before he could think of what to do, the front door flew open and slammed back against the house. Raffianello stormed out, another unsavory looking character on his heels. Instinctively, Devon started the car and tugged down the brim of his hat.

"Let's get out of here," Sy barked, sliding into the back of the limo. The other man got in with him. "Take us back to the estate."

"Yes, sir," Devon managed, his voice weaker than he intended. "Right away, sir," he added, this time more assertively.

Devon drove carefully, trying to appear calm while every nerve in his body screamed. He knew beyond any doubt that someone had been shot in that house, that someone lay bleeding or dead on the floor. This was exactly what he'd been warned to ignore.

Once, on a movie set, he'd witnessed a murder. A fake murder, one committed by an actor with a gun filled with blanks. The victim lay in a pool of movie-blood. Although he knew it was all a matter of good acting and props, Devon had shuddered at the vivid image of the character who lay suffering under the big lights.

This, however, was different. He couldn't pretend it was fake, couldn't turn his thoughts to something else. No distraction was strong enough, not the thought of his upcoming paycheck or his dreams of Ashley Pierce. He couldn't unhear the gunfire or unsee his real boss's face in the window. Sitting at a red light, his blood turned cold; could Christian be the man who lay dead or dying in the Reseda house? He shuddered again, wishing he could stop the tremors, praying his upset wouldn't be obvious to the men in the back seat.

When at last they arrived back at Raffianello's palatial home, Devon quickly walked around to open the door for Sy and his "associate." Normally, the client would hand him a sizable tip and send him on his way. Not so, tonight.

"Devon. Come in with us. Come in and have a drink."

Devon forced a smile. "Uh, that's very nice of you, sir. But I'm, uh, you know, on the job. And I'm sorta not old enough."

"Never bothered me when I was your age."

"Didn't matter," his friend quipped, slapping Sy on the back. "Back in Italy, you can drink when you're a kid!"

"True, true ... but never mind that. I insist. Come in and have a Coke or something. It's been a long day."

"Thanks, but ... my mom is expecting me and —" Devon stopped talking when he saw the look on Sy's face. It was a look that repeated the words he'd heard coming from the window: *or else.* "Well, I guess it couldn't hurt." Devon closed the back door of the limo and stepped up to join the two men walking into the house.

·♥· ♥· ♥·♥·♥·

Christian tossed his leather jacket across the back of the couch and headed straight for the well-stocked bar in the living room. Without breaking stride, he swiped a bottle of Scotch from the counter with one hand while reaching for a glass with the other. He poured out two generous splashes and drank it down.

Still standing just inside the door, Megan tilted her head and watched. "Bad day?"

"I'm sorry. Did you want a drink?"

"Only if you have a good red."

Christian perused the wine rack before pulling out a bottle of Pinot Noir. "This okay?"

"Sure. Looks fine. Are you okay?"

"Today was just … brutal." He poured out the wine and handed it to her. "I'll be okay in a bit."

"Something in particular?"

Christian drew in a breath, considered the amber liquid in his glass. "Unexpected problems. Conflicts. More than usual, I guess."

"Can we fix it?" Megan sauntered closer, touched him on the shoulder. "How about a dip in the hot tub?"

Christian turned to face her, his expression unreadable. Megan felt unsure and tried again. "The hot water could be therapeutic, and afterward, maybe a little massage?" She placed her palm against his chest and could feel the strong beat of his heart.

His grin was obviously forced, and he covered her hand with his own. "That sounds great. Just … after this." He held up the half-finished drink.

Megan nodded and went back to the doorway to retrieve her overnight bag. Without another word, she went to the bedroom to change. Christian clearly wasn't himself, and it set her on edge. The role of seductress was a new one, and she tried hard to make it seem natural when it couldn't be more foreign. His lukewarm response made her stomach hurt. Perhaps the impromptu date was a bad idea; she'd called him only an hour before to suggest they get together. He'd agreed and offered to swing by to pick her up. Now, changing into her swimsuit, she wished she hadn't called.

"God! You look damned hot in that."

Megan spun around and picked up her discarded dress from the bed. Christian leaned into the door frame, drink in hand.

"Only in the dark," Megan muttered. Momentarily buoyed, she dropped the dress and went to him, fingers finding the top button on his dress shirt. "Want some help?"

Christian smiled and allowed her to unbutton his shirt. Megan took his empty glass and put it on the dresser, then returned to remove his gold cuff links. She paused, turning his wrist to look at the upper part of his sleeve. "What's this? Something brown."

"What? Where?"

Megan tugged at his sleeve and he shrugged out of the shirt. She held up the stained area. "This is weird. It looks like dried blood. Did you kill someone today?" she asked, smiling as she looked over the rest of the shirt.

Christian frowned and whipped the shirt from her hands. "Crap. That shirt's done. I, uh, cut my arm today. I thought I had it bandaged enough that it wouldn't get on my shirt." He balled up the ruined dress shirt and launched it into the bathroom wastebasket. Megan frowned, seeing the dark stained bandage on his upper arm.

"That needs changing. What happened to you?"

"Stupid thing. I was carrying some boxes down to my car, to drop off at the resale shop, and I kicked the gate open, a little too hard, and it swung back and the latch nailed me. Tore a big hole in my shirt and in my arm. Bled like a sonuvabitch. I cleaned it up and thought it was done bleeding, but apparently not."

"I'll put a fresh bandage on there after our dip in the hot tub."

Christian's expression softened. "Yeah. Cool."

Once in the tub, Christian seemed to relax. Or perhaps it was the second glass of Scotch, Megan mused. Either way, he was better, and she also let her anxiety go. She looked forward to getting into bed and letting Christian do his magic. Six weeks had passed since their chance meeting in front of the gallery, six glorious weeks of dining, drinking, parties and hot sex. Watching Christian drag the rim of his drink slowly across his lips, Megan wondered if it really was hot sex or just average sex. How would she know the difference? What was hot to her might be tepid to other girls. Zoe – Ashley – probably had legitimately hot sex with guys.

Why Ashley? How were they so different? Ashley was less inhibited, more free, easy to adapt. She'd run off with gypsies, after all. Ashley seemed to not care which way the wind blew, while Megan not only needed to know which direction but also the velocity, the temperature, and the humidity of that wind. *I'm so hung up on things.*

Like Chris's shirt. Why did it keep bothering her? Why did she keep envisioning the gate to the parking garage, trying to understand how the latch – a smooth round ball peen knob – could rip a hole in his shirt? But to question meant she suspected Christian of lying, and that just couldn't be. That just –

"Meg? You there?" Christian waved a hand in front of her eyes. "You want any more wine?"

"Sure. Yeah. Sorry, I was daydreaming."

"Obviously." He'd brought the wine bottle to the table beside the tub and now poured her another glass. "I got this up in Paso. You like it?"

"It's perfect," she murmured, watching while her ... companion? Is that what Christian was? Certainly not a boyfriend. Again distracted, she watched him pour another glass of Scotch and bring it to his lips. She'd never seen him drink so much, especially not hard liquor. *Is it me? Does he need alcohol to be with me?* "I'm ready to get out," she said quickly. "You can stay in if you want. I'm going to take a quick shower if that's okay with you."

"Fine. I'll be in soon."

Megan showered off the smell of chlorine and put on her short, silky robe. Her hair was a little damp from the shower, so she took up Christian's hair dryer, then touched up her makeup. A tiny spot of perfume on her wrists and below her ear. Turning from side to side before the mirror, Megan sighed. Ready or not.

She emerged into a dark bedroom. The drapes were still open, and the light from the hot tub illuminated the deck. It took a moment to realize that Christian lay sprawled across the bed, still in his swim trunks. His light snore told her all she needed to know. Back in the bathroom, she got dressed and wrapped her wet suit in a dry towel, then quietly left the suite. She called a cab and debated about whether to leave a note. "Nope." *He'll call if he wants to see me.*

Ashley stood looking out her bedroom window. Lifting one foot, she absently ran it down the inside of her opposite leg, trying to relieve an itchy patch of skin. She'd lounged too long in the bath, pensive, reflective, wondering if coming home had been a good idea after all. "Of course, it was," she murmured at the moon, low in the dark sky. Even though she had not made amends prior to Rita's demise, her mother's death had somehow brought Ashley closer to her estranged siblings. Alex's surprising vulnerability left him saddened and distraught. He'd come around several times since the funeral. Despite Melissa's immediate reaction to the tragedy, she'd shown strength in the ensuing days and had met with her father and stepmother to discuss her future.

Ashley heard movement in the hall and went to her door, quietly turning the knob and then peeking out. Devon was just entering his bedroom. "Hey," she whispered. "You're out late."

"Yeah, had a late passenger." He hesitated, looking down at the doorknob in his hand. "I'm wiped. See you tomorrow."

"Okay," Ashley said. She started to close her door but then stuck her head back out. "You okay?"

"Fine. Good night."

Ashley frowned and closed her door. Perhaps her mother's horrible "accident" had affected Devon, too. The pall over the Pierce household had to lift soon. Otherwise, she couldn't trust herself not to take off again. Here, she had no job, no plans, and no ambition. No real schooling. No man.

She got into bed and picked up the new iPad Dane had bought her. It hadn't taken her too long to get the hang of social media, and she lately dabbled while passing the time. She tapped on the now familiar "f" in the blue icon and started scrolling through her timeline. She didn't have many Facebook friends and found the ones she did have mundane and narcissistic for the most part. But at the top of her page was a disturbing post.

DevOnTop "*is feeling scared*" began her stepbrother's status update, posted only moments before. "What do you do when you find out that someone is not who you think they are? When you trust someone who is hiding a dark secret? This is so not cool."

Ashley frowned. Maybe it wasn't Rita's death that was troubling Devon. Who could he be writing about?

Melissa hunkered down beneath the covers and slipped a protective arm around her sleeping son. The small night-light plugged into the wall near the door lit the open suitcase on the floor. She smiled in melancholy. Most of her possessions lay in and around that suitcase, but it somehow didn't matter. Could it be, the shock of Rita's dramatic end hadn't yet sunk in? Melissa closed her eyes and breathed in the shampooey scent of Brady's still damp hair. A decision had been made tonight, and despite all the mistakes in her checkerboard past, this one felt right. The Pierce mansion boasted six bedrooms, and beginning on Monday, two would be hers.

Melissa had no doubt that Jessica's influence would be good for Brady. In years past, Rita had spent countless hours of indoctrination, convincing her daughter of the "other woman's" evil and subversive ways. Yet whenever Melissa truly recounted her dealings with Dane's second wife, she could recall nothing but positive feelings. Jessica MacKendall Pierce had always treated her with kindness. Go figure; the movie star mom is the good witch; the suburban birth mom is the dark and twisty one.

Melissa's gut clenched a little. This was no time to be critical of Rita, a woman who'd shown remarkable strength during her daughter's worst time. Hadn't her mother held her hand and mopped her brow during Brady's violent entry into the world? Wasn't Rita the one who'd thrown out all the pills and spoon fed her drug-addled daughter back to health after Mr. By-the-Way-I'm-Married had changed his phone number? Melissa issued a heavy sigh. "I'm sorry, Mom. I'm so sorry your life wasn't happier."

Squeezing her eyes tightly closed, Melissa forced her mind on to happier thoughts. Roxanne had offered her full-time hours. Her father and stepmom would care for Brady, get him to school and back, get him on to his homework. Such a blessing! Because she needed to make money, needed to further build her life – now more than ever. She wanted to be able to pay her father back, if in no other way than to make him proud of her. She could do this.

She caressed the top of Brady's head with her lips. Things were going to be okay.

EIGHTEEN

Debts Never Incurred

Christian peered into the bathroom mirror with chagrin. He needed to shave but couldn't manage to hold his razor steady. It had been many years since he'd driven the porcelain bus, a time when he'd run with a rough bunch back in London. *"Black Dog is our friend,"* Derek had slurred, his reddened eyes jolly.

"Scotch is not my bloody friend," Christian moaned to himself. He'd stopped vomiting around 3 a.m. and had fallen into a comatose sleep. Now, his headed pounded and with every beat, his vision shook. He wanted to go back to bed, but it was almost eleven and he had too much on his mind to sleep any more. He grabbed a bottle of ibuprofen from his medicine cabinet and shook out three tablets. After throwing them back with some water, he braced himself on the sink counter. "Oh, God." The nausea reared from the depths of his gut, and he closed his eyes, taking a deep breath. He then staggered back to his bed and fell onto it, dragging a pillow over his eyes.

The pain was like a big black balloon in his head. The images he knew hid behind it weren't welcome. Something bad had happened yesterday, something he could barely fathom. Like a scene from a nightmare. As his head began to clear, he tried to reconstruct the events that had led to his shocking discovery. First, the email, and then the anonymous text message. The drive across town to meet the sender, and the dark, threatening stranger. How had the guy known so much? His demands made simple identity theft look like a walk in the park. Christian wasn't one to give in to idle threats; he'd proved as much on the streets of Paris, where he'd been regularly targeted by thugs. But this – this was different. This particular thug knew things, details and locations and names. Ignoring him meant putting everyone Christian knew and loved at risk.

He struggled to stand. On the sink counter was a wine glass with just the faintest purple stain in the bottom. *Megan's glass. Crap. Megan was here last night. I brought her here on my way home.* He stumbled to the living room, looking around for signs of her. A note, perhaps, but nothing appeared. On the corner of the bar lay his cell phone, and he swept it up, squinting at the small screen while he pressed the power button. No response. Battery dead. He walked on to his small office, glad for once for his landline. He dialed and listened to her voice mail message. He cleared his throat, tried his best to sound normal.

"Man did I blow it last night. I'm sorry, babe. Let me make it up to you. How about ... how about Morton's on Saturday? Get us a couple of steaks?" Christian paused, hoping she would answer. When he realized she was not going to pick up the call, he sighed. "Call me. Bye."

In the kitchen, he poured a glass of tomato juice and forced it down before heading back to the phone. He dialed, and this time his call was answered quickly. "Hey, Dev. It's Chris. How did yesterday go with the man?"

"It went bad. But you know that already."

"What? How so? He didn't lodge any complaints. That I know of," Christian added, remembering his dead cell. "I just wanted to make sure you ... made it through the day okay. He can be a tough customer."

"Tough, you say? Oh yeah, he's tough. He invited me in. To his house. He gave me a beer."

Christian's temples began to throb again. "A beer? You can't be drinking and driving, dude."

"Tell me about it. He insisted. Practically dragged me into his palace even after I said no. Not sure I like this guy, Chris. There's something dark about him."

"We discussed this, yes? About how you weren't going to worry about what Raffianello does for a living, or does in his free time? It's none of our business, right?"

"True, as long as it doesn't involve killing people."

"Killing people? You saw him kill someone?" Christian sat down, rubbed his hand across his forehead. "You saw it happen?"

"Not in person. But *you* were there, so what did you see?"

"I was there? I think you're mistaken, Dev. I was nowhere near the guy today. I had a meeting of my own over in Pasadena."

"But ... never mind."

"No, Dev, say it. What did you see?"

"I saw ... you. Through the window, at the house in Reseda. You looked right at me. And then I heard it. The gunshots. And Raffi and his friend come rushing out of the house and tell me to head back to his place. This is scary stuff, Chris. I'm not sure I'm cut out for it."

Christian shook his head. "I swear to you, I was not in that house. And I also promise you, you do not need to work for Sy again. I'll get Gustov next time. You – you did nothing wrong, Dev. Just forget about it. Sy, he gets a little coked out now and then, nothing to worry about. I'm sure what you saw or heard was all a big ... misunderstanding."

Devon was quiet on the line for a few moments, and Christian silently prayed that his explanation was enough. But Devon spoke with just the slightest quiver in his voice. "When we went back to his house, he had a lot of questions."

"About?"

"Mostly about you. He wanted to know how long I'd known you, and where you came from, and if you had family, that kind of stuff."

"What did you tell him?"

"I didn't have much to say. Because honestly, I realized that I don't know you all that well. I didn't know where you came from, or who your people were. My sister brought you to a party once. You could be ... anyone. From anywhere. And that was the truth, so it was easy to say."

Christian let out a breath. "Okay. Good. You did good. Like I said, don't worry about it. And I want you to take a few days off, okay? I'll still pay you."

"I like working for you. I like driving the stretch. Don't make me quit."

"I'm not making you quit. Just giving you some time off. And as for me, Dev, I'm just a regular guy. I don't have any skeletons in my closet; I don't have any hidden debts or creditors looking for me. I'm clean, okay? So please don't worry." He forced a chuckle. "Your sister is safe with me."

"But why would he be asking?"

"Because ... even though I said we'd never talk about it, you do understand that this man deals in sensitive product. He has to worry about whom he deals with. He watches his exposure. From time to time, he checks things out. It's sort of routine with him. Okay?"

This time Devon only paused a moment. "Okay. I got it. And I guess, it was getting dark, and the guy in the window, maybe he just looked like you."

"Right. Had to be. And the sound you heard, well, backfire?"

"Coulda been. Yeah. Okay." Devon huffed out a sound of relief. "Okay. Thanks, Chris. I'm sorry I flipped out."

"No sweat, pal. Now I gotta see to your sister. I kinda flaked out on her last night."

"Good luck with that, man."

Christian hung up the phone and noticed the drops of sweats spotting up his desk. He grabbed a sport towel from the gym bag on the floor beside his desk and ran it across his damp forehead. What the hell was Raffianello doing, and did it have anything to do with the blackmailer?

Worse, who was it that Devon had mistakenly thought was me?

· ❤ · ❤ · ❤ · ❤ · ❤ ·

According to the office calendar, Christian had Devon scheduled out twice in the coming ten days, both times on easy assignments involving teens. The kid needed a break, and he liked driving young people because he could relate to their teenage jargon and passions. Today, Christian taught him about limo maintenance and emergency maneuvers. He also had planned a few errands for Devon to run. It would keep him out of trouble while Christian addressed his bigger problems.

"It looks like I'll take the Harbor Freeway, right?" Devon sat in front of Christian's laptop focused on Google Maps.

Across the room, Christian dug through a file cabinet. "Yep. You'll get off at 11th. Near Staples. Pay attention though, it's easy to get tangled up on one-ways."

"Been down there a million times to see the Lakers and the Kings."

"Right. But most of the time other people drove, I'll bet?"

Devon nodded. "You seen my sister lately?"

Christian didn't pause but continued to pull files out of the drawer. "Seeing her tomorrow night. Why?"

"Just wondered. Are you guys, like, a real thing?"

Now Christian stopped and turned to look at Devon. "I'm not sure what you mean."

"Yes, you do. It's called GET-TING SER-I-OUS. Like, hooking up for good."

Christian returned to his work and chuckled. "I don't think Megan is SER-I-OUS-LY looking for something like that. And frankly, neither am I."

"So, what, it's like friends with benefits? I mean, is that fair? Megs isn't getting any younger."

Christian again paused but did not turn around. "Has she said something to you?"

"No, not really. I mean, no. She hasn't. It's just that, like, I think you two are so cool together. You make a great team, right? And it would be totally sick for you to be in the family."

"Sick. Right." Christian shook his head. "You'll need to gas up before you go. Take the Shell VISA. The Chase card is maxed out."

"I thought we just paid it off?"

"*We* didn't pay anything off. I needed a cash advance. Nothing to worry your pretty blond head about, junior."

Devon blushed. "Sorry. I'm too nosy sometimes."

"Nonsense. I like it when you take an interest in the business. Maybe one day we'll be partners."

"Can't imagine that I'd ever be good enough for that." Devon pocketed the credit card and headed for the door.

"You won't be if you keep thinking that way," Christian called after him.

Christian pondered Devon's words after his protégé left the office. Could Megan be expecting more from their relationship? He hadn't been paying attention. He had bigger fish to fry, a cliché he hated but one that came to mind as he logged in to his bank account for the third time today. The balance wasn't quite there; he was still a few thousand short, but if the bank came through on the short-term collateral loan, he could meet the blackmailer's demand. His hand hovered over the phone; should he call the bank again and risk annoying them? "Probably not," he muttered.

Issuing a heavy sigh, Christian closed his eyes. He had to keep his head. He couldn't mess this up – too much was at stake. But he also couldn't get past the questions plaguing him. How did this Corfu guy know so much about Christian's past? He'd been careful not to talk about his background, his roots, to anyone. As Devon had pointed out, Christian was just a guy without family, without history. Even Megan, the only woman he'd become even remotely close to, knew little about him. Yet Salvatore Corfu lodged threats, serious threats, asking restitution on a debt Christian had never incurred. Christian would have shrugged off such claims as nonsense. But Corfu knew about Robbie. About Martin and Mari and exactly where the gypsies were camped. Vulnerable, helpless, unsuspecting, the Duprés were like sitting ducks.

Christian put his head down on his desk and closed his eyes. He tried to remember every detail of his meeting with the slime bucket who'd met him in the dimly lit parking garage.

"You still owe us, man. With interest and, oh, some for the aggravation. Big time."

"I've told you before. I didn't borrow any money from you. This is crazy."

"You think we're stupid or something? You're standing right in front of me, Mr. Collins. You borrowed the money from me, for your poor, sick, derelict family who lives hand-to-mouth out in the swamps of the South. Did you think you could just take the dough and we'd look the other way? That we wouldn't thoroughly vet you?"

"It had to be someone else, impersonating me."

"Your brother, maybe? We know your brother is dead. And they say you probably killed him yourself, by the way. Do I care? No. But the cops might care. You wanna risk that?"

"I didn't kill anybody. And I didn't take any money." Christian paced behind his car, shaking his head. This was insane.

"You know pal, I don't give a flying fuck if you killed him or not. You get me the dough, and your family, what's left of it, lives. You don't and, well, I might spare that little sister of yours. What a hot piece of ass she is! But is it true gypsy girls don't shave their –"

"That's enough!" Christian was suddenly back on the mean streets of Paris, defending the honor of a young girl who'd been dragged into

the shadows in front of him. He lashed out at Corfu and clipped him on the chin, unaware that the thug wielded a knife. The blade caught him below his shoulder and Christian leaped backward.

"Aw, did you get hurt? 'Cause I'm good to go some more if you want." His attacker made a show of wiping the knife on a handkerchief.

"I'll get you the money. Just stay away from my family. They don't need any more grief. But I need guarantee that this is the end of it. I pay off this supposed debt and you disappear from our lives."

"If you're lucky, sport. But hey. It's not up to me, is it now? Surely you realize this is much bigger than just us."

"Who is it? Who's behind this? If you know who's setting me up –"

Corfu got into his car and lit a cigarette, then blew the smoke out the window. "What does it matter, kid? There's bad people in the world, and shit happens, and sometimes you step in it. And maybe you walk away and maybe you don't. You just do your best. Like I do."

Christian watched as the late model Lincoln drove away. It was too dark to read the license plate. That didn't matter either, he realized. He couldn't go to the cops, not without talking to his father first. There were too many secrets, too many unknowns. Like, who'd actually killed Robbie? Was this somehow related to Robbie's debt? Everyone had thought it was a group of common drug dealers; but this ... this extortion smacked of something "much bigger" as Corfu had pointed out. Organized crime? Could Robbie have lied about the amount of money? He'd told Christian it was fifty K, but these guys were tapping him for four times that much.

The memory of the meeting stung. Devon's story about Raffianello's questions came back to him. Was there a connection? Raffi had not returned his call.

Corfu's comment about Mari worried him. Maybe he'd fly out to Louisiana the minute the money transferred hands and persuade Martin to move the band. Perhaps even break it up, go their separate ways, hide out for a while. He could bring Maricela to California, protect her. Of course, that would mean exposing himself to Ashley.

He'd cross that bridge later. If he were going back to the Bayou, he'd better be prepared. There was a little operating capital left in his checking account, enough for a plane ticket. Regardless of the outcome with Corfu, it was time he'd paid his family a visit. The next available flight to Louisiana was tomorrow morning.

Nineteen

Accusations

Ashley sucked in her upper lip and tried not to bite it. Devon opened the driver's side door for her, then made a little flourish with his hand. "Step inside. Your carriage awaits."

It was her own car, dammit. She should be able to at least drive it to the store and back. She slipped behind the wheel and Devon closed the door, giving it a smart smack and then a thumbs up before getting into the passenger seat. "I'm not going to give a step-by-step. You know how to drive. I'm just here for comic relief," he said while snapping the seatbelt into place. "But ... the ignition button is right there."

Ashley slapped away his pointing finger and pressed the start button. When nothing happened but instrument lights, she turned back to Devon, who again pointed; this time at the dashboard message, reminding the driver to press down on the brake before starting the car. Ashley huffed out a sigh and put her foot on the brake. "My little Honda had a damned key," she muttered. Clearing her throat, she looked around at the vast, empty parking lot around them. Overhead, a flock of pigeons crossed the sky enroute to their next big arbor.

"If you do this, I'll buy breakfast," Devon said, crossing his arms.

"I'll do this. Just give me a minute."

"Breakfast is only served until 11:15."

"Shut up." Ashley moved her hand to the gear shift and moved it into "D." Looking around again, she reasoned that with nothing to hit, she was safe to drive around the lot. She eased off the brake and the car began to move.

"There you go."

"Yup, here I go," Ashley whispered, reluctantly moving her foot to the gas pedal. The car lurched and she quickly applied the brake, nearly sending them both into the windshield. "Sorry! This thing is fast."

"Just takes practice. Go again."

Ashley complied, this time easing the pressure and creating a smoother start. After a few moments she was crossing the parking lot toward the nearest large warehouse.

"Not so bad, right? All coming back to you? The thrill of driving?"

"Wouldn't exactly call it a thrill," she said, carefully moving the steering wheel and getting a feel for the turning diameter. "But it works. Especially nice without rain."

Devon chuckled. "I drove around the ranch once. Dad has a Denali up there. Whoa, you wanna talk about fun? Snow flyin' everywhere, tires spinning ... "

"I don't need that kind of visual right now, Dev."

After ten minutes of driving in circles, Ashley parked the car and got out. Such a simple activity, and yet she was sweating and shaky. She walked away from the Acura and turned to look at it from twenty feet away. "It's kind of sexy, I guess."

Devon soon joined her. "You did awesome. Now we can get some big ol' honkin' omelets. You wanna drive?"

"No, not yet. Maybe next time. I –" Ashley's eyes were drawn to a black Mercedes speeding toward them from the street. "Who's that?"

Devon frowned. "Don't know but whoever it is, they're in a hurry. Let's get back in the car."

Ashley got into the passenger's side and closed the door. Before Devon reached the car, the black luxury sedan had swerved to a stop in front of them. Two men got out. Both wore older, ill-fitting suits. One of the men leaned against the car and lit a cigarette.

"Out for a little joy ride, Mr. MacKendall?" the second man asked, tugging upward on his belt over his protruding stomach. "Funny, so are we. Why don't you join us?"

"I don't think so. We were just leaving."

"Then you can leave with us. Who's your friend? She can come, too."

"She's ... no one. Just a girl I met. I'll come with you but leave her here."

"Aw, let's bring her along. For company. She might even know something about our mutual acquaintance."

Ashley listened to their words, her mind racing. Clearly, these thugs were trying to abduct Devon! Without considering the consequences, she started to get out of the car, but her step-brother's voice stopped her.

"Go! Just — go!"

Panicked, Ashley looked from Devon's alarmed expression to the driver's seat and then back. One of the men grabbed Devon by the arm and dragged him toward the Mercedes; the other approached the Acura. She had a choice to make: either go with them or try to get help. She'd made many such decisions while traveling through the South – the fight or flight kind of decisions.

"GO!" Devon managed one last directive before being shoved into the backseat of the abductors' car. As quickly as possible, Ashley lifted herself over the gearshift and into the driver's seat. *Foot on brake. Press button.* With a quick glance toward the kidnappers, she slammed the car into reverse and pressed the gas pedal. The car jerked backwards. In a moment of clarity, she tried to see the Mercedes' license plate but realized it had been removed. The last thing she saw was Devon nodding at her while the mobsters slammed the backseat door of their car.

She hit the brake and the car skidded. Back into Drive, and the car turned easily around as she headed for the parking lot exit. She turned out into traffic and sped down the boulevard, keeping an eye on the rear-view mirror. If they'd followed her, she'd already lost them, but she kept driving, turning corners, watching the mirror. Finally, she pulled into a gas station and parked to the side. Pulse pounding, palms sweating, she tried to catch her breath. With shaking hands, she reached for her purse on the floor and withdrew her cell phone. She hesitated; 911 or her father? She chose 911 and said a silent prayer.

After giving the 911 operator the details, she hung up and pressed her hand over her eyes, hot tears leaking out between her fingers. She could barely comprehend what had just happened. Devon, her sweet, dare she say innocent, brother? Kidnapped by guys the likes of which she'd only seen in Godfather movies? How could this happen? Why? Her mind raced to come up with any possible reasons but could find none.

I have to calm down. I have to call someone. Alex! Of course. Her brother was a cop! "What am I thinking?" Brushing the tears from her cheeks, she quickly scanned the phonebook in her cell, eventually found "ALEX" and pressed "SEND."

"Hey, sis, what's up? I'm here with Dad, we just finished a round of tennis –"

"It's Devon! He's been taken! Two guys came, they grabbed him and took him!"

Ashley wasn't sure how to get home. Considering what had happened to her stepbrother, she could hardly ask anyone to come and get her from the gas station. Alex had assured her Devon would be found, but his hollow promise hadn't brought any measure of hope. She edged the car down the driveway and put her blinker on, taking a moment to wipe the tears from her face before turning out onto the busy boulevard. Sobs harnessed her ribs, making it impossible to take a full breath.

Was it this way? Ashley looked left and right, seeking a familiar landmark as she waited at a red light. When the light changed, she hesitated to lift her foot from the brake, watching closely all the cars around her until the one behind her honked. "Okay, dammit!" Hands and arms shaking, she moved into the intersection and across it while voices in her head screamed at her to stop, to pull over, get out of the car and call a cab.

Everyone else seemed to be going so fast! Cars passed her on the left and on the right, some of them frowning in her direction and others making obscene gestures as they sped past. She drove several blocks before she caught sight of a small photography studio she recognized on the right. Without thinking, she pulled to the curb and parked, crossed her arms on the steering wheel, and bent her head to cry. "Oh, Devon, Devon ... why?"

Ashley didn't know how long she'd been parked. Rummaging through the glove box in search of a napkin or tissue, her hand closed on a small stack of brown Taco Trail napkins. The fact that Devon had stashed them there was not lost on her, prompting a fresh wave of grief. Movement on the sidewalk interrupted her impending meltdown. Megan MacKendall was just leaving the photo studio. Ashley quickly looked away, but soon Megan tapped on the passenger window.

"Zoe! Dammit, I did it again. *Ashley*, I'm sorry. I – hey, are you all right?"

Ashley turned her head and stared through swollen eyes at Devon's sister. She shook her head, then hit the "unlock" button. Megan got in.

"What's going on? What is it?"

"Oh, Megan. I don't know how to – it's Dev. He's ... he's been kidnapped!"

The color drained from Megan's face. "What do you mean, kidnapped?"

"We went out this morning for a drive. He was – was teach-teaching me stuff about my new car. We were in this b-big parking lot, and these two guys drove up real fast, and they grabbed him and put him in their car ... they wanted to take me, but I got away." New sobs choked her speech. "I-I called Alex, and they are going to find him, they have to find him, oh God ..."

Megan's eyes darkened. "Why? What would they want with a sweet guy like Devon?" She frowned and turned to stare out the windshield.

"I can't imagine. I-I can't think of why."

"Does this have something to do with you? With those people you ran with? Those heathens?" Megan twisted around and leaned closer to Ashley.

"What are you talking about? Of course not!"

"It has to be! He's never done anything wrong in his life! You, on the other hand, ran away from home, fell in with common thieves, then came crawling back to your wealthy family. Those people, they followed you here, didn't they? What do you have that they want? Did you steal something?"

"Are you crazy, Megan? It was nothing like that! Nothing! They were good people, kind and very normal. They weren't thieves. They work for their money, like anyone else, just in different ways. How can you – how can you even talk like that when our brother is missing?"

"*My* brother. Not yours. Just because Jessica made the questionable decision to marry your father, it doesn't mean any of us are related." Megan huffed out a breath and pushed back her hair.

"You just left him there, with those criminals. Took off, did you? Coward!"

"No, that's not true. I did it so I could get help. He told me to go! He yelled at me to go. What good would it have done for me to go with them? We'd both be missing, and no one would even know yet! Alex said, he said it was good and the right thing to do."

"Of course, he would say that ..." Megan mumbled. "But he's being nice. Why did you even stop here?"

"I got lost. I'm upset. I saw your shop and I just stopped here."

"Fancy car like this, you could use your nav to get home. Unless you're too ... challenged to use it," Megan said. She briefly covered her eyes with her hand and groaned. "You should have stayed with him. Now Devon's alone and helpless. He's just a kid! *You* brought this on, I know you did."

Ashley sniffed and raised her chin. "Get out. Get out of my car. You can't talk to me that way. Not now." *Maybe you got away with it when we were kids, but not anymore.*

"But—"

"Just go. Someone, other than me, will call you as soon as we know anything."

Without another word, Megan got out of the car and walked purposefully back to the studio. Ashley started the car, punched her home address into the navigation screen and began a long, harrowing drive back to Malibu.

The thirty minutes it took Megan to get home seemed more like hours. She went straight to her small bar cart in the living room and poured herself a glass of something dark amber. It didn't matter what if it dulled the stabbing pains in her chest. Devon, the one person she valued more than any other, taken by criminals while stupid Ashley Pierce stood by and watched! How could something so tragic happen?

Two messages left for Christian, one for Alex. A tearful conversation with her mother, and a confusing one with Jessica, who ended up handing the phone over to Dane.

"She's sedated," he told Megan. "And I wish I were. They're doing everything they can. Ashley is here at the station giving the sketch artist details. She's understandably shaken. She says Devon has been acting a little strange lately, something about his Facebook posts. Do you know anything about that?"

"No, I-uh, don't go on Facebook much. I'll check, though. Anything else?"

"Not that it means anything, but Jess says he had a bad nightmare a couple of days ago. Not like him. I've been trying to reach Collins to see if he knows anything."

"I have a call into him as well. Dane, please – let me know if you hear anything, or if there is anything I can do."

"I will, Megs. I promise. Alex and his guys have our phones all rigged up in case ... in case there is a ransom call."

"Ransom. Yeah. I can't believe I hadn't thought of that already."

"Let's hope they do. At least then we'll know he's okay."

"Right."

Megan hung up the phone and poured herself another Jack Daniels.

TWENTY

Memories and Mobsters

C hristian stopped pacing and stared again at the phone in his hand. The text messages displayed troubled him.

Meg MacKendall: *"Please call me back. It's urgent."*

Meg MacKendall: *"Chris, this is an emergency. Please call me as soon as you can!"*

He couldn't imagine something being important enough to divert his thoughts from the blackmailers. Christian slammed his fist against the door jamb of his office. Two hours had passed since their last text message. When he tried calling the originating number, he got a blind electronic voice saying that the person he'd called was away from the phone. If only he knew for sure that his family was safe, he could take different action here in L.A. But his inability to check on his father and Maricela clouded everything. These guys had the wherewithal to attack from anywhere. Anytime. They'd described the camp exactly as he'd remembered it, almost as if they'd seen inside his mind. His father's characteristic red neckerchief, the pink and turquoise dragonfly tattoo on his sister's wrist. The rotting wooden barges they used to move upriver; the canvas tents and the old Ford Ranchero that barely ran.

He fell into his office chair. He could see that old Ford now, struggling along the riverfront to get to the road leading into town. His mother, moaning, wrapped in an old blanket and himself trying to hold her still in the shimmying, filthy truck bed. The cold stars overhead. Then, the pitying faces of the nurses as they stood by while doctors tried to break the news to Martin and his young son at his side.

"Salmonella," they said. "It's an e-coli infection. It probably started somewhere else, but it's gotten into her brain. I'm sorry."

"Sorry for what? What are you telling me? Can you fix my wife or not?"

"Mr. Dupré, it's too far gone. We advise you to take your wife home and make her comfortable."

Christian moved closer to his father and held tight to his pants leg. At nine, he fully understood what the doctors meant. "C'mon, Dad," he whispered. "We need to take Mom back."

"No. They can do something. They would if we had money," he said, shaking his head. "But their greed makes them no better than murderers."

"Mr. Dupré," the second doctor said, stepping forward. "If you'd brought her in sooner, we could have treated her. But as it is, her organs are already failing. I assure you it has nothing to do with money." He placed his hand on Martin's shoulder, but the older man shrugged it off.

"Liars."

Christian watched quietly as they brought his mother out in a wheelchair. He waited at the door with her while Martin brought the Ranchero around. The same group of nurses stood watching as Christian climbed into the back and spread out the blanket.

"You can't put her back there," one of the nurses called out. She rolled the wheelchair forward and opened the Ford's passenger side door. "Get in here and hold her on the way home," she said, this time more gently. Christian obeyed, wrapping his small arms around his groggy mother. The nurse smiled, leaned into the car, and pressed a small bottle into Christian's hand. "One, every six hours. Can you remember that? It will make it less painful." Christian nodded, his eyes wide.

She spoke once on the way home. "Take care of Robbie and Mari, Chris," she whispered, kissing his forehead. "I love you."

"I love you, too, Mama."

By the time they got back to camp, Lizbeth Dupré was dead.

The buzzing of his cell phone dragged Christian back to the present. Another text message.

2135559099: "Well look at this. Maybe now you can find the money you owe us?" then, "Bring the money to 18748 Laramie Street, Reseda,

8 p.m. Come alone. NO COPS. Don't make the mistake of thinking this isn't serious. Guns are pointed at heads."

Two photos were attached to the message; the first practically stopped his heart: Maricela hanging laundry on a rope line tied between trees. While he hadn't seen her in years, the young woman laughing and reaching up to secure a clean shirt was clearly his little sister. He almost smiled, but then remembered why the photo had been sent. The second one was similar but taken from a different angle. Christian stared hard at the snapshot. In the corner, almost hidden by bushes, stood a man watching.

His gut clenched. His hands grew damp as his mind raced. His thumbs rapidly typed out a response. "I need a little more time. I don't have all the money yet. Another 24 hours."

He'd barely hit send before the response appeared. "You can buy 12 hours with half the money. 8 p.m. Alone or a gun goes off. Not sure which."

Christian squeezed the phone in his fist as if the slim device could transmit his rage. A wild man fraught with both anger and terror, he uttered a growl that grew from his gut and echoed across his small office. How could this be happening? For the hundredth time he cursed Martin for not investing in a cheap, emergency use cell phone. Christian knew no one in the area, no one that could go out and check on the vagabonds who walked into the small towns and quietly did menial jobs for sustenance. Even if he could convince the local cops to look, he couldn't name any of the possible communities they frequented. The last he'd heard they were somewhere not far from Shreveport.

At the bank, Christian withdrew 111,000 dollars from his account. Barely more than half. Enough to stall them for a little while, and maybe long enough for him to get to Louisiana and warn his family.

He drove to Reseda in a stupor. The traffic around him seemed fake, as if he were driving through a movie of celluloid cars and trucks. None were a threat because they just weren't real. He'd studied a map before leaving and had burned the route into his brain. Now, pulling up outside the small, post-war cracker box, he frowned. Reseda. Wasn't that where Devon had claimed to have seen Christian? On the very day he'd met with Corfu?

Christian grabbed the zippered bank bag from the passenger side floor and got out of the car. Stepping up to the sidewalk, he unconsciously straightened his tie before moving to the porch. The door opened before he could knock.

Megan could not wait another moment. She could only check her phone so many times a minute. No word from anyone! Hadn't Alex received her messages? And where the hell was Christian? Even that worthless Ashley had promised that someone would call. Dane's phone was apparently off, a fact that enraged her; what if the kidnappers tried to call him?

"I can't do this." Grabbing her keys, she was out the door and on her way to Malibu. Driving as fast as her law-abiding mind would allow, she considered the possible scenarios. Devon's social media entries showed something had rattled the normally laid-back kid. But why hadn't he come to her, confided his problems? Had she been too busy, unavailable as she worked on her makeover? As she tried to become a sex goddess?

Blushing, Megan blew out a breath and tried a different line of thought. Perhaps she'd been too harsh with Ashley, let her past emotions color her thoughts. In retrospect, her accusations seemed silly and baseless. When this was all over, she'd apologize. When Devon was back, and his captors locked up. She'd pay better attention, too, once he was safe. She would abandon her plans to become someone she was never meant to be. Christian wasn't her perfect man. Her perfect man would be driving the car right now, holding her hand, assuring her that everything would be all right.

She approached the hilltop mansion, typed the code into the gate keypad and parked on the driveway. When no one answered the doorbell, she tried the knob and found it unlocked.

"Hello? Anybody here?" She peeked into the massive kitchen and broad family room. Empty. "Hello?" she called again.

"In here," a man called back from the sunroom at the rear of the house. "In here." The voice was weak. Megan hurried through to the back and found Dane sitting in a recliner. His face wet with perspiration, he grasped his left shoulder. "Thank God," he whispered hoarsely.

"Oh my gosh, Dane, what's wrong? Have you heard from the kidnappers?"

"No."

"Where is everyone?"

"Jess is upstairs asleep. Everyone else is still down at the police station. Megan, I need your help. I think I'm having a heart attack."

"Why, Mr. Collins. How nice of you to join us." Corfu held the door open, and Christian stepped inside. The mobster led him to a small living room sparsely outfitted with worn, mid-century modern furniture. Christian sat on the couch and looked around; his breath hitched at the sight of a black chauffeur's cap on the coffee table. A small, bronze, double-D emblem adorned the bill. "Where did you get that cap?" he demanded and started to get to his feet. Corfu moved to stand in front of him, too close for Christian to rise.

"Sit down, smart guy. We have no interest in the kid. Let's just say, his usefulness was limited. Now, where's the dough?"

"Here." Christian slapped the vinyl cash bag into Corfu's outstretched hands. One-hundred eleven thou. I'll have the rest to you tomorrow."

"I told you half would get you twelve. This ain't even half."

"It's more than half of 200K."

"Oh! You think it's still 200K? Got news for you pal, we upped it. You now owe us 300K. The price went up." Corfu took a banded packet of bills and fanned it. "And don't think we're going to hang around here. We're outta here in an hour. We got places to go. We'll get back to you on where you can bring the rest."

Christian watched in awe as Corfu and two other thugs shuffled out the door and toward a car in the driveway. "Wait! Where are you going?"

"You don't hear so well, pal. I just told you we'll be in touch. And don't try to follow us." Corfu pulled a revolver out of an arm holster and waved it toward Christian. "You get the picture?"

"Yeah, yeah. I get it."

I get it, all right. You want me to believe you're going after Mari. He waited in his car around the corner and watched for the black Lincoln to pass by before pulling out and following a couple of car-lengths back. *Well, I'll get to her first. After I make sure Dev is okay.*

TWENTY-ONE

The Heart of a Hero

Alex stared at the composite drawings made by the precinct artist. Neither man looked particularly familiar, but Ashley said the likenesses were fairly accurate of the two middle-aged thugs. While Alex's emotions roiled, his intellect stayed intact. His training in Missing Persons had prepared him well if he could keep it impersonal. Devon may have been a spoiled Hollywood brat, but he was Alex's brother, nonetheless. A brother ill-equipped to stand up to criminals like the ones who held him captive.

Ashley continued to turn the pages of the perp book, perusing every face. "Nothing so far. Is this typical, that they are waiting so long to contact us?"

"I can't say it's typical or atypical. Every case is unique. Have you been able to raise Dad yet?"

"They must both be sleeping. Jess was a wreck and that pill they gave her knocked her right out."

"We're tracking any incoming calls that are not from any of us." His own phone rang as he started to walk away. He peered at the screen before answering. "Pierce."

"Alex it's Megan. I --

"Meg. I'm sorry. Man, I should have called you back. We don't know anything yet or –"

"That's not why I'm calling. I'm with your dad. We're in an ambulance on our way to the hospital."

"What? What happened?"

"His heart. I stopped by the house and he was in distress. I called 911. The strain about Devon probably brought it on."

"Dammit! Is he okay? Is he conscious?"

"Yes, but they have oxygen on his face and an IV in his arm."

"Okay, okay." Alex blinked and then turned back toward his sister. "What about Jessica? Is she okay?"

"I didn't wake her. She's there alone. Someone should go there and explain when she wakes up."

"Right. Um, okay, can you stay with Dad until I can get there? I'll get Mimi or Aunt Rox to head over to the house, and I'll meet you at the hospital." Alex hung up and slipped his phone back into his pocket before rubbing his eyes. He'd just buried his mother, his brother had been abducted — and now Dad was sick? Not at all sure how he would handle this new turn, he cleared his throat and approached Ashley. "Hey. That was Meg. She's with Dad. They're on their way to Los Robles Hospital. Something about his heart. Can this day get any worse? I'm going to get over there. Can you call Melissa or Roxanne and ask them to go to the house and stay with Mom? She's alone there and won't know what happened."

"What about Jill? And Brady?"

Alex rolled his eyes. "I completely forgot about them. Are they at school?"

"I suppose so ... I'll call around. While we're on our way to the hospital. I'm going with you."

·♥ · ♥ · ♥ · ♥ · ♥ ·

Ashley held a death-grip on the passenger door handle as Alex sped across town toward Los Robles Hospital.

"Good thing you're a cop," she muttered, and tried to calm her breathing. Neither of them knew what to expect. A heart attack? Dane Pierce was in good – if not great – shape. Or at least she'd thought. He'd given up smoking over a decade ago, and while he enjoyed a good drink and an occasional prime rib, he took better care of himself than he ever had. It was possible, she considered, that his earlier years of indulgence had damaged him.

Megan was alone in the cardiac unit waiting room. She got quickly to her feet when they arrived. "He's in surgery. I would have called you, but I knew you were on your way. Something about an emergency by-pass?"

"Fuck," Alex said, turning away, arms akimbo. Ashley gulped back a sob.

"I'm sorry," Megan said softly. She reached out as if to touch Ashley, then withdrew her hand. "I – I didn't know what to do. He was sweating, and in pain, and he told me he thought he was having a heart attack. I called 911 immediately. I sat with him in the ambulance. I ... I held his hand."

Alex turned back around and nodded. "Thanks. That means a lot."

"He was scared. I could tell. But all he could talk about was ... was Devon." Megan drew in a quick, shuddering breath and blinked. "I never realized how much ... how much he loves my brother."

Ashley snatched up a box of tissues from an end table and handed one to Megan, then wiped her own face. "Of course he does," she muttered. Megan's earlier tirade still stung.

"Thanks." Megan dabbed at the corners of her eyes. "I don't suppose you've heard anything? I, um, took the liberty of bringing Dane's phone, just in case someone calls."

"We have it cloned already but thank you. That was smart. It's not a perfect system."

"Oh. I'm not up on all the techno-stuff. I just want him back. He's still so naïve, you know? I mean, who could want to hurt him?"

Alex shook his head. "I have to tell you; we have zero leads. I wish we could get a hold of Collins. He's not answering."

At the mention of Christian, Ashley started. Was he missing, too?

"I've tried him a few times myself. I can give you his address in case you think something's happened to him, too." Megan said.

"I already have a squad on their way over there."

"Oh."

Ashley frowned with conflicting emotions. "You don't think he's involved in this, do you?"

"No. It's just that Dev works for him, and we have to interview anyone and everyone who's been around him lately. Who might have seen or heard something unusual."

"There's something about him. I'm not sure what it is. Not sure I trust him," Ashley murmured.

"Chris? He's absolutely trustworthy!" Megan said. "You just don't know him."

No, I don't. So why am I so worried?

No sooner had the words left her lips than Megan regretted them. Did *she* even trust Christian? The story about the shirt and the injury came to mind. She'd lately wondered, too, about his family, where he came from. He'd never shared. And why had he gotten so blitzed a few nights back? It wasn't like him. While she'd been mad at the time, she later found it disturbing and odd. He wasn't one to pass up a night of passion and lust. Until Alex had called attention to Christian's disappearance, Megan had thought little about it. Now she was worried.

Time in the waiting room dragged by. Megan didn't know where to focus her attention, where to spend her time. Having arrived via ambulance, she had no transportation but considered calling a ride to take her down to the police station to await news. Alex, she knew, was as – if not more – conflicted than herself; here, waiting for his father to come out surgery, or at the precinct, waiting for news of his stepbrother. His phone rang from time to time, and with each interruption, she and Ashley both looked up; each time, Alex shook his head. "Nothing," he'd murmur.

Megan took a brief nap, necessitated by her utter exhaustion, and awoke as a surgeon strode into the room. He addressed the three of them together.

"Your dad is in recovery. He'll be there for a while. It was touch and go, his heart stopped twice during surgery, but I feel confident he'll make a full recovery, if he can adhere to a strict regimen. Diet, exercise, you get it. He won't be able to see anyone until morning. He's critical but stable, so I suggest you all go home and get a good night's sleep."

Ashley dropped back into a chair and covered her eyes as sobs erupted from her chest. "You're sure? He's gonna be okay?"

"As sure as I can be at this point. There can always be complications, of course. I will personally call you if there is any change you should be aware of."

Alex nodded. "That's good enough for me. Thanks, doc. Thanks a lot. He's a pretty important guy."

"Yes, he told me that just before we put him under." The doctor smiled and left them.

Alex shook his head and turned to Megan. "Let's get out of here. I need to get back to work. I'll drop you at your place on the way."

"No. Take me with you."

"Me, too," Ashley murmured, standing.

Alex sighed. "There's not much either of you can do at the station. It would probably be best if one or both of you waited at the house. Jess is going to need your support. What with Dad, and Dev ..."

"Okay. Of course, you're right." Megan picked up her purse and dipped into it for her phone. Surely Chris had called back by now. The message light blinked, and she quickly tapped her text screen. The message was short and heart wrenching: "It's Dev. Can you pick me up?"

TWENTY-TWO

An Armed Ally

Christian's bag was already in the trunk of his car. Traffic was a bitch on the 405, as usual, but he made decent time to LAX. His stomach churned and his head throbbed – he didn't remember if he'd eaten today. After checking in for his flight, he tried Devon's phone again, but didn't bother to leave a message. He recalled the hurried note he'd left at the office, on the off-chance Devon showed up there. "Some family business, nothing serious, will be back on Friday."

He still had twenty minutes before boarding. Slipping onto a barstool, he ordered a glass of Malbec and issued a heavy sigh. No matter that it was morning; he needed something to "steady his nerves" as his brother used to say. As much as he dreaded doing so, he knew his next call would be to Megan, and he'd have to dodge her questions as best he could.

Where have I been? Why haven't I called her back sooner?

I lost my phone.

I slept all day.

I fell into a sink hole.

I was dealing with murderous thieves. Yeah, that's the one.

Christian practically gulped down the wine and ordered a second. He stared at the screen of his phone and wished as hard as he could that it would ring and it would be Devon, and everything would be okay. When that didn't happen, he found Megan's contact info and pressed SEND.

"Hey. It's me. I, uh, just got your messages. I was down in Signal Hill on an appointment and damn if I didn't leave my phone at home! Imagine me, without a phone."

"Imagine that."

"What's up? Your messages sound urgent. Is everything okay?"

"No. Everything's a mess. Where do I start? Where are you? Can we get together? I'm a wreck."

"Umm ..."

"Devon was kidnapped today, by some thugs looking for you! *You*, Chris. You need to tell me what's going on."

"Me? Whatever for? I –"

"And if that isn't enough, Dane's in the hospital. He had a heart attack when Dev went missing."

"Oh, no. No! Is he okay? Is Devon still –"

"Dev is fine. I picked him up about forty-five minutes ago at a mall in Woodland Hills. Dane's out of surgery and they're saying he'll be okay. Triple by-pass."

Christian bowed his head and covered his eyes. Devon was safe. He couldn't begin to process the news about Dane. "I can't believe this. But you're sure – Devon is okay? They didn't hurt him?"

"Apparently not. Look, he thinks you're involved somehow. So does Alex. Can I come over?"

"I'm not home. I'm actually ... at the airport. I have some family business I must take care of. My, uh, father is sick. Back East."

The silence on the line exacerbated the pounding in his forehead. His sudden departure upset Megan, especially considering all she'd been through today. "I'm sorry, I have to do this. I wish I could be there for you, Meg. I'm so relieved that Devon and Dane are both ... okay."

"Does this trip have something to do with those guys who took Dev?"

"I don't know anything about that. I can assure you ... Is Dev there? Can I talk to him?"

"He's making his statement to Alex right now. He said these two guys took him to some house in the Valley, a house he'd been to before. He said he thought he saw you there once. They asked him all kinds of questions about you, where you were from, what you did before you had your business. Do you owe these gangsters money, Chris? Are they loan sharks?"

Christian closed his eyes tight and ran his hand over his mouth. "I swear, Megan, I don't know anything about these guys. Maybe they're extortionists. Are you sure they weren't looking to get money from Dane? I mean, did they contact Dane before he had his attack? Does anyone even know?"

"Dane was alone when I found him. He didn't say anything about a phone call, only that he was in pain. He was upset about Dev, of course. But I'm sure he would have told me if he'd received a ransom call. And anyway, those guys dumped Devon off when they were through questioning him." Megan paused, and her next words bore an accusatory tone. "Alex works in the MISPER department, you know. He'll get to the bottom of this."

"I see."

"When will you be back?"

"Not exactly sure. My dad, he's ... he's kind of stubborn and my sister can't handle him by herself. I just need to make sure he gets some medical attention."

Megan went quiet again, and Christian heard her exhale. "Okay. But will you call me? Where are you going? Where in the East?"

"Look, Meg ... they're calling my flight. I will call you, I promise, and give my best to Devon. Tell him I'm so sorry for all that went down today. We'll talk when I get back. Be safe!"

"Okay but –"

Christian hung up before Megan could lodge further protests. His fingers shook as he dropped the phone onto the bar and picked up his wine glass. Where *was* he going? He didn't even know. Baton Rouge, a rental car, a guy he knew who had guns for sale.

He wanted to sleep on the plane, but every time he dropped off, he'd awaken with a start. He finally gave up and ordered a cup of coffee. Washing down a couple of Advil, Christian leaned back in his seat and thought about his destination. Would he even remember the narrow, quiet roads leading to the camp? The camp that might now be only a bare acre of land with the remnants of fire pits and tent stakes? He hadn't been back in, what, three years?

There was someone who'd been there more recently. Zoe Pierce left the Bayou less than a year ago, and she surely knew more about the band's locale than he did. How many times had he wished he could ask her about his father, his sister? But doing so would reveal himself. Bring back memories she may wish to keep hidden; buried. He could only imagine the embarrassment they might both experience. *Hey, remember me? I'm the guy who ... who possibly popped your cherry?* Christian uttered a sardonic chuckle and shook his head. His random thoughts had him wondering about the men who'd followed. Surely, she'd had other lovers, especially after maturing into such a hot babe.

Hot babe? The term was an insult. Ashley was a beautiful woman, every bit as beautiful that first night in the tent as she was today. He remembered seeing her for the second time, that afternoon at Pierce's estate, when he'd arrived with Megan for Ashley's birthday bash. There was something about her, a magnetism that drew him. His eyes sought her out wherever she went, and he fought the urge to leave Megan's side and pursue the guest of honor.

Now, months later, it occurred to him that his relationship with Megan, so brand new that day, hadn't had a chance. Seeing Ashley changed everything, and discovering her identity changed everything again. It was either tell her immediately who he was or hide the fact forever. When immediately had come and gone and he hadn't mentioned their mutual past, Christian was forced to abandon his attraction and live the lie. The lie that would prevent them from ever becoming anything other than polite friends. And yet, she was the one person who might have been able to help clear his name. For he was almost certain he was with Zoe Pierce during the exact moment that Robbie Dupré was murdered. Not just with her, but *with* her. In the throes of her first sexual experience.

"Oh, the irony." Christian huffed out a sad breath. None of that mattered, now. Robbie was dead, and his debts had outlived him. It was all-in time. He had to protect what family he had left or die trying.

The black, nondescript SUV came to a stop in front of the run-down coffee shop with an oversized catfish sign above the door. The sun had been up for an hour or so, and Christian stretched his legs, glad the fog had lifted. The hotel in Baton Rouge wasn't half-bad, but he would have slept on the ground he'd been so tired upon his arrival. After downing a cup of black coffee, he asked the woman behind the counter if Rudy was around. She fixed her narrowed eyes on his. "Whachu want with Rudy?"

"He's an old friend. We went to school together. Tell him Chris Dupré is here."

"Dupré? You related to the old man on the river?"

"Might be," Christian said, looking down at his mug before holding it up for a refill. The waitress filled his cup and then disappeared through the swinging saloon doors into the kitchen. Soon, a man with shoulder-length, white-blond hair and a beard came back through. Squinting, he peered at Christian before breaking into a grin.

"Chris-chun-dooo-preee! As I live and breathe!"

TWENTY-THREE

A Cry for Help

Ashley pulled a clean, white t-shirt over her head and gathered her hair back into a ponytail. She peered into her bathroom mirror, barely registering her own, tired reflection.

"What a day." She washed her face, brushed her teeth, and shuffled back to her bedroom where her bed already waited, covers turned down. After everything, Jessie had straightened out her bedclothes for her and left a note.

"Everything will be okay. Your dad is strong and will come out of this ornerier than ever. Love you. Mom II." Beside the note lay a sugar cookie on a napkin.

"Hmm." Ashley sat down on the bed and broke off a piece of the cookie. She savored the morsel on her tongue, closed her eyes, and thought about her stepmother's own strength. Jessica was outraged, upon awakening, that the doctor gave her such a strong sedative. Sure, she was upset – traumatized – over Devon's abduction. And yes, she'd acknowledged, a little something to calm her down would be nice. But Dr. Brown had "slipped her a Mickey," she complained, rendering her useless to Dane when he'd needed her the most.

"I hope I can be half the woman you are someday," Ashley murmured, reflecting that with Rita gone, Jessica Taylor MacKendall Pierce was no longer *Mom II*.

After slipping between the sheets, Ashley stared into the darkness, eyes wide with sleeplessness. What had started out to be a fun outing with Devon had rapidly evolved into the worst possible day. You'd think after all this, she mused, I'd be comatose by now. Her father was resting comfortably, she'd been assured, and Devon lay in his room across the hall, free of his captors, the memory of his ordeal rapidly fading.

But what if it wasn't? What if he was also awake at 2 a.m., unable to shut off the ugliness of the day? With a sigh of mild self-recrimination, Ashley got out of bed and tread lightly to Devon's room. She tapped lightly.

"Come in."

"I wanted to make sure you were okay."

"I'm not sure what 'okay' means anymore, but I'm probably going to live," Devon remarked. "You?"

Ashley closed the door behind her and sat down on the edge of Devon's bed. "I'm sorry. I shouldn't have left you there."

Devon swallowed hard and looked away. The dim light from his nightstand lamp cast shadows of doubt on his youthful face. "No," he whispered, then cleared his throat. "You did a very brave thing. Besides, I told you to go. And as they were stuffing me into that car, all I could think about was, look at that girl go! She's driving that damned car away by herself!"

Ashley felt her eyes brimming – again. She sniffed and tried to laugh. "You crazy nut." She took his hand and squeezed it. "They didn't hurt you?"

"Naw. Assholes just wanted to know about Chris. The second time I've been grilled about him. Something's up with his past. I wish I knew. Here," he said, moving over on the bed. "Stay and talk to me a while. Bore me to sleep. Sister."

Ashley lay down on her side and propped her head on her hand. "There *is* something strange about Christian. I've felt it since I first saw him at the party. I can't explain it, it's like he's got some kind of polarity going on. Like I want to know more, but I don't. And he seems familiar, in a way. Did Megan say anything? Does she know anything?"

"Nope. And to tell you the truth, there isn't much to the Chris-Meg thing anyway. He's not in it with her."

"In what?"

"My bet is, my sister is looking for someone kinda permanent. Chris is more a Teflon guy."

"Did he say that?"

"In so many words, yeah."

Ashley recalled a moment, earlier in the evening, when Megan had grown quiet after a phone call. "I just assumed ... they were, probably, hooked up."

"Depends on your definition of hooked up. Megs is getting something that's put a shine on her, that's for sure. But for Chris ... I think it's fun and games."

"I'm surprised." Why did this news put a tingle inside her?

"He didn't even mention to her that he was going out of town. What kind of guy does that to his girl? A guy that isn't committed. In any way. He gave her some lame excuse about forgetting his phone when he went to Long Beach. Ha!. I work with the guy. He never, ever, *ever* is without his phone. It's like glued to his ear."

"Glued."

"Yeah. Glued."

"Hmm."

"Don't get me wrong. I like Chris. A lot. He's a stellar boss. He's honest and he treats our customers fairly. He buys my lunch all the time. He puts up with the crazy ass things I do. He'd probably give me his shirt if I asked for it. But I just don't get that he's into Meg. It's a shame."

"Maybe she's using him, too. Did you ever consider that?"

Devon frowned, a hurt creeping into his brown eyes. But after a moment, his face cleared, and he chuckled. "You could be right about that."

"Are you bored enough yet? I have to get to sleep." Ashley stood up and went to the door, then turned back around. "I'm glad you're okay, Dev. And thanks for the driving lesson."

He blew her a kiss.

With a new worry replacing an old one, Ashley tossed in her bed for another hour. Devon's revelation about Christian had her reeling. Was she allowed, now, to feel the attraction? What if Dev was wrong about the situation, and they were really into each other? She couldn't afford the embarrassment, nor could she incur more wrath from Megan. The woman already misdirected all her anguish over her father's death to the Pierce family. If Ashley made overtures to her boyfriend, world-war-three would likely ensue.

Ashley sighed and punched the side of her pillow. She reached for her cell phone on the nightstand to check the time: 3 a.m. Just before putting it back down, she noticed a missed call and voicemail pending. The call had come in at 2:15. She quickly pressed the 'listen' key and put the phone to her ear. A woman's voice; hushed and distressed.

"Zoe! It's me. Mari. I'm sorry, I didn't know who else to call. I'm in trouble. We're all in trouble. There's some awfully bad guys here. They're fighting with my father! They're trying to get money, they say Robbie is still alive ... can you call me back, please? Zoe, I wouldn't call you if there was anybody else left to call. Honest. Please. They said if we get the police, they'll ... oh, God. I gotta go. This is Ronnie's phone. Call me!"

TWENTY-FOUR

Two to Louisiana

By late Thursday morning Ashley was seated in coach, a fat envelope in her backpack. Her early phone call to Maricela had put a chill into her bones that wouldn't go away with any amount of coffee or number of blankets. What was she doing? Although the money was hers, she felt like a thief drawing it from her trust fund at a bank branch near the airport and lying to Jessica about her quick trip to Louisiana. She had an unfair advantage; Jessica was preoccupied with Dane. Her stepmother would normally have seen Ashley's lie from a mile away.

As the Boeing jet's wheels folded in on lift off, Ashley allowed her doubts to surface. There was no turning back now, but the ice in her veins grew. No one knew where she was truly going, a fact that stabbed at her responsible side. If the plane crashed, if the rental car went into the bayou, if the marauders shot her down, no one at home would have a clue. They'd hear about it in the news. ACTOR'S DAUGHTER FOUND FLOATING IN MISSISSIPPI TRIBUTARY.

"Ha!" She laughed out loud at the absurdity, then covered her mouth when another passenger looked her way.

She'd almost told Devon but realized he couldn't be trusted when it came to his relationship with his mother. And she could not, would not worry Jessica right now. So instead, she'd told them both the story of a friend in need – not a complete lie. *"I'll only be gone two days,"* she assured them. *"Please kiss Daddy for me."*

The friend in need had warned her to park at the abandoned farmhouse a mile from the camp and walk through the wooded area.

There are three guys, Mari told her, and they have guns. "They've come because they think Robbie is still alive and that we somehow have the money to pay off his drug debts. They seem to be waiting for something. Or someone."

"But Robbie is dead! We all saw his body."

"Yes, but no one knows where he is buried. Our father won't tell. He's afraid they'll dig up Robbie."

Guns. Three men. What if she didn't have enough money? What if they wanted more than just the cash? Somewhere over New Mexico, Ashley's anxiety went into high gear.

The drive from the airport rental car lot to the hotel was only a couple of blocks. Ashley self-parked and checked in, relieved to be off the plane and out of the car. In her room, she put the envelope full of cash in the ~~room~~ safe and sat down on the bed. Between the five-and-a-half-hour flight and the two-hour time difference, it was past 7:30 p.m., too late to do anything today.

"What am I doing here?" she asked aloud, sitting up straight with her hands clasped in her lap. As a kid, she'd always loved travelling and couldn't wait to see what each hotel room looked like. Did it have little bottles of shampoo, conditioner? Body lotion? Some fancier places had shower caps and mouthwash, and fluffy terrycloth robes in the closet. Daddy was always impressed with the honor bar. Today, however, the room was just a place to sit down, regroup and plan her next move.

Remorse overwhelmed her. She'd acted impulsively and possibly quite stupidly. Like the first time she'd fled L.A. and ended up at a high school friend's college dorm in New Orleans, then accepted a new friend's invitation to become a gypsy.

"A gypsy? Are you kidding?" Ashley had stared at the young woman who was digging through the same basket of used clothing.

"Yup. We live down by the river. We used to live in Natchez, I went to elementary school there, but at some point, my folks decided to 'live off the land' and we went with a bunch of my father's friends to camp out. It was supposed to be for one summer but, well, we stayed." Maricela had an open friendliness about her that Zoe immediately loved.

"So, you call yourselves gypsies. That's interesting. I can totally appreciate wanting to get away from society. Back where I grew up, it's all about how expensive your house is or how new and fancy your car

is, and how many pairs of shoes you have, and everybody needs to be skinny to have friends." Zoe paused and her face colored. "Sorry. I guess I'm a little sensitive about that stuff."

"You'd love our people. We never judge. We just enjoy life and keep on; the river is there, giving us transportation and food and a sense of peace. You wanna come down there with me?"

They'd become fast friends and confidantes. Maricela was funny and loving and a loyal friend. Yes, sometimes she talked too much or got a little silly, but Zoe had put Mari right into her own personal family, taking the place of her fussy and immature biological sister.

Becoming Ashley had pulled the curtain on Zoe's life, but when Mari had called, panic-stricken the night before, Ashley's love for her friend had resurfaced in a big way. After making sure her brother was safe and her father stable, she'd not hesitated to pull together the cash Mari said she needed. Now, in the dim lamp light in her hotel room, Ashley questioned her sanity. She was no match for drug dealers and thugs. How could she possibly go through with delivering the money to them?

Frowning, she thought about the trauma of yesterday's events. The kidnappers who'd followed her and Devon to the parking lot. How was it possible that the very same night, Maricela would have her own encounter with criminals? Could they be related somehow? With startling clarity, Ashley realized there was one common denominator: herself. Yet the heathens who'd abducted Devon didn't seem to even know her identity. Was it all a crazy fluke?

But what if it wasn't. What if these guys had made a connection, somehow, and were looking to profit from her family? A chill passed over her, and it became stunningly clear that she'd screwed up. *I'm not as smart, or as strong, or as courageous as I thought I was. I need to call Alex.*

"It's a Beretta 84. Holds thirteen rounds in a double-stack magazine. The first round you shoot is double-action and follow-up shots are single-action. Here. It's loaded."

Christian took the .38 pistol from Rudy and pulled the slide. "Nice. You have more ammo, I assume?" Rudy gave him a look of disgust, and Christian chuckled. "Sorry. Dumb question."

"Here's another dumb question. Who you goin' after with this piece?"

"If I told you, I'd have to kill you, too," Christian quipped, holding the gun to eye level and peering down the barrel.

"Fair enough. Just don't get popped, hear? Now go ahead and practice a few rounds. I want to make sure you can handle this bad boy."

Christian took aim and fired off five shots, hitting two of the glass mayonnaise jars Rudy had set up several yards away. "Not bad for a pansy-assed Californian," Rudy said, clapping Christian on the shoulder. "But seriously, Chris, I hope you don't use it."

"Me, too. I need to get going. I'll bring it back, tomorrow, with any luck. If I don't get offed myself." Christian blew out a breath. "Oh, and I need a pair of binoculars if you have them."

Rudy found him a pair, dirty but serviceable field glasses. "You take care. You sure you don't need help with this situation?"

"I know where to find you if I do."

Christian got in the rental, tucked the revolver into the glove box and got back on the road, Rudy's hen-scratched map on his lap. Nothing looked particularly familiar once he left the main road, but Rudy had penciled in a few landmarks for him to watch for. An old cypress tree with a pair of red Converse high-tops dangling from a low branch. A small wooden hut with a headless, pink plastic flamingo stuck into the ground in front. A stack of old tires with plants growing out of the center, like some elaborate, dystopian flower vase.

He stopped when he came within view of the camp. His breath caught in his chest at the sight of the dozen or so dirt-brown tents set up in a haphazard fashion around a tiny wooden shack. The shack was new to him; he wondered if his father had built it for himself. He pulled out the binoculars for a closer look. The building looked to be about twelve feet square. He saw no one around, and other than the thin ribbon of blue smoke coming from the morning's fire, the camp appeared abandoned.

Christian placed the pistol on the passenger seat. He wondered if he could buy some time. If Corfu wasn't already here, he could swoop right in and round up his family; but if he was, he could be walking into a trap. He should at least attempt to find out. He retrieved his phone from his backpack and dialed the number Corfu had called him from.

"Mr. Dupré. How's the rest of that money coming? I hope you didn't go looking for us in Reseda."

"I have the rest of the money. I can meet you tomorrow."

"Why tomorrow?"

"I assume you're in the Bayou."

"Right you are! What a lovely place to grow up. You must miss it."

"It will take me a while to get there," Christian hedged.

"I'm feeling magnanimous. I'll give you until noon tomorrow. I'll do my best to keep my ... associates from bothering sweet Maricela."

Christian's heart quickened. "I want to talk to her."

"She's a little busy right now."

"I need to know she's okay. Otherwise, why would I bother to come all that way?" Christian clenched his teeth but waited. There was a short delay. He saw movement in the camp as an unknown man emerged from the hut and went to the nearest tent, where he went inside and returned with Maricela. Christian's breath caught in his throat. There she was. His little sister, being hurried along toward the shack. And a moment later, she was on the line.

"Chris?" Her voice was small and uncertain.

"It's me, Mari. Are you okay? Have they hurt you?"

"No. But – are you coming? Don't come unless you have money, Chris. Don't c – "

"That's enough. See you tomorrow." Corfu spoke and then the line went dead. Christian watched as Maricela was led back to the tent in which she was being held. Her wrists were bound.

Christian lowered the binoculars. Gun or no gun, he would not be able to storm the shack by himself. It was walk in on his own and try to negotiate or go back and get a posse together.

TWENTY-FIVE

Meganalex

Alex dropped into his chair and leaned onto his desk, his head propped by his hands. Despite what the doctor said, he wasn't convinced that his father was out of the woods. Jessica seemed almost too optimistic, all smiling assurances and acting as if the clearance of Dane's three blocked arteries was merely a walk in the park. He reminded himself that she was, after all, an actress. Alex himself couldn't pull off that kind of role; he'd barely been able to hide his feelings in front of Megan. Such irony. He'd seen her more in the last forty-eight hours than in the last forty-eight months, but all due to the hellacious events plaguing their two families.

The thought brought him around to Devon. When his little brother had gone missing, all Alex could think about was the fact that he'd been so mean to Devon. What if the unthinkable had happened and the kidnappers had killed the only brother he'd ever had? Rita was dead; Dane was in critical care; no way could Alex lose Devon, too.

An involuntary shudder rippled across him. He needn't go there because Devon was alive and apparently unharmed. Yet there was a stone left unturned. Collins was now missing, and according to Devon, the same thugs that had taken him were also after Christian. Alex clenched his teeth at the thought of the dark and mysterious player who'd managed to coax Megan out of her cocoon. "Jerk," he murmured, picking up a ballpoint pen and twisting it. "He's behind this whole rotten mess. If we find Collins, we'll find the root of the crime."

Alex looked through the windows of his glassed-in office. A few others worked at their desks, but overall, the room was quiet. He didn't quite know what to do next, so taxed was his brain. He knew he should be digging around, trying to find out where Christian had gone in such a hurry. Both Devon and Megan had reported that Collins had a family matter "back east," but it sounded lame to Alex. Hell, the dude could still be in L.A. for all they knew. Had he been a bonafide person of interest, they could delve into his credit card records and look for a plane ticket, but it would be a push. Collins had done nothing wrong.

Blowing out a frustrated breath, Alex pushed back from his desk and let the chair roll a bit. Maybe he'd go get a bite to eat. As he contemplated what could get him motivated enough to leave the office, Megan walked into his office.

"Busy?" she asked, grasping a small handbag to her chest.

"No. I mean, not too ... I was just thinking about getting an early dinner. Can I ... can I help you? Is everything okay?"

"You probably have me identified with problems now, huh? I mean, my brother, your father ..."

"Not at all. What's happened in the last day or so doesn't ... doesn't take away all those other years we've been ... friends."

"May I sit down?"

"Oh! Yeah, please!" Alex stood up so quickly his legs slammed against the front of his chair, launching it back against the wall with a crash. He rushed over to drag the client chair closer to his desk, then retrieved his own chair, chuckling under his breath. "Such a douche," he murmured.

"What?" Megan settled into the chair and crossed her legs. "Did you say something?"

"No. I, uh, never mind. You were saying?"

"No, you were saying. About us being friends. All those years."

Alex looked away for a moment, scratched at his forehead before looking back toward Megan. "I got this picture in my head of you falling out of a tree in your Dad's front yard. It was some holiday, Thanksgiving? Anyway, you went tearing into the house and he was so ... so good to you." He shook his head. "Don't know where that came from. Sorry."

"Sorry?" Megan sucked in her upper lip, then smiled. "I'd forgotten about that day. Yeah. I do remember. Everyone was there.

Jessica, and my grandmother, and Roxanne and Tom, and Uncle Dane ... he had that horrible woman with him. The one with black hair. I forget her name. She wasn't nice at all."

Alex frowned. "Jackie? God. I'd forgotten about her, too. Those were bad times, when she lived with us. She was just after Dad's money and fame. He never loved her."

"She got shot, right?"

"Yeah. She threatened to kill Jessica and then said she was going to kill herself. Dad tried to stop her, and I guess they were tussling over the gun and it went off. What a nut case."

Quiet ensued while they each recounted the dark days of the past.

Alex broke into their silence. "Hey. You, uh, wanna go for some Italian? There's this place over on Melrose ... unless ...?"

Megan's face flushed rose. "Sure. That would be great. I don't remember when I ate last."

The "place on Melrose" had checkered tablecloths and straw-covered Chianti bottles hanging amidst plastic grapes in the corners. They ordered a pizza and a pitcher of beer.

"This is great. I haven't had pizza in, like, forever," Megan said.

"We had so much of it when I was a kid, but then when you grow up it's sort of verboten in certain circles. I decided I missed it."

"My dad didn't let us have it much. It was a guilty pleasure. He was kind of a health nut."

"Yeah, I sort of remember that about him. But I was always jealous of you. You had an attentive father and two genuinely nice mothers. I had an absent father and an even more absent mother. Until one of your mothers became my mother, and my father came back. Then things kind of evened out, but by that time, you were ... gone."

Megan's smile faded and Alex cursed himself inwardly. He'd said something wrong, just when things were going so well.

"Jessica was never my mother."

"Really? It seemed like it to me. I remember she decorated a room for you in Uncle Mac's house. She made you clothes and took you on shopping trips. The three of you were always going places; you always looked like the perfect family. She was so proud of you and Devon." He watched as Megan absorbed his words, his memories. "She missed you."

"I missed her, too. But she had a new life. One that often didn't include me."

"I'm not so sure about that. But I am sure about one thing. She is the one woman, the only woman, according to my dad, whoever truly loved him. The only woman he ever absolutely loved. I know their relationship was – *is* – crazy and complicated ... convoluted, for sure. I hate to speak ill of the dead, as they say, but Mom, she wasn't the best wife. She tricked my Dad into marrying her, and she did nothing but complain in all the years they were married. He wasn't perfect either – he should never have stayed and had us kids. But he had some sense of duty, I suppose."

"So, you're saying Jess loved him and not my Dad?"

Alex tilted his head and frowned. "No, not saying that at all. Clearly, Jess and Mac, they had something special. I don't know if you know this or not, but Jess and Dad, they dated before Jess ever met Mac. When Jess met your father, it was all over for her and Dad. And then Dad and Mac became friends. They hated each other because of her, and they loved each other, too. He probably wouldn't want me spreading this around, but Dad made a promise to Uncle Mac that he would keep his distance. That he would never try to get next to Jess again, as long as they were married." Alex took a long draught of beer and then moved the pitcher to clear space for the arriving pizza. "This looks *sooo* good."

It was Megan's turn to frown. She took a sip of her own beer and slid a slice of pizza onto her plate. She stared down at it without taking a bite. "So, he actually promised Daddy he wouldn't pursue Jessica. That's ... just ... weird."

"Mmm. Yeah. So, he confided in me once, when I went to him about some woman I was seeing ... he told me that he was seriously conflicted after Uncle Mac died. He was heartbroken. They'd become close friends, and business partners, you know, all that. And Jess was so miserable. He wanted badly to comfort her, but he kept remembering the promise. He was committed to honoring Mac's memory and the pact he'd made."

"But ... Daddy was dead. Did it even matter?"

"It did, to him. But finally, I guess, they were both so miserable, and Jess – and this part is confidential, Meg – Jess felt like Mac visited her, from beyond somehow, and he told her to go ahead and be with Dane and to be happy."

Megan's lips parted in awe. "And you believe that?"

"I do. I honestly do. Hey – I'm not particularly spiritual or anything, but I know Jessica well enough to know she's not some crazy knucklehead who goes around seeing ghosts or spotting the shape of the Madonna in her French toast. If she says she had a vision of Mac, in whatever way, I believe her. It makes perfect sense to me that Mac would want his two best friends to be happy."

"That's so ... strange. Wow." Megan shook her head slightly as if to clear it. "I'm glad you shared that. I guess," she said, breaking into a brief smile. "I need to digest that along with this pizza."

Alex started to respond, glad that his words had been taken in a positive way. The vibration of the cell phone in his pocket interrupted his response. He stared at the screen before answering. "Devon! What's up?"

"I found something in the office. The printer was jammed, and when I fixed it, this boarding pass thing popped out. It says Chris took a flight to Baton Rouge."

"Very interesting. Wow. That's, uh, that's good intel, bro. Can you take a picture of that with your phone and text it to me?"

"Sure. Hey, have you heard from Megan?"

"Might say. Why?"

"Just making sure she's all right."

"She's quite fine." Alex peered Megan, his mouth curling up on one side.

They finished their dinner, the talk of the old days put away in favor of catching up on more recent times. Alex apologized for not attending her gallery showings. Megan regretted not keeping up with Alex's professional career. "I didn't even know you worked Missing Persons. What a way to find out, huh?"

"It's nothing glamourous, believe me. I mean, I like it, I just wish I could sell my screenplay."

"I understand. Covering weddings and retirement parties isn't glamourous, either. Getting the award helped, though. Something might come through because of that."

"The waiter is staring. Do you think they need the table?" Alex said, noting the full waiting area in the restaurant lobby.

"What – two hours is too long?"

"Wanna see my place? It's not far, and fortunately my cleaning lady came yesterday."

"I'd love to."

"It's similar to mine," Megan commented, looking around Alex's contemporary apartment. "But nicer. Two bedrooms?"

"Yeah. It was a strain on the budget at first, but over time, I've gotten a couple of bumps in pay, so, it's affordable."

Megan slipped off her coat and draped it over the back of the couch. "You've lived here, how long?"

"Oh, I don't know. Five years? Maybe? It's comfortable. No view or anything, but it's close to nightlife. Care for a drink?"

"Sure." Megan stood in the middle of the living room, feeling awkward. She'd imagined, many times, what his place might look like, and could hardly believe she was now there.

"Uh, sit down. Sorry, my coffee table met with an unfortunate incident a while back."

"Can I use your restroom?"

"Oh, of course. Right there, off the hall."

Megan stared at her reflection in Alex's bathroom mirror. His mirror. The one he undoubtedly peered into every day. Now, her face was in that same looking glass. Their dinner had been like a modern-day fairytale. Or a Hallmark movie. Childhood friends grow apart and then reconnect and find out that ... that they, what? Like each other? Maybe want to get close? Become more than friends?

She'd certainly felt that during dinner, in the dimly lit restaurant, when Alex had smiled and reminisced and made her feel special. But now, in his apartment, without the table between them and the purpose of eating dinner behind them, what would they talk about? How would the evening end?

Megan emerged from the hallway and Alex handed her a drink. She sat down on the couch and smiled. "So, tell me again, what happened to your coffee table?"

Alex smiled, and Megan could tell he was weighing his response. "In a moment of unrestrained emotional turmoil, I may have gotten a little aggressive with a soccer ball. My next coffee table will be of the wooden variety."

"Have a bad temper, do you?"

"It's gotten better. Let's just say it was a particularly challenging day."

"Tell me about it." Megan took a sip of her drink, leaned back, and crossed her legs. "I want to know what she did."

Alex narrowed his eyes. "She walked out."

"And why?

"She knew something I didn't know ... yet."

"Which was?"

"She wasn't the right woman."

Megan smiled and looked down toward her lap.

TWENTY-SIX

The Cavalry

At 5 a.m., Alex's phone began to ring from the pocket of his discarded khakis on the floor. Untangling himself from the limbs of his bedpartner, he reached over the side of the bed and felt around. He tried to answer quietly.

"Ashley! What's up? I tried to call you earlier. Where are you?"

"Alex, I've done something incredibly stupid, and I need your help. I'm in Louisiana and I might be in seriously bad trouble."

"Louisiana? What the hell – what kind of trouble?"

"It's a long story. I have friends here, the ones I used to live with, and they're being blackmailed. I came here to try to help them." Ashley's voice lowered, as if someone might be listening nearby. "I have a big wad of cash. But now I'm afraid, what if it's not enough? And I'm wondering if ... if these are the same people who kidnapped Devon!"

Alex didn't respond immediately as his mind sifted through his sister's words. Coincidence? Hardly. "You could be right. There might be a connection. Are you in a safe place?"

"A hotel."

"Look, you stay put and don't go anywhere. I'll call you back in a few minutes, okay?" Alex sat up and tucked his pillow behind his back.

Beside him, Megan stirred, then sat up and rubbed her eyes. "What was that all about?"

"Ashley." He shook his head slowly. "She's in Louisiana. Her hippie friends asked her to bring them money. There's apparently a blackmail going down."

Incredulous, Megan's eyes widened. "Louisiana? Isn't that where Chris supposedly went?"

"That's what I'm thinking. There's a link. He's somehow mixed up in this. And now Ash is involved. She's carrying ransom money or something. I need to get local P.D. in on this. She'd be crazy to walk in on this alone. I need to get to the office." Alex started to get out of bed, then paused and turned back to Megan. "I, uh, hate to go," he murmured, reaching to caress her cheek.

"I hate for you to go, too."

"Last night was ... if I say unbelievable, would that be too cliché? It's just that I thought it would never happen between us."

Megan smiled and slid down beneath the covers. "But it did."

"When this is all over, what will you tell Collins?"

"It won't matter. Trust me."

"I'll probably end up flying back there. I wish you could go with me, but it's not safe."

"It's okay. I have some people here I need to be with while you're gone."

They would part ways in the parking garage. Alex shuffled his feet while Megan unlocked her car. "Can I ask you something?"

"Sure," she said, tossing her handbag into the car and turning to face him.

"Is this real? Because I'm actually ... kinda ... scared. I'm scared because my sister is in a dire situation two thousand miles away, and all I can think about is, when will I see you again?"

Megan blushed but slid her hands up his chest and around his neck. "I'm a little shaken, too. I've never believed in fairytales or happy endings. But ... I'm not going anywhere. You go and get *Zowashley* and then come back to me." Standing on tiptoe, she kissed him briefly on the lips. "I'll keep an eye on your parents while you're gone."

"You have no idea how much that means to me."

Ashley was torn. Alex had called back and told her to meet him at her hotel. He wouldn't be in, however, until late in the afternoon. She forced down a granola bar and some orange juice from the hotel buffet, then got into the rental car. And there she sat, filled with indecision; until the text popped up from Maricela.

"Scary things happening. Two of them are okay, but one is evil and keeps making nasty advances at me and Ronnie. They are keeping us captive. Ronnie won't stop crying. I think they are beating on my father."

Ashley uttered a soft gasp and covered her mouth. She looked around the parking lot, where cars sat with dew running down their windshields and other cars rushed by on the nearby interstate. Just a normal morning in a hotel in a big city. But only miles away, a horrible drama was played out, where people were scared and crying, and others were exacting violence on innocent people.

Perhaps she should just go. Just walk in, hand over the money, and get Mari, Martin, and Ronnie the hell outta Dodge. That's all they wanted, right? Money? And she had it, right here in her lap. Maybe she shouldn't have bothered Alex.

Even though she followed Mari's directions explicitly as she made her way to the Dupré camp, it occurred to her that she'd never driven in this part of the backcountry. That she'd only traveled briefly between the big city, the river, and the small towns in the vicinity. She didn't know, as a driver, what to look for; she'd always been a passenger.

After an hour or more of travel, she reached the area where Maricela had told her to park. Ashley packed her small bag and got out of the rental car. "I can do this," she murmured. As quietly as she could, she approached the camp, picking her way through the moss-covered trees, occasionally tripping over a fallen log or an exposed root. When she caught sight of the tents and the little building in the center, she stopped and stared.

This is it. I'm here.

She wasn't ready. She sat down on a rotting tree trunk and tried to calm herself. "I can do this," she repeated softly. She knew she'd have to force herself up; she'd come too close to turn back now. But before she could fully stand, a hand clamped over her mouth and an arm grasped her around the waist. She tried to scream.

"Shhh! Don't scream. It's okay." Her captor turned her gently around.

"Chris?" she asked quietly when he'd removed his hand. "What's happened to you?"

He looked like he'd spent nights, possibly weeks, living in the wild. His hair was disheveled and longer than she'd remembered, and a thin scar lined his forehead above his eyebrow. His clothes were tattered and stained. He smiled, a sad, soft smile that broke her heart. Not Christian, after all. But familiar...

"Don't you remember me, Zoe?"

Ashley blinked and stared hard at his face. A memory formed, a hazy one, but one that grew clearer as she looked. "Robbie? Is it really you?"

Robbie nodded. "Yep. It's me. And guess what? I'm not dead."

"No, you're not," Ashley said, feeling stupid for the comment. "What happened?"

"It's a long story, and we don't have time for it right now. There're some awfully bad people in there, and they are holding my dad and my sister hostage. And it's all because of me." He lowered his head. "I assume that's why you're here?"

"It would seem so," Ashley said softly. "I brought money."

"It'll never be enough. There's only one thing that will fix this. I need to give myself up."

"What? Are you crazy?"

"It's me they want. I'm the one who took their money. Such an ass. I needed to support my habit. I ruined everything. Because I didn't go the night Mama died. I could've helped Chris. I turned away, I got into dope because I couldn't bear what a failure I was. The best thing I could do was just ... die. But I couldn't even do that right. Five years of hiding, and they're after me again."

"Wait; what do you mean, you could've helped Chris? Who is Chris?"

"Thought you knew. You called me Chris. He's my brother. My *twin* brother."

Ashley brought her hand to her mouth. "Christian Collins is your brother? How is that possible? Mari would have told me. She never said a word about... about any of this." The thought of Maricela's coming joy was muted by her confusion of Christian's role.

Robbie tried to brush the hair from his eyes. "She doesn't know I'm alive. And Chris made a new life for himself after all that happened. The less anybody talked,
the better."

"But...even before that! He wasn't at the camp. I never met him. How could I not have known?"

"He was there the night I...died."

"I don't understand. I—"

"Shh! Someone's coming."

Christian returned to the same spot he'd parked the day before. This time, Rudy sat beside him in the SUV. A small, white compact was already parked around five yards away. Suspicious.

"I don't condone killing," Christian murmured, getting out of the car, and sticking the Baretta inside the back waistband of his jeans. "Just so you know."

"Absolutely, brother." Rudy nodded, carrying his own rifle at his side. "But sometimes a man's gotta do what a man's gotta do. You say there's women in there that need protecting."

"True, that," Christian responded.

"How old's old Martin anyway?"

"Sixty-nine or seventy. Not sure. Never was."

Rudy nodded. "And not in good health."

"Can't say he is, no. He's no match on his own in there. And the others, I have no idea if they're even around. They tend to scatter like deer when a mountain lion comes around. But I know Mari's there, and perhaps some of the other girls."

"Reason enough." Rudy squinted his eyes. "So, you got a plan?"

"I believe the girls are in the tent on the left. They might be in there alone, I don't know. The hit men are probably in the shack with my dad. Just a guess, but it looks like there's a fire going in there."

"So's you want to sneak into that there tent and see if those little gals are in there?"

Chris considered. "It's risky. Let's hunker down and watch for a bit."

They found a vantage point from which they could watch without being observed. After twenty minutes, Christian saw movement on the far side of the building. Two people moved slowly through the tangles of moss hanging from the cypress and tupelo trees. A woman and a man. Christian dug into his backpack for the binoculars and trained them on the couple.

"Holy shit."

"What?"

"I don't fecking believe this."

Rudy tugged the glasses away from him and looked for himself. "Well, I'll be damned. That looks like Robbie."

"And Ashley Pierce."

"Ashley who?"

Christian huffed out a shuddering breath. "A girl I know. She used to live here. She's a friend of Mari's."

"But your brother is dead."

"Apparently not. This explains a lot. All those years, all that guilt. That bastard. If he's behind this, I'll ..." Christian stopped himself before saying words he would later regret. "We need to stop them. Come on."

They were forced to backtrack a distance to stay out of view of the hut. They were almost close enough to get the attention of the others when the door to the shack flew open and three men came bounding out. Christian and Rudy both ducked down; Christian hoped that Ashley and Robbie had also done so.

The men were arguing. "I say we off the old man and take the women with us. That asshole isn't gonna show up here. He doesn't have any more money; he was just stalling for time."

Christian recognized the speaker as one of the men from the Reseda house. Corfu raised his arms in the air. "He'll be here. By noon. He knows we coulda offed that MacKendall kid and what we'll do to his sister if he doesn't show. I believe him. I got a sister, too."

Ashley heard the words being spewed. Enlightenment dawned and twisted her stomach painfully. These were the same guys who'd taken Devon! How was that possible? That the hoodlum had a sister was irrelevant, but the fact that she, too, had sisters buoyed her. Mari was like a sister to her, and the thought of her falling prey to these heathens chilled her, and simultaneously strengthened her. "We need to get in there."

"I have a gun," Robbie said. "But by itself, it's not enough. They'll take me in trade. Me, and your cash. Let's do this."

"No. You can't give yourself up."

"What do you expect me to do? That's my family in there."

"And this is your family out here, too," A voice said from behind them.

Ashley turned suddenly and came face to face with Christian. She frowned. "You've got some serious explaining to do. No wonder you looked like Robbie. All this time, and you never said a word. What madness are you two involved in? I can't believe this."

"And I can't believe you're here. Do you have any idea how dangerous this is for you? And *you*. I don't know whether to hug you or kick you in the balls." Christian said to Robbie.

"Look, kids. This isn't the time. We gotta come up with a plan," Rudy said. "Y'all can duke it out later. If we make it outta here alive."

Christian groaned. "You said you have a gun?"

Robbie pulled a small .22 caliber Colt revolver out of his waistband. Christian and Rudy exchanged a glance, and Christian pursed his lips. "Better than nothing. And what did you bring, *Zoe*?"

"Two hundred thousand dollars."

Christian's jaw dropped. "Are you nuts?"

"Mari and Martin are like family to me," she mumbled.

"Okay. Give me the cash. The three of us will go in and negotiate the release. Do you have a phone?" Christian asked Ashley.

"Yes, but it doesn't work out here. And I want to go in with you."

"Nonsense. Too dangerous. And besides, we need you out here. If things go sideways in there, you'll need to go for the police."

Ashley had trouble arguing. She reluctantly handed over the tote filled with money. Christian slung it over his shoulder.

"I say we try to sneak up on them, throw the door open and point the guns at them," Robbie suggested.

"Sure. Just burst in, guns blazing. We don't even know how many of them are in there."

"Three men. Plus, Martin," Ashley said.

Christian frowned. "How do you know this?"

"Mari told me. And I'll bet two of them are the ones who took Devon. There's some connection and you need to tell me what it is." Ashley stepped forward and jabbed two fingers at Christian's chest.

Christian scowled down at her and tried to grasp her hand, but she turned away. "This is not your business, Ash. You need to get out of the way."

"Chris, look," Robbie interrupted. "It's me they want. Just walk me in there, be the hero, give 'em the dough. Take Dad and Mari and go." He folded his arms resolutely.

"Not that you don't deserve that, but I left you once before and I won't do it again. You might be a sorry excuse for a brother, but I won't let them have you." Christian looked at his watch. "It's almost noon. We should plan for each of us to take out one of them. We'll sneak up and try to get a look at what's going on. There are a couple of windows. And when I say, 'take out,' I'm talking about debilitating them, not killing them. If possible."

"You mean like, shoot 'em in the legs?" Rudy asked.

"I mean, no need to use deadly force. We're not killers. Let's go."

Robbie started walking slowly toward the hut, with Rudy behind him. Christian lingered and turned back to Ashley. "That your car I saw back there?"

"Yes."

"Go sit in it. Watch for trouble. You understand?"

"Yes," she repeated.

"And be careful." He looked her sternly in the eyes, but he would have preferred taking her into his arms. He was standing in ankle deep mud; his brother,
sister and father were in dire jeopardy, yet all he could think about was this crazy, stubborn, compassionate woman. This complicated little gypsy who'd cleaned out her savings, flown across country and walked herself into the middle of an organized crime throwdown. All to save his sister. Now Ashley, too, was in jeopardy. He grasped her shoulder. "Okay?"

"Okay."

Christian left to catch up with the others. Ashley waited until they were a safe distance, then began making her way around the perimeter of the camp, staying well hidden among the foliage. Eventually, she found herself behind the tent where she believed Maricela was being held. She crept closer and pressed herself against the back of the rough canvas. She heard nothing. As stealthily as possible, she slipped her fingers beneath the bottom edge of the heavy, dirt-crusted fabric and lifted.

The space inside was dark, but Ashley could clearly see Maricela was alone in the tent. She turned suddenly and gasped. "Zoe!" She whispered hoarsely. "You came."

"Come. We have no time. Hurry!" Ashley led Maricela back the way she'd come, rushing her through the underbrush and around the encampment until they reached her rental car. They got in and locked the doors.

Maricela began to cry, hard, until her sobs were uncontrollable. Ashley held her close and gently rocked her as best she could in the close confines of the car. "You're safe now. I've got you. You're safe."

"But – but what about — Daddy?"

Ashley ignored her question and asked one of her own. "Where is Veronica?"

"Sh – she got away. Last night. I hope she's okay."

"If she got away, why didn't you go with her?"

"I wanted to. But I couldn't leave Daddy. And it's miles to the next anything, and I was so scared..."

"All right. Hopefully we'll find her. Look, Mari ... did you know about Robbie?"

Maricela tried to quiet her sobs, rubbing her eyes on the rough fabric of her denim jacket. She sniffed loudly. "What about Robbie?"

"Mari, he's alive. And he's with Chris and another guy. They're out there," Ashley said, gesturing toward the small wooden building. "They have money. They're going to get Martin out."

"Robbie can't be alive. I saw his body. He was dead."

"You said yourself you never saw where he was buried. Martin ... must have lied. To keep Robbie from being killed. But somehow, they found out he was still alive."

Maricela's eyes were wide with shock. "They'll kill him if he walks in there. They have guns! They're mean, rotten criminals."

"Chris and Robbie have guns, too. And the other guy with them has a rifle. They'll figure out what to do. Hopefully, they'll take the money and let everyone go."

"Don't believe it, Zoe."

Just as the words exited Maricela's mouth, shots were fired at the shack.

TWENTY-SEVEN

Showdown in the Bayou

Twelve noon had come and gone. Christian, Robbie and Rudy quietly took refuge inside one of the tents closest to the hut. Again, they witnessed Corfu and his henchmen exit the building amidst a fresh argument.

"Go get her, then," Corfu conceded. "Bring her inside. Perhaps another call to her brother is in order. God knows her daddy isn't gonna last much longer." On the boss's order, one of the thugs broke away and headed for the tent. The others returned to the shack.

Christian pressed a finger to his lips and gestured with his other hand for Rudy to get ready. The flap to the tent flew open and the man stepped in, blinking in the dim light as he looked for his prey. Before he could react, Rudy struck a heavy blow to the man's head with the butt of his rifle, knocking him out cold.

"Nice," Robbie whispered. Chris pulled a roll of duct tape from the pack Rudy had prepared and quickly covered the man's mouth and secured his wrists and ankles.

"One down," Rudy murmured. "Two to go."

It wasn't long before Corfu sent his second man to look for the first.

"You better not be havin' your way with that gypsy whore," he called as he crossed the expanse of cleared earth between the shack and the tent. "I'm comin' in." But something tipped him off; his buddy's lack of response must have concerned him, because he drew his handgun and aimed it at the tent.

"Come outta there. Right now," he called.

Robbie started for the tent opening.

"Where do you think you're going?" Christian whispered. "Do you want to get killed?"

"They've got Dad. They'll let him go if I trade myself."

"No, they won't. And anyway, you don't need to do this."

"If he starts shooting at the tent, we'll all be dead. Let me go." Robbie pulled the .22 revolver out of his waistband and held it out in front of him with a shaking hand.

"Give me that," Christian growled, grasping the gun by the barrel and quickly wresting it from Robbie. He set the safety and then stuffed the weapon into the back of his own jeans. "You're just as crazy as ever, bro."

"Maybe so, but you can't stop me."

Christian tried to block his brother's path, but Robbie shoved him roughly aside. Christian retaliated by punching Robbie in the face. Robbie fell backward but regained his position quickly, just as the first bullet pierced the heavy tent wall and exited through the back.

"Guess we're on," Rudy shouted. He quickly fed the barrel of his rifle through the tent opening and aimed. He popped one off just as the gangster fired again, causing the latter's bullet to go astray. The man grasped his thigh and cried out. Robbie took the moment of distraction and raced from the tent, passing the limping man who was trying to slow the bleeding with his hand. They both disappeared into the hut.

"Judas Priest! What was he thinking! What an idiot." Christian stormed about the tent, looking for something to take his anger out on. He stared down at their captive and squinted. "You!" He pulled his foot back and the lashed out, kicking the man in the hip. "That's for Devon! And for Ashley!" He kicked again. "And for my sister, you lousy scum!"

Rudy chuckled. "A little mad, are ya? We should just storm the place. I mean, all's that's in there is the one you called Carfoo, and that piece of shit with a bullet in his leg."

"Thanks to you. Good shot. He would have nailed me otherwise. Let's see if we can wait this out because it's likely they'll have to get medical help for that asshole."

"Good point. Hate to bring this up, but do we know where your sister is?"

Christian scowled. "No. But she's not in there, at least, or they wouldn't have come to get her. Maybe she got away."

The gunshots sent a new wave of fear over Ashley. She had to find out if Christian was okay. "I'll only go far enough to see if anyone has left the shack," she promised, warning Maricela to stay in the car. As she retraced her earlier steps, the clearing and the ramshackle hut came into view. There was no one in sight. She needed to get closer. She kept thinking about the men and the gunshots. And if she was honest with herself, her thoughts were focused on Christian. She prayed he'd not been hurt. Unable to stop herself, she kept walking until she was directly behind the building.

A large, low window was slightly open. She crouched beside it, trying to ignore the once-familiar bugs and earthly smelling soil around her feet. Voices wafted out, one of them moaning in pain. Ashley cringed. "I need a doctor," he cried out. The voice was too young to be Martin's.

"You're gonna have to wait. We step foot outside the door, they'll pick us off like they did you, you lunatic." This, most certainly, was the boss.

"We have a car. I can take him into the city," said another man, and Ashley suspected this voice belonged to Robbie Dupré. "They won't shoot me if I bring him out."

They. Christian and his friend. Ashley slumped down with relief. Christian was alive and had possibly shot one of the bad guys. But where was he? And why was Robbie inside the shack? Not knowing what to do next, Ashley stood and inched closer to the window. It had gone quiet inside, save for the occasional moan from the injured man. She wanted to get a glimpse of the situation; how many were inside, and whether Martin was okay. Slowly, she began to inch toward the opening. There, inside the tiny room, were four men. Robbie, of course, kneeling beside his father who sat slumped at the end of a rickety bench. A man lying on the floor, bleeding. And another man, pacing anxiously, grumbling to himself.

As if fate deemed it, Robbie turned to look at the window and caught her. Ashley quickly put her finger to her lips, but in her haste, she lost her footing in the slimy ground beneath her and she uttered a little cry, reflexively grasping the edge of the windowsill for support. The pacing man was approaching the window when she gave away her position. With a maniacal laugh, he threw open the window and grasped Ashley by the shoulders. His surprising strength caught her off guard and he was able to drag her into the room and drop her to the floor.

Her involuntary scream as she hit the floor filled the small room. Robbie rushed forward to help her up. "Why did you come? I told them I could handle this."

"And have you? Handled it?" Ashley asked, examining a new cut on her forearm.

"Dad's very sick," he said quietly. "It's like pneumonia or TB."

Ashley set aside her chagrin and went to Martin.

"That's right, you get to play nurse now that you're here," the boss said. "Only you need to look at Squiggy here, first."

"Squiggy? You can't be serious," Ashley replied, lifting her chin. "And believe me, I'm no nurse."

"Well, we all like to change our names around here. Squig's a little shy. Now get down there and see what you can do about all that blood. This might be a long wait."

·❤·❤·❤·❤·❤·

The scream from the shack drew Christian's attention. "Did you hear that? They've got a woman in there after all." Concern clouded his thoughts. Surely it wasn't Ashley; they would have seen her entering the hut. Unless there was another entrance they hadn't seen? "Waiting's over."

"Well, let's see here. Once again, they got Ol' Martin, Robbie, the bleeding sot, and the boss. And a chick. How hard could it be for us to get in there?" Rudy nudged their prisoner with his toe. "This guy ain't goin' nowhere."

"It could be all three of the girls in there." Worse than he'd imagined. Christian checked the magazine and the chamber on the Baretta and then motioned to Rudy. "It's time. Cover me." He picked up the pack full of money.

Rudy nodded, and Christian stepped out of the tent and ran toward the closed door to the shack. He listened carefully, but the only sound was of his own heart pounding in his ears.

You can't stay holed up in there forever. Taking a deep breath, he kicked the door open and rushed inside. It took only a fraction of a second to identify Corfu and train the pistol on him. It took only half that time for Corfu to press his gun against Ashley's head.

Christian took a step back. There was no way he could get off a shot without risking Ashley being hit. Corfu was using her as a shield. Still, he kept his gun pointed. "Let her go."

"And why should I do that, Mr. Collins? Or should I say, Mr. Dupré? I'm having trouble with my scorecard here. One of you two lookalikes is in a lot of trouble, but you know what? I don't care! You didn't bring the money. Big surprise. And as it turns out, I don't have your sister. But I got something just as good. I'm quite sure this sweet young thing is a good bargaining chip."

"I did bring the money." Christian used his free hand to pull the small day pack from his shoulder. "It's all here."

"Drop it on the floor and kick it over here." Christian did as Corfu instructed. He assessed his brother and father, sitting together on a long bench against the wall. Dried blood surrounding the corners of Martin's mouth alarmed him. His ragged breathing was not a good sign.

Corfu snagged the bag with his foot and dragged it to him.

"Look," Christian began. "You've got the money, and there are two people in here who need medical attention. Why don't you just take the money and go. I can load these two into my car and get them to the nearest hospital."

"And how far do you think I'd get? You got a sniper out there with a thirty-aught-six pointed at my head. Am I right? My vehicle is parked two hundred yards away in a tangle of putrid river muck. My comrade here, Mr. Squigworth, he's not looking so good. So, it looks like we got ourselves a Mexican standoff. Unless you want to take the risk that I'll get nervous and shoot off this young lady's ear, you'd best put down that piece and go sit down with your equally lame family members. Gypsies, indeed. Huh."

Christian knew he had little choice but to comply. He very carefully placed the Baretta on the floor and walked to the bench where his brother had his arms wrapped around Martin. What Corfu didn't know was that Christian had Robbie's .22 Bearcat revolver stuffed into his pants.

"Are you okay? How's Dad?" Christian whispered.

"Not too good. He's been coughing a lot. He needs to be in the hospital."

"Nonsense," Martin croaked. "This is all nonsense. He then launched into a coughing fit that wracked his thin frame.

"Water. Is there any water in this place?" Christian demanded.

"I'll get some." Ashley surprised them all by suddenly wresting herself free from Corfu's grasp and going to the make-shift kitchen counter, where a plastic bottle of water stood. She found a coffee cup and wrinkled her nose. "This isn't exactly clean, but it will have to do." She poured the water and brought it to Martin.

Corfu kept his semi-automatic pistol aimed at her as she moved about. She handed the water to Robbie, who brought the cup to Martin's lips. Still coughing, Martin tried to wave it away, spilling some. Ashley lingered, her eyes eventually seeking Christian's and she held his gaze.

"*Sit down,*" he mouthed, and she obeyed, sitting next to him on the bench.

"Hey, I didn't say you could sit there," Corfu hollered, gesturing with his gun. "You gotta finish fixing him up." The man he'd called Squigworth moaned and turned his head.

"I've done all I can for him. I wrapped the wound as tightly as I could to stop the bleeding." Ashley paused, then spoke up again. "Chris is right. You should take the money and go. He can tell his ... associate to hold his fire and let you pass."

"You think I'm that stupid?"

"Well, what's going to happen if you stay here? The police have been called. It's only a matter of time before they get here and surround this place. Then, you'll be arrested, and you won't get the money."

Corfu seemed to ponder Ashley's words. He looked from the four people sitting on the bench to the man on the floor, then to the open window on the back of the building. He picked up the pack of money and slung it over his shoulder, then squatted down.

"I hate to do this to ya, Squig, but I don't think you're up to the trek. At least you'll get fixed up."

Squigworth growled. "You're leavin' me and Chuck here? And takin' all the dough for yourself? You bastard!"

"Sorry, buddy. Gotta go." Corfu picked up the Baretta and turned to the Duprés. "Don't come after me. I can pick any of you off at fifty yards." And with that, he climbed out of the window and was gone.

Christian stood and pulled the Bearcat out of his pocket, checking the cylinder for bullets. Robbie jumped to his feet, took the gun from Christian, and headed for the window.

"What are you doing?" Christian yelled. "I swear, you have a death wish!"

"I can't let him get away with your money," Robbie called over his shoulder. "I know these woods better than anyone. I have to stop him." He turned after climbing through the window. "Besides, if I don't take him down, he'll be after me forever."

"It's not my money," Christian called after him, shaking his head.

No longer forced to be strong, Ashley began to quiver. The enormity of what had just transpired washed over her and she found it difficult to stand. Martin leaned back against the wall and closed his eyes.

"You okay?" Christian asked her. "I should go after him."

"You have no gun now," she murmured. "I left Mari in my car."

Christian stared hard at her. He took her hands and helped her up, "Thank God. Look. I'm going to get Rudy to watch out for you until I get back. It's not safe to walk back to the vehicles right now – that thug could be anywhere. Just ... take care of my Dad, okay?"

"Of course." Ashley swallowed and mustered her strength. "I can do that."

"Thanks." He took her face between his hands and kissed the top of her head. "This will be over soon."

After duct taping Squigworth's ankles together, Christian left through the front door. Ashley was relieved to hear no bullets being fired on him. She sat back down to wait.

·♥·♥·♥·♥·♥·

"Zoe Pierce," Martin said, his voice hoarse with pain. "Never thought you the type to sign up for a rescue mission."

Ashley patted Martin's arm. "No, not my usual gig."

"My boys are good. They mean well. Didn't have a proper upbringing but they got good family sense." Martin coughed.

"Don't talk. And yes, they mean well. I'm so glad Robbie is alive."

"You – you understand why ..."

"Yes, I do."

"There's something about Chris you should know."

Ashley turned to look into Martin's eyes.

"What?"

"He blames himself –" Before Martin could put together his words, other words from outside rang out through a bullhorn.

"WE HAVE YOU SURROUNDED. COME OUT, ONE AT A TIME WITH YOUR HANDS ON TOP OF YOUR HEAD."

Ashley frowned. Although obscured by the megaphone, she knew the voice behind the demands. How did he get here so fast?

"My brother," she assured Martin. "He's brought the cavalry."

Ashley sat with Alex on the bumper of the large van emblazoned with the words "Special Response Team" on the side. His arm draped around her, Ashley closed her eyes and rested her head on his shoulder.

"No one could ever say you live a dull life, Ashley Pierce," he murmured.

"Mmm."

"When I look around here and think about you living here for, what, over three years? In this muck?"

"Mmm-hmm. I did." She opened her eyes and watched two ambulances being loaded. Detectives interviewing Robbie and Rudy. A squad car had already whisked away Corfu and his remaining henchman, Chuck. And Christian, not far away, stood with his arm protecting his younger sister. Why hadn't she seen it before? Christian and Maricela's features were so similar, anyone would have recognized them as siblings. And Robbie, while not identical, was still nearly a clone of his brother. Had Ashley simply left Zoe's memories behind?

Alex brought her back. "I'll drive you to your hotel." She started to protest, then thought better of it. Driving wasn't her strong suit to begin with, and right now she'd be hard-pressed to maneuver a shopping cart.

As they began the trek back to her rental car, Ashley turned once and peered at Christian, who lifted his chin in a subtle nod. Maricela broke free of his embrace and rushed after Ashley, giving her a fierce hug.

"I would be dead. I would be on the way to the morgue if you hadn't come."

Ashley shook her head, but she kissed Maricela on the cheek and promised to stay in touch. Somehow.

On the way back to the hotel, Alex described how they'd found Corfu, mired up to his knees in swamp mud, screaming about alligators. He was literally begging Christian to get him out of the swamp Robbie and Chris had chased him into. He'd handed over the money and the guns in exchange for assistance in escaping the reptiles, real or imagined.

"Oh, they could easily have been real," Ashley assured Alex.

They flew back to Los Angeles the next day on the same flight. Despite her assurances that she could make her way home, Alex delivered her to the Pierce estate and stayed to visit with his father. Ashley went upstairs to her room to unpack her bag and met Jillian in the hall. "Hey, baby girl," Ashley murmured.

Jillian wrapped her arms tightly around her big sister and looked up. "I'm so glad you're back," she said. "Mom was a wreck, and Daddy said, 'don't worry, Ashley is a tough cookie.' And I said, 'I'm a tough cookie, too, right?' And Daddy said, 'of course you are, half pint'."

Ashley squatted down. "You absolutely are. You're a Pierce. We're all tough cookies, didn't you know? Oh my gosh, you should have seen our brother out there, rounding up all the bad guys there in the Bayou, with alligators and giant mosquitoes, and slime and moss on everything ..."

"Ewww! For reals? Alligators?"

"For reals." Ashley looked at her sister fondly. "How would you like to go out for some girl time? Maybe get some ice cream? Or we could stop at the mall for some earrings. Or nail polish." Ashley spewed off a list of things she suddenly had a huge appreciation for. Going back to the river had given her a swift kick in the butt, a reminder that unlike those left behind, she could have almost anything she wanted.

Anything, except perhaps Christian Dupré.

TWENTY-EIGHT

Resolutions

It would take a while to get her money back. Still, Alex told Ashley he was satisfied with the way his Louisiana associates had handled the Salvatore Corfu case. Squigworth insisted there was another man on the scene, whose thirty-caliber rifle round pierced his thigh; no evidence of the gun could be found, and Christian Collins had suggested that Charles Pink had taken the shot in a "friendly fire" mishap. Chuck denied the story, of course, but he was a thug, after all. Christian's hints that Rudy's possible priors could make things messy convinced Alex to persuade the Baton Rouge PD to accept Christian's recollection as fact, and the matter was closed.

Louisiana's open carry laws meant that Robbie Dupré's handgun was legal but would be held in evidence during the trial phase of Corfu's case, along with Ashley's money. The Baretta had conveniently disappeared. It had been weeks already, but it would be months before anything more happened. It would all shake out in the end.

Ashley looked out her bedroom window, which faced the driveway and the street below. Movement caught her eye as Melissa and Dane returned from their morning walk. They were laughing and acting every bit the father-daughter they should be. Melissa had made Dane's rehab her personal quest, getting him out for walks and swims, even dusting off Dane and Jessica's bicycles for rides around the hills surrounding their Malibu home.

Bringing up the rear was Brady on a pair of in-line skates. Dane paused to help his grandson navigate the steep driveway, with Melissa standing by and shaking her head. Ashley sighed. This is how it should be. They'd reached the front porch when the garage door opened and Devon walked out, keys in hand. Although she couldn't hear them, Ashley knew Devon was off to school and was touching base with his father about dinner plans. It was the new routine now that Devon had enrolled in community college.

"I need to learn how to be a businessman," he told his sisters one night the month before. "I can't learn everything I need to know from Chris. If I'm going to have my own company one day, I need to get a degree." Ashley was delighted with his decision, as were his parents. It was his first show of ambition. "Did you know Chris went to school in Paris?"

No, she hadn't known. In fact, she didn't know much about Christian at all. Not nearly enough. They hadn't spoken since returning from Baton Rouge.

"I haven't told you, but I'm living with Rudy," Maricela had confided over the phone. "He's really cool."

"Mari, he's like forty years old!"

"He's thirty-five. He's extremely sweet. We're talking about moving to Arizona and opening a café there, together. The dry climate would be better for Daddy, whatever time he has left. And Rudy and I are sick of the swamp."

"Well, that's good, I guess." Ashley rolled her eyes. "When are you making this move?"

"That's what I'm calling about. We're having a party to end all parties. To give Daddy a proper send off. And I want you to come."

"Where? Not ... back there?"

"Sure, yeah, at the camp. Everybody who's ever been with us, all up and down the river, and those who got away, like yourself, will all be there. It's going to be the best ever. You'll come, right?"

Ashley squeezed her eyes shut. There was a part of her that never wanted to see or smell the Bayou again. Too much horror, too many strange and painful memories were attached. But Maricela was compelling. "Daddy would want you there."

"How is he?"

"He's dying, Zoe. He won't last a year. The doctor said he needs full-time care now. The conditions at the camp aren't healthy for him, and I can't, I won't go back there. I have a life now, with Rudy."

"Can I let you know?"

"You have to think about it? Wow. That's sad."

Ashley sighed. "I'll come. Of course, I'll come. Email the details."

"Yay! I knew you'd say yes."

"Will, uh, Chris be there?"

Maricela paused. "Not sure. I haven't heard from him since he left. I thought, maybe, you had."

"No. I haven't. My brother quit his job, so I don't hear much."

"Well, if you do, tell him he'd better get his butt out here for the party!"

Ashley wondered if this was a good enough reason to call Christian. Would it be expected? Acceptable? Maybe not.

Alex hit print and waited for his document to finish filling the output tray. He took a sip of iced tea and leaned back in his chair. Megan walked up behind him and began massaging his shoulders.

"It's sensational. I mean, I could see a bidding war in your future."

"Ha! You are biased, my love. But keep it up."

"I brought your phone in. You had a missed call."

Alex stared at the small screen and raised his eyebrows. "Jess?"

"Dane okay?" Megan asked, concern diminishing her smile.

"As far as I know ... but I did email her a copy of the updated script yesterday."

Megan grabbed the corners of his chair and spun him around to face her. Alex smiled and pulled her onto his lap. "What if she liked it?" Megan cooed.

What if *she liked it?*

He'd added all the new material, inspired by the takedown in Louisiana. The first-hand experience of collaring a perp on the FBI's most wanted list proved invaluable. The writing was tighter, the characters stronger, the plot solid. After Megan had moved in, his inspiration had grown tenfold.

Not completely moved in, he reminded himself. She still had her apartment but had commandeered two dresser drawers and a vacant rod in his closet. Her smoothie maker graced his kitchen counter, and he'd cleared out the second bathroom for her lotions and potions. And apparently, their budding relationship posed no problem for Christian Collins.

Collins, he suspected, was a loner. He himself had been a loner for so long. Until the right woman had opened her eyes to him. Perhaps that was all Christian needed, too. The right woman. But now that

Alex's brother was no longer working with Destiny Drives, Christian had faded away. *So be it. We never saw eye-to-eye anyway.*

<><><>

Melissa was making sandwiches when Alex walked in. "Hey, you staying for lunch?" she asked after giving her brother a brief hug.

"What was that for?" he asked, a surprised smile appearing.

"I have a helluva lot of hugs to make up," Melissa explained. "Sometimes a hug can change someone's whole day. Now, do you want a roast beef sandwich?"

"Love one. Mom and Dad are expecting me."

"They're out on the patio."

"Dad doing okay?"

Melissa nodded. "More than okay. We're doing four miles every other day. He's lost twelve pounds; his heart is in great shape."

"You look pretty good yourself," Alex said, also nodding. "Side benefit of fixing up Dad."

Melissa shrugged. "I'll bring the sandwiches out in a bit."

"Thanks for the hug, Mimi."

She threw a dish towel at him but smiled to herself. She was thinking that a year ago, this scene couldn't have taken place, but she amended her thoughts. She and Alex had never had the kind of relationship they now fostered. What was a simple tease today had been serious antagonism in the past. She wondered about his upbeat mood. That he and Megan were getting it on was no secret, but there was more. Maybe the sense of contentment that comes from getting your life in order. She knew it well.

Melissa ran out of roast beef and opened a package of turkey for Brady's sandwich. She stopped to listen and could barely pick out the sounds of a video game coming from the den where her son played with his Aunt Ashley. That had been a surprise. But everything was a surprise these days, right?

Devon, whom she'd never had anything to do with, lived in the room next to hers. When she and Brady had moved in, there'd been polite coexistence as they passed in the hall or jockeyed their cars in the driveway. He seemed polite, funny, warm even, but aimless. He was just a kid, after all. But enrolling in school had been another happy Pierce surprise. And Devon, too, had developed a fondness for Brady, treating him like a little brother rather than a distant nephew.

Melissa went to the intercom on the kitchen wall and took a moment to figure out which button to press. "Ash? You okay with turkey?"

"Sure," came her sister's answer. "No mayo. Well ... maybe a little."

"You got it." Melissa was reminded of the many years her sister had fought weight issues. Mayonnaise was an enemy. "Hmm." Melissa still harbored a bit of uneasiness around Ashley. Perhaps it was because she, herself, Alex and Devon, and even Megan – whose photo business was on the rise – had all emerged from their troubled times. Ashley was still a wild card.

"I'll help you carry these out," Ashley said, lifting one of the two sandwich trays Melissa had prepared. "Brady? Can you get the door for us?"

Jessica, Dane, and Alex sat at the largest of the patio tables on the far side of the pool. The girls placed the trays and distributed plates of sandwiches, cole slaw, and fresh vegetable sticks.

"You guys all set? Can I get you some more tea, or water?" Melissa asked.

"All set," Dane answered. "Why don't you join us?"

"Oh, we were going to sit over there. Thought you guys were talking," Ashley said.

"We are talking. It's all in the family." Dane seemed in no hurry to depart the subject matter and took a big bite of his sandwich.

Jessica laughed. "Right. Just hint at something and then fill your mouth." She shook her head comically, and her contented smile immediately calmed the small bit of anxiety growing within Ashley. "Your brother has written quite a screenplay. We're just negotiating a price."

"What? That's wonderful!" Ashley exclaimed, and Melissa shared her excitement.

"Are you kidding me? For real?"

Brady tugged on Melissa's arm, and she bent over to listen. "Can I be in Uncle Alex's movie?"

Ashley looked around the table at all the smiling faces. So much joy. So many new directions for everyone. Except herself. Her grandiose plans – to get a job, to get out more, make new friends, maybe take a class – had gone by the wayside. Her bedroom had become her safe, yet drab, sanctuary. Since returning from the traumatic incident in Louisiana, Ashley had thought of nothing but Christian Collins. So many questions, unanswered.

Why, for example, hadn't she known that Robbie had a twin? Why had Christian left the commune? Why hadn't he gone straight to the police when he clearly knew Devon's abductors? They'd never met, but how was it that he – the brother of her best friend – had walked into her birthday party with Megan? Coincidence?

And Robbie. Not dead, but in hiding for over five years, evading the drug dealers to whom he'd sold his soul. He resurfaces and sets off a string of events affecting all her loved ones. No wonder she felt so lost.

"Ash? Hello?" Dane was beckoning.

"I'm sorry, what did you say?"

"I asked if you want a role, too, in our new film?"

"Ha! My life is enough of a drama already."

Jessica reached for Ashley's hand. "You need to do something fun, sweetie. You've been moping around for weeks."

"I'm going back to the Bayou. In two weeks. They're disbanding the commune and having a party to celebrate. Mari and her dad are moving to Arizona and it's kind of a goodbye for Martin. He's not going to live long."

Their silence and expressions told Ashley that her family was not in favor of her upcoming trip.

"Are you sure you want to do this? You don't have to go, you know," Dane told her. "Don't feel obligated."

"I don't. I want to go. I feel like it might put some things to bed."

Alex scoffed. "If you ask me, and I know you didn't, that swamp isn't any place I'd like to visit ever again. But if you feel like it'll help you deal with what happened –"

"I do. It'll be a short trip. And thanks to you, all the bad guys are locked up."

TWENTY-NINE

Return to the River

D evon drove her to the airport. After hoisting her small suitcase from the trunk, he moved in close and hugged her, rocking her and nestling his cheek against her hair.

"Don't worry about me," Ashley said. "I won't be alone."

"I can't help but worry about you. You're my sister. Keep in touch, will you?"

Ashley kissed him on the cheek. "I will. It's only a few days."

Devon pulled away but lingered, looking into her face. "I got this feeling that something is going to happen. Something ... good."

"I hope so. We've had enough of the other kind of somethings. You stay out of trouble."

Ashley pondered Devon's words as the jet gained altitude over Southern California. Her flight was uneventful, and the weather was predicted to be mild. She chose a different hotel this time. A different color car. She brought different clothes, having the option to choose this time. And she arrived a day early, hoping to get in a little alone time.

Living in the Pierce household was comfortable, but crowded with her parents, three siblings and a nephew always on the move. Having a quiet, uninterrupted evening, complete with bubble bath and a glass of champagne, was on top of her to-do list. She even bought a sketchy scandal magazine in the hotel gift shop and thumbed through it in the tub. She smiled at the memory of a time when her father's face had graced the cover of the very same publication.

The memory sparked another. There was someone she wanted to talk to, someone she'd not connected with for years: Katrina Vidal.

She answered while laughing. Music blared in the background. "Zoe? Is that you, baby?"

"It's me," Ashley confirmed, smiling and trying not to drop the phone into the bath water. "Are you at work?"

"On a break. How the hell are you?"

"I'm soaking in magnolia water and drinking Prosecco. And I'm in Baton Rouge."

"Oh! That sounds heavenly. Only you must be solo or you wouldn't be wasting time calling me. What's up, cookie?"

"Just missed you." Ashley tried to envision Trina tending the bar in the fancy club where she now worked. "Feeling a little alone."

"Sweetie, it amazes me that you haven't hooked up with some uber hot guy who's taking you to Provence for lunch and Paris for dinner and then Venice for dessert, of course. And afterward, rockin' you all night in bed."

Ashley chuckled. "If you know where that guy is, please let me know."

"Baby girl, you got something on your sweet little mind? Something Auntie Katrina can help you figure out?"

"Aw, well, there's this guy. And he *is* uber hot. And smart, and he has his own business. He's got some deep secrets, and I want to know what they are. He was dating Megan, but they broke up, and she's now latched onto Alex."

"What? Hold on a minute, baby cakes –" Katrina turned her mouth away from the phone to deal with a customer. "I'll be there in a minute! Keep your tighty-whities on, lover boy! – Zo? You there? Okay, so, whoa, Meggie and Alex are finally hooked up? Did he finally grow a pair?"

"I'm happy for them. And yeah, it's about time, right?"

"How's your daddy? Does he miss me yet?"

"He's recovering from a recent heart attack. I know, I should have called you."

"Holy Mother of God!! Yes, you should have called me. Is he okay? I knew I shoulda never left him to his own devices."

"He's going to be fine. Mimi has made it her life's work to make him exercise and eat kale."

"Wonders never cease. But tell me about this hot guy."

"I can't stop obsessing about him. He's mysterious. He's sexy. He looks at me like he knows what I look like without my clothes. I can't talk when I see him."

"Now, Zo, listen to me. You are letting yourself lose power over this dude. Stand up, straighten your crown, and remember, as they say, who's unofficial niece you are. You walk right up to Mr. Mysterious, tuck your pretty fingers into his belt, plant your boots on either side of his Nikes and look him in the eye. Then you ask him, flat out, what's taking him so long. Does he want to hook up or doesn't he? It's that simple."

Ashley giggled, a silly, girlish laugh she'd not uttered since that night, so long ago, when she'd fallen so completely in love with the stranger in the dark. "What if he doesn't wear a belt?"

"All the better, my sweet. Then you stick those red, manicured nails right into his waistband. And don't underestimate the value of a V-neck sweater. Honey, I gotta go. You call me again, okay? Let me know how it goes. Love ya."

"Love you, too," Ashley murmured. Happy that she'd called her longtime mentor, she tossed her phone onto the rug and sank down in the hot water. Why had she thought about her gypsy lover, tonight? She'd realized, long ago, that the encounter in the tent was a fantasy. Just a dude looking to get off for free with a self-acknowledged virgin. What guy wouldn't hit on that? She'd made him out to be a prince on a steed. He and his stupid guitar. He'd ruined her, and not in the physical way one might expect. He'd ruined her expectations, her future potential for love. Who could ever live up to the tender and attentive way he'd made love to her? To the sweet sound of the song he played? To the caring way he'd said goodbye?

A fantasy, indeed. Truth was, she hoped to never see him again. Because surely, in the light of day, the guy would be a flat-out fraud.

Ashley ordered a full breakfast in the hotel coffee shop. She'd slept well and late; it was nearly lunchtime. For want of something to occupy her thoughts, she looked over the brochures of local attractions she'd picked up in the lobby. She marveled at the tourist sites available – things she'd had no idea existed while living on the river. It had been like a step back in time.

Maricela had asked her to come by 2 o'clock, to help set up and to have a chance to chat. There wasn't anything to do in the meantime, so she decided to head out to the camp. She'd packed a bag of necessities – a jacket, spare shoes, wet wipes, bug spray, lip balm, bottled water from the room. Her hairbrush and makeup. And pepper spray.

She walked across the lobby and paused before exiting the hotel, peering out at the partly cloudy skies. It should be a fine evening for a party. The doorman opened the door for her, but before she could step outside, someone tapped her on the shoulder.

"Ashley?"

She turned and nearly collided with Christian.

"Sorry," he said, taking a step back. "Wasn't sure that was you."

"Oh, it's me. Here for the party, I guess?"

"Yeah. Wouldn't miss it. My dad, you know."

"You staying here?"

"Yeah. Got in last night. Didn't know you were here; we could've connected for dinner."

"Hmm. Maybe another time." Ashley looked away. Christian cleared his throat.

"Why don't we ride out there together? I wouldn't mind some company."

Ashley thought over his offer. Now that she was more comfortable driving, she preferred the autonomy of her own vehicle. She didn't like being dependent on others in case she wanted to bounce. Looking down, she noticed Christian was wearing Nikes, but she couldn't tell about the belt. "I'd like that," she finally responded. "Thanks."

"Were you ..."

"Yes. I was just leaving."

"Then let's go."

This trip bore no resemblance to the one two months ago, when Christian had broken all laws getting to his father, unsure if he would even be found alive. Still, he was again nervous. This time it was a honey-blonde girl with green eyes. The girl who looked at him expectantly, when he had no words coming from his usually silver tongue. He'd asked her to ride with him but had absolutely nothing smart or witty to say.

"So, what flight were you on?" she asked.

Safe subject. "I got in around 6:15 on American. You?"

"Five-thirty, on United."

"Ah." How could he talk intelligently with her, when all he could think about was the fact that he knew her intimately. That he had touched and enjoyed her curves, her flesh, her secret places. The memory made him warm up inside, but the fact that she knew nothing chilled the heat.

"So. You and Robbie."

"Yeah. We're twins." Christian stared straight ahead, not trusting himself to look at her.

"You weren't there when I was there. Where were you? No one ever mentioned your name to me. Not even Mari."

Christian sighed. "They were all mad at me, I guess. Because I left. I got out. It wasn't the life for me. My father apparently put out an edict that no one ever speak my name again. I tried to get Robbie out, but he … we may look alike, but we're just not the same."

"When did you go?"

"As soon as I could. I was around sixteen."

"Where did you go?"

He finally stole a look. "Twenty questions? Is that what we're doing here?"

"You're right. Sorry." Ashley turned to look out the window. "My stepmom is a twin."

"Jessica? Didn't know. Identical?"

"Yes. Super sweet woman."

Christian nodded. "How's Dev like school?"

"Surprisingly, he's eating it up. I wasn't here when he was in high school, but Dad says he was a lazy student who didn't care about his grades. But now, he's hitting the books hard."

"He's motivated. That's good. I'm proud of him."

Ashley seemed unimpressed with the extent of Christian's pride in her brother, so he opted to keep his mouth closed for the next several miles. Apparently, the quiet suited Ashley as well. They spoke little the rest of the way to the river camp. Christian was happy to note the celebration would be held in a different camp than the one that held such recent, heinous, memories.

Maricela rushed out to greet them. "Carpooling?" she asked, arching one brow.

"Made sense. We realized this morning that we were in the same hotel," Christian explained.

"I see. Okay. So, I could use some help setting up the tables. You guys ready?"

People started showing up at 4 p.m., in cars, on motorbikes and in boats. The grounds filled up quickly, and by sundown a raging bonfire provided light, heat and excitement. A Zydeco band tuned up from a flat barge docked close by and people got up to dance. The drinks ranged from Planter's Rum Punch to moonshine.

Christian sat with his father for the better part of an hour, helping him to greet the people wishing him well. Many wanted to know, 'where the hell is Azirona?', and those that did know loudly proclaimed that the Colorado River had nothing on the Bayou. Martin tired early and Christian got him to Rudy's motorhome to lie down. After assurances from his father that he'd be fine, Christian returned to the revelry and finally accepted a plastic cup of Rudy's best rye.

"Guess this is it, huh?" Rudy asked, as they stood on the fringe of the merriment watching.

"It, how? For Dad, yeah."

"No, I mean you. You'll have no reason to ever come back here, now."

Christian grinned. "You could always come out west. I could show you some good times, man."

"I'll bet you could. As it turns out, your sister has invited me along for the ride. Long as I don't run into any trouble with my priors."

"Shave off that animal growing on your face, get a pair of proper specs so's you can see where you're going, you might have a chance at evading the long hand of the law." Christian took another sip. "This isn't half-bad, man." But his eyes were focused on the girl; the woman, laughing and gossiping with Maricela and Ronnie, their forms silhouetted by the blaze behind them.

He had to get next to her but didn't see how he could without somehow divulging his secret. Maricela knew. Martin knew. And chances are, even Robbie knew. It was a miracle it hadn't gotten back to Ashley by now. He could take his chances and tell her the truth. Isn't that what he'd advise someone asking his advice? Always tell the truth. No matter how much it hurts, it will always be better than the repercussions of lying.

Ha. If I believed that, I would have told her by now. And not telling her is akin to lying.

The whiskey was beginning to dull his senses. When Rudy turned away to seek out Maricela, Christian dumped his cup on the ground, then tapped his friend on the shoulder. "I'm gonna go shake down my brother."

Robbie was surprisingly sober. The brothers sat down together.

"So, what are you going to do when they leave for Phoenix?" Christian asked. "You're not staying here?"

"I'm going with them."

"You are? I didn't know that. Wow. What will you do? Dad's not going to last long."

"I'll get a job and help support. Mari and Rudy are talkin' about starting a business. They're going to need help. And no one knows me there."

"Very different there, you know. Dry, hot, you'll be trading Cajuns for Comanches."

"Ha. Don't care. I'm up for different. Will you come out, you think? It's not far from L.A."

"Of course, I will."

"Look, Chris, I'm sorry for the shit I got you into. I never meant to. I laid low, for a long time, up in Idaho. It was hard, I cleaned up. I honestly did. I met a girl. We were good together. But last year, there was this accident. She died."

Christian could see the grief was still fresh in Robbie's eyes. "What happened?"

"It was so stupid. We had a little house. Not much else. It was so cold, I put a propane heater in the house."

"Fire?"

"Carbon monoxide poisoning."

"That's rough. I'm sorry."

Robbie mustered a sad smile. "Of course, knowing me, I fell off the wagon and hit it hard. I came down to L.A. I started sniffing around for a good high. I met some guys. Right? Don't I always? But anyway, somehow, one of these guys knew about my dealings back here. And he was working for some fat cat dealer, who turned out to be someone who knew you. In fact, he thought I was you."

Christian closed his eyes for a moment, knowing what was coming next. "And you let him believe you were me."

"It was wrong, I know. It seemed like a good idea at the time. You were respectable. You had a good reputation. It was only supposed to be a quick thing. Then I would disappear again. But it didn't work out that way."

"They figured it out."

"I was there, at that house in Reseda. That was me your driver saw."

My driver. Devon. It all made sense now. Christian frowned. "Go on."

"I don't know exactly what happened next. These guys all talked, and they put together a plan to extort money from you. I tried to talk them out of it, told them I'd get the money somehow. But they were done with me."

"Was Sy a part of this deal?"

"I don't know any of their names. But the boss man, the one riding around in the limo, he didn't want any part of the deal and he left."

"But there were gunshots."

"Oh, that was nothing. One of those jerks thought it would be fun to shoot at a cockroach crossing the floor."

"So, Robbie, why didn't you come to me about all this? Don't you think I deserved to know what was going on? My employee – he's just a kid – was kidnapped. I cleaned out all my bank accounts. Our sister was taunted and held captive, our dad roughed up ... man. I get it about needing a fix. But you totally screwed up, brother."

"I know. I know. I don't know how to make it up to you. I'm sorry, bro."

Christian huffed out a breath. "Turns out I'm supposed to get back whatever's left of my money. Ash will get all of hers back. Dude. You gotta promise me you'll stay clean this time."

Robbie looked at the ground. "I'm not much good at promises. I'm gonna try, real hard, Chris. And I'm gonna take care of Dad as long as he needs me."

Christian considered his brother's confession, apology, and plans. Looking at Robbie, he realized how much he'd missed those days, so long ago, when life was climbing trees and catching lizards. When their mother had not-too-successfully tried to dress them alike and had run interference with their grumpy father. Her death had been the fork in the road for them. Guilt was a powerful thing, and it had latched onto Robbie's soft and vulnerable soul. He couldn't stand up to Martin's iron fist. He gave up, and the fragile bond between two very different brothers had unraveled. Frayed, but not severed. He slapped Robbie on the thigh, then stood up. "I guess that's good enough. You need to take care of yourself, too. You got that?"

Robbie nodded, but Christian was scanning the partiers for Ashley, whom, he discovered, was dancing in a circle with several other river folks. The firelight lit her features, once again setting off feelings within him he wished he didn't have. This woman was complicating his life. He'd never felt complications or encumbrances with Megan, which still pained him to acknowledge.

He didn't know anyone else at the party. He decided to hunker down and wait for Ashley to signal she was ready to go back to the hotel.

THIRTY

Confessions in the Dark

"Are you sure? Chris is around here somewhere, and if he's not, we can get someone to drive you back to town," Maricela said, her voice a little thick with rum.

"No. I just want to lie down and clear my head. Is there a bunk I can have?"

"Of course, there is. If you want quiet, that tent at the end is where Ronnie and I are bunking, until tomorrow. We kept the layout the same when we moved the camp."

Ashley nodded and gave her old friend a brief hug. "See you in the morning. Maybe we can catch up a bit then."

She made her way with the help of a tiny flashlight on her keychain. Once inside the tent, she lay down on Veronica's bedroll and closed her eyes. Just over a year ago, she'd spent her last night in this humid, earthy jungle. So much had happened since. Her return to the Pierce fold, affluence, society, and family. It was supposed to all calm down then, but chaos had followed her home. Her father's heart attack, her stepbrother's kidnapping. The terrifying ordeal with the gangsters. Now, it all seemed like a scene from the worst part of a storybook.

She turned onto her side and reached for the neatly folded blanket at her feet, pulling it up over her shoulder. Her life had taken some serious turns during the past few years, but never in her craziest thoughts would she have expected to return to the Bayou, never would have believed she'd lay down again in a frigid tent in the backwoods of Louisiana. So bizarre. What had been her dreams, her aspirations, upon leaving the South? Had she run from, or toward? Were there any formed expectations?

Ashley wasn't sure about those expectations. She'd been bored, for sure. She'd been restless. And ... lonely. She had friends, of course; Mari and Ronnie and a handful of others. But she'd seen her future in the eyes of the older women in the tribe. Quiet, hard-working but drab women with no excitement in their days or nights. And while she'd never wanted the kind of life her mother had, she did feel a renewed appreciation for the excitement of Hollywood, prosperity, and her wacky, extended family. The comforts of living in a home, with choices of what to eat, what to wear, places to go, and people to meet. Nothing like that would happen in the camp. Excitement, joy, and ... dare she think it? Love.

She sighed out a breath. She'd certainly experienced excitement. And yes, joy. She thought about Dane and Jessica, and their loving acceptance of her craziness. About Devon and his sweet charm, his adoration and devotion. But love? Had she ever even come close to feeling that elusive, all-encompassing, mind-boggling sea of emotion? Craved a man's touch, wanted a look into his mind, felt a desire to never leave his side?

Maybe. Maybe once, long ago, and that experience had not occurred in Los Angeles. It had happened ... right here. Here, in the dark, on a chilly night not unlike this one. "Ha," Ashley muttered, rolling onto her back and throwing her arm across her eyes. "What a joke."

"Excuse me? Did you say something?"

Ashley nearly choked at the sound of a man's whispered voice. He had to be lying not five feet away from her. Instinctively grasping the blanket to her chest, she sat up. "Who is it? Who's in here? I'm sorry, I didn't realize –"

She heard the man moving about and sensed he was closer now.

"It's okay. I just needed a place to chill. If you don't mind sharing."

Wide-eyed in the dark, Ashley slowly laid back down. The voice belonged to Christian. "No. It's okay."

"I doubt I can sleep, though. After today."

"No argument there," Ashley mumbled, frowning. He was still moving about, and she heard him mutter an oath as he tripped over something. Something tuneful.

"Wow. I can't believe this is still here. She kept it."

Now Ashley again sat up. He was strumming a guitar. The notes were hesitant at first, then rhythmic. "You might remember this," he said softly.

She did, indeed, remember the tune he carefully picked out with gentle fingers. "I Belong to Us," she whispered, her voice hoarse with emotion.

He continued to stroke the guitar strings and hum intermittently. "You never knew it was me, did you? I had the distinct advantage, that day at your party. Megan called you 'Zoe' and mentioned you'd run off with gypsies. It didn't take a lot of brain cells to put it together."

Ashley opened her mouth to speak but her words all jammed into her throat. The realization that Christian Collins was her unknown lover took her breath away. She swallowed hard. "I knew it all along," she murmured, drawing a chuckle from her troubadour.

"Yeah, right you did."

"And you never mentioned it because?"

"Because ... I wasn't at all that sure it would be a happy memory for you. Presumptuous of me to bring up a past you'd clearly left behind. You aren't the same girl I ... I spent that time with back then."

"Fair enough, I guess. But now I feel totally stupid."

The strumming stopped and the guitar slid away. Christian moved to sit in front of Ashley. She felt his warmth and allowed him to take her hands. "On the contrary. I'm the stupid one, here. To think I wasted all that time, hiding the way I felt, even from myself."

"I'm not sure what you mean."

"I told myself for years that our encounter – if that's what we call it – was just a silly fluke on a crazy night. A night when my life changed forever in many ways."

"Well, my life certainly changed."

"Of course. But for me ... so much happened ... finding, then losing you, losing Robbie, abandoning Mari –"

"What? What about Robbie? And Mari? You have a lot to tell me, Chris. Because you are the only one in the light, here. All I know is that a man came into this tent and gave me the night of my life. Stars exploded in the darkness. I felt truly alive and beautiful for the first and only time. And the next thing I know, you're gone, and I'm left with this ... this huge hole in my life, where none existed before. Nothing felt right after that."

"Zoe, I –"

"And then you walk in with my arch-nemesis, a woman who's hated me my entire life, and when I saw you across the pool, I felt like I couldn't tear my eyes away. Did I know you? Of course not. But I did. Somehow. Yet I wasn't about to fight her over some remote, bizarre connection I couldn't justify."

"It's weird, I know. I –"

"And now, you show up here, tonight, in the midst this emotionally charged time, and start playing that stupid song, the song that has haunted my dreams for the last four years. And you say you've known all along it was me. I don't know what to –"

Her words were clipped by Christian's sudden kiss. A kiss so immediate and desperate and still wanting of more. "Stop," he managed against her lips.

Ashley pushed him away. Hard. "Don't even. You have no idea what I've been through. And you, so smug, looking at me, knowing we ... did that. It's humiliating." Her words spewed from the long-sheltered pain in her heart, but her lips still hummed from the power of his kiss. She wanted more, and yet, she wanted to slam her fist into his face.

"There will be time to sort it all out. I'll explain, I will, about my brother and sister, and my mother ... and how I had to flee. About how I regretted so much for so long." Christian moved in close, again, cupped her face gently. "But tonight, let us be gypsies. Be my gypsy."

He took her mouth again before she could protest. Protest that she was angry. That she'd been spoiled by him for any other man. That she dreamed, still, of their night together, and only survived by imagining that he'd died somehow before he'd been able to come back to her. But she said nothing and lay back on the thick bedroll. She made half-hearted efforts to thwart him, not because she didn't want him; she did, badly. She just needed him to feel her anger.

"Stars exploded? Truthfully?" he inquired, gently tugging at her t-shirt. "That might be a hard act to follow."

"Try," she whispered, her fingers finding the buttons on his shirt and making quick work of them. "Make it up to me. All this time.

Remind me of the gypsy girl I was."

Quickly shedding the rest of their clothes, Christian launched a sexual, loving assault on Ashley's body, unable to pause for even a moment to reflect. It was nothing like the first time, when he'd been so careful to usher a young girl into womanhood. That girl was now a woman of experience, of talent and carnal knowledge. Yet there was more here than simple lust. There was no question that Ashley was truly a gypsy at heart, a passionate, erotic but loving partner who made his own stars explode.

He normally would have rolled away and let his body cool alone. Tonight, however, was different. He kept Ashley close, their slickened bodies touching from cheek to ankle. "That was ... man. That was incredible."

"I didn't believe it was possible. I didn't think I would ever feel like that again," she murmured, and he sensed it was more of a personal revelation than an admission.

"Quite honestly, neither did I."

Ashley stirred, looked up at him in the darkness. "What about Meg?"

"What about Meg? We broke up. It was fun, she needed to feel valued, but she and I? It wasn't meant to be."

"You made her feel valued? Is that your lot in life, to go around fixing damaged girls?"

"Hmm. Maybe so."

"She's never been happy."

"She might be now."

"Why? Because of your tutelage?"

"No. Because she's finally with your brother."

"Are you serious?"

"I gave her the confidence to go after him."

"Your modesty is overwhelming." Ashley pulled away and started to dress. "I'd like to go back to the hotel now."

"Wait. Why the hostility? Can't we just...be together? I don't know about you, but for me, this is a lot to absorb."

"It is a lot. More than I can handle. And by the way, I'm the one doing the absorbing. If you think that us having sex will fix it all, you're clueless, and honestly, off planet." Ashley stood up and straightened her shirt. She moved to the tent door. "Look. I'm not okay with this, with any of this. I grew up in a dysfunctional family and frankly, I ended up here because of that. There's no room in my life for secrets and lies. Now, if you'll just get me back to the hotel. Please."

Christian got to his feet and pulled on his jeans. He wanted to apologize, wanted to take the pain away, to somehow reset time. But Ashley was in no mood for conciliatory efforts.

"I'll meet you at the car. I need to check on Martin before I go."

THIRTY-ONE

Becoming Sisters

Ashley spoke little to anyone from the time she left the tent that night until she was back at home in Malibu. New memories conflicted with what she knew to be true: Christian Collins was a callous, insensitive man who utilized a "smash and grab" modus operandi when it came to women he wanted. She couldn't fathom any reasonable explanation for his behavior.

He'd tried to initiate conversation on the way to the airport and during the flight back to L.A., during which they'd sat together. Ashley wasn't having it. She took a separate shuttle home, acknowledging a vague promise to get together soon. She needed time to process what she'd learned and what she'd experienced.

In the days that followed her return, Ashley was quiet, perhaps sullen, if she was honest with herself. With Melissa working, Devon and Brady both at school, and her parents in meetings at the studio, she had the house to herself but found she didn't enjoy the solitude. She roamed from room to room, looking for something to gain her interest. On the kitchen table was a stack of Devon's textbooks, and she perused the titles: College Algebra II, English Literature, American History, and a thin booklet detailing the rules of archery.

Why didn't I go to college? Oh, yeah. I was busy living in a bug-infested swampland.

Beside the textbooks was a scratch pad on which Melissa, she assumed, had listed items she needed to restock at work. Threads, bobbins, bias tape in emerald green.

Why don't I have a job? Oh, yeah. I have no skills and clearly, no ambition.

On the counter below the microwave was a dog-eared script for Alex's film.

Why am I not in the movie business? This is getting ridiculous.

Her self-recrimination went on pause when Melissa walked in, a tote bag slung over her shoulder. She opened the refrigerator and found a liquid yogurt drink.

"Whatcha up to today?" She dug into the pantry and found a granola bar.

"Let me check my busy calendar," Ashley said with a huff. "I thought you were at work."

"Took the day off. We finally have a few days' breathing room. I have a couple of personal things to get done."

"You like working for Roxanne?"

"She's a dream boss. I mean, look at me, I've never done anything, like, skilled, in my life. She gave me a chance. Turns out I'm not as worthless as I thought."

"Of course, you're not worthless. That would be me."

Melissa opened and took a sip of the yogurt. She appraised Ashley and wiped her mouth with a paper towel. "Wanna come with me? Just ride along?"

"Where are you going?"

Melissa drew in a serious breath. "Mom's headstone came in. Finally. I'm heading over there to ... visit and check it out. After that, I've got a little shopping to do. Brady's birthday is coming up. Might get lunch."

Ashley's lips parted in surprise. She could not remember her sister inviting her anywhere, ever. She did recognize the look of impatience growing on Melissa's face, and knew she had to decide quickly. "Sure," she blurted. "Let me run upstairs and grab my jacket."

"I don't have all day," Melissa called after her.

Talk enroute to the cemetery was cursory. Brady's birthday party, Dane's progress, a gown commissioned by a big name in Hollywood. Ashley marveled at how normal they seemed. Almost like two sisters spending a day together. She thought Melissa's demeanor would change once they reached their destination, but her matter-of-factness remained predictable and not difficult.

"Wow. It's nicer than I thought it would be," Melissa said, when they'd reached Rita's grave. "Next time I'll bring some flowers."

Ashley felt a lump grow in her throat. It wouldn't have occurred to her to bring anything at all. She stared down at the polished granite, etched with Rita's name, her birth and death dates, and the phrase, "Forever in Our Hearts."

Whose hearts?

This was her mother's final resting place. The woman who'd given birth but little else to her. Still, unbidden tears flooded her eyes and she turned away.

"Hey, you okay?" Melissa asked.

"Sure." But she wasn't, and her sister touched her lightly on the shoulder.

"What gives?"

"It's nothing."

"Oh, so it's normal for you to burst into tears without warning? Because truth is, I wouldn't know that about you. Hell, I don't know anything about you."

"I can't explain. I don't know."

Melissa frowned and licked her lips. "Okay, change in plans. Lunch is next."

Ashley was in no condition to agree or disagree, so Melissa decided on the restaurant and ushered her sister into a booth in the most private corner. She ordered Bloody Marys for them both.

"Now. The waterworks. I'm kind of an expert in that area, so I know when the heart is bleeding, that stuff comes out of the eyes. You wanna talk about it, or just let it stew and then boil over again? And next time, it'll be in front of Jess, and she'll needle you until you feel like a pin cushion."

Ashley uttered a shaky laugh. Melissa was dead on with that one. But she still didn't know what to say. "I'm going through something. I'm not sure what it is. This morning I was mad that I never went to college. I don't even remember going to high school. You think you have no skills? I have less than that."

"Hmm. You might lack experience, but it doesn't mean you lack skills. But I suspect there's more on the table than your vocation. You spend a lot of time alone. No boyfriend? A hot chickie like you? No obvious baggage?"

Ashley couldn't help a lopsided smile. "I've got plenty of baggage and it's not a matched set."

"A particular guy giving you some hormonal imbalance, is that it? I mean, not that I know anything about that. I've been with, what? Let me count how many guys. Um... one, ..."

Ashley waited for Melissa to count off her lovers. But her sister stopped and took a sip off her drink straw.

"Yep, that's right. One. Brady's daddio."

"But ... you're pretty. You're smart, you have confidence."

"Sheesh. Have you fooled, do I? C'mon. Who would date a woman like me. I'm almost twenty-six, with a kid. Who lives with her parents. Who has no experience with men and just recently learned how to balance a checkbook. Yeah, I'm in demand."

Ashley didn't know how to respond. She'd never considered her sister undesirable. "I'm sure there are guys out there who ... who ..."

"Oh, they're out there, all right. There are those who don't care about the kid, or the economic status, or even the future. They're only interested in hooking up for a night. Been there, almost done that."

The waiter stopped by to take their order.

"They have a Southwest salad here that's the bomb," Melissa said, ordering that and a basket of popovers. Ashley ordered the same. Curious, she ventured back to the conversation. "You've never talked about Brady's father."

"I guess it doesn't matter now, does it? That he was married? He never knew. I saw no point in telling him. I mean, he was *really* married. And I was a foolish, sixteen-year-old girl. But you knew, right? I mean, everyone knew."

Ashley considered her words carefully. "There were whispers, maybe some overheard conversations. I wasn't ever sure what happened. I was only twelve, and I was living with Dad."

"He was a high school tutor. I was failing pretty much everything. He was young, handsome, so together. He invited me out for coffee after our sessions, we talked about worldly things. Travel, politics, places he'd been. I was flat out in love. Talk about a teenage crush. He was everything. We had sex in his car once, and at his friend's house once. And a third time at our house when Mom was out cold. Then, Mom got an email that my sessions were being transferred to another tutor. A middle-aged woman was taking Ricardo's place. And I, I was stunned to realize I had no way to reach him. All of our 'dates' had originated at the learning center where he taught. I had no phone number, no email address. He just disappeared on me. Do they call that 'ghosting' now? You have no idea how devastated I was. I tried to subtly ask the new teacher questions without sounding too obvious."

"What did she say?"

"That his wife had just had a baby and they'd moved away to live with her parents. His *wife*. And *baby*. Are you getting this? He was screwing me while his wife was pregnant! Poor little me. And then, of course, I found out I was pregnant, too."

"That seriously sucks."

Melissa drank down the rest of her cocktail and signaled the waiter for another. "Mrs. Garbanzo, or whatever her name was, said she had Ricardo's address in Tucson if I wanted to send them a card. Ha! What I wanted to send him was a letter filled with Anthrax. Or a box of scorpions. With a copy of *Lost Season*." Melissa broke into uncontrolled laughter at her own little joke.

Ashley smiled. "Have you ever watched it all the way through? I thought Daddy made a decent rogue."

"Mom bought several copies just so she could smash them to pieces with a hammer," Melissa explained. "And yes, I've seen it. It's not half-bad."

"Does Brady know about his father?"

"No."

Ashley nodded and finished her drink just as their second round arrived. "Look, I'm glad you told me. I'm glad to know what happened and I think you're incredibly brave. You kept your baby. That means a lot."

"Actually, Mom kept my baby. I wanted to get an abortion. When that wasn't an option, I wanted to give him up. I didn't want to see him when he was born. Didn't want to touch him, or nurse him, or diaper his little bum. It was Mom who pushed me, taught me, made me become a mother. Weird, huh? She wasn't a good mother herself, but she forced me to become one."

Ashley had trouble envisioning Rita as a positive maternal influence. "Wasn't she drinking?"

"She stopped when Brady was a toddler. She was dry until earlier this year."

"I can't imagine what you went through."

"So, meeting men hasn't been a priority for me. But let's talk about you, chickie. Tell Big Sis what's got you chewing your fingernails down to nubs and causing those dark circles under those gorgeous green peepers."

Ashley took a long sip off her Bloody Mary and drew in a deep breath. "Okay, so, there's this guy. He's under my skin. I can't take a breath without thinking about him. And he's just ... out of reach. I can't come to terms with some things he's done."

"Eh. Sounds typical. Is this your first love or just a current attraction?"

"Um, both?" To Melissa's confused look, Ashley continued. "My first was a guy I couldn't see."

"Couldn't see? What does that mean? He was invisible?" she jibed.

"No. I couldn't see anything."

"Blindfolded? Kinky."

"Not blindfolded. It was just very dark. I couldn't see him. I didn't even know him."

Melissa frowned. "You weren't raped?"

"No! Gosh, no. It was an arranged thing. I was nineteen and hadn't ever, you know."

"Hadn't been laid? At nineteen? Shit, girl. What happened?"

Ashley wet her lips. "Most likely, after what happened to you, Daddy had me locked into a virtual chastity belt. And don't forget, I was tipping the scales at a hefty weight. My self-esteem was in the gutter."

"Sweet mother of sin, no wonder you ran away. I would have, too. So, who was this mysterious lover? This was in the gypsy compound, I assume? Wow, an unknown gypsy lover. I'm fairly sure I've read this plot in one of my romance novels."

"It was an incredible night. I had put the word out that I wanted someone to, um, have sex with. He came to me in the dark, and he was so romantic. He played guitar. He was tender, and gentle, and slow. He said sweet things, then he left. He took my heart with him."

"Oh puh-leeze. Now you're channeling one of the heroines. It's a little sticky. So, what, you never saw him again?"

Their lunch arrived, and Melissa grabbed a popover and slathered it with honey-butter. "These are to die for."

"I still hesitate to eat good things."

"You got no problems, hon. You got a cute, sexy little body that any man would kill to hit. Now, you did, or didn't see this traveling Casanova again?"

"I did. He came to my birthday party. With Megan."

Melissa stopped short of stuffing a loaded fork into her gaping mouth. "Not Christian Freaking Collins?"

Ashley pressed her lips together and nodded.

"He was your hot gypsy lover? But you didn't know him, right?"

"I didn't know he was the one. No clue. But he knew it was me. Megan told him my name was Zoe and that I'd been living with the gypsies. He put two and two together. But he didn't tell me who he was."

"Let me think about this."

The girls worked through their salads. The vodka had loosened Ashley's lips, and she felt an unusual level of relief at having confided in someone. But she hadn't told Melissa the whole story.

"So, when I went back to Louisiana, during that whole fiasco –"

"Oh, you mean when you were almost kilt dead?" Melissa pushed her glass away. "No more for me. I need to be clear on this."

"After that. When they had the big party. He was there, of course. And we were back in that dark tent again, and –"

"Oh, lord. Don't tell me. He made love to you again in the dark and this time you turned on the freakin' light!"

Patrons turned to stare, and Ashley briefly covered her eyes.

"Sorry," Melissa said.

"No, you're mostly right."

"So, I'm not seeing a real problem here. He's hot, God, uber-hot, he's got money, his own company, and if he did you again, he must like you even better now, but ... the look on your face says you're pissed at him."

Ashley pouted. "It was humiliating, Mimi. He knew, all those months he was dating Megan, that he and I ... that I was ... that poor, fat, inept virgin living in a swamp. And he was screwing a woman who hates the ground I walk on. He the same as told me he was lusting after me while he was in a relationship with her."

Melissa began to giggle. Her giggle prompted a snort, and she covered her mouth with her napkin.

"What? What's so funny? Ashley demanded.

"It won't mean anything to you, but this is sounding like history repeating itself. You and Megs, Dad and Mac. I mean, not entirely the same, but still ... you're a Pierce, she's a MacKendall."

Ashley shrugged. "I guess. Yeah. Hmm."

"How long since you've seen him?"

"A few weeks. We haven't spoken since we got back."

"So, you still haven't explained the problem. What's stopping you from becoming Christian's special girl?"

"I don't know."

"Okay." Melissa stabbed a cherry tomato with her fork and popped it into her mouth. "You good if we hit Party City on the way back?"

THIRTY-TWO

The Gypsy in Me

Melissa pulled into the driveway and parked near the porch. She had the trunk open in seconds. "Can you stash these in your room? I'm cutting it close."

"Sure. Does he get out at three?"

"Yup." Melissa threaded five white plastic bags over Ashley's arms. She started to turn back to the car, which was still running. Instead, she paused, clearly hesitant but determined. "Look. I know that even if Mom were still here, she wouldn't tell you what you need to hear. She was hardened and no-nonsense. The light from the greatest love of her life had been extinguished a long time ago. And we've already established that I'm no role model. Huh. Can't tell you what to do. Jess might. All of her bones are romantic ones, but I'm not real clear on your relationship with her."

Ashley stared, unable to respond, so Melissa continued. "All I can say is, if I were you, I'd go for it. I know you're thinking that this is a fantasy and couldn't possibly be real. You might be right. But you won't know unless you ... unless you try. Another cliché, I know. Just think about it, Ash. What have you got to lose? Your heart is still aching. It'll continue to ache. If you jump into the pool and swim with this guy, you'll at least find out if he's the real deal. If he isn't, you walk away and let it go. Blow out the torch."

"Mm hmm," Ashley murmured.

"Then there's the other scenario. You don't jump in, and Mr. Wonderful gets tired of waiting."

"But what if he's supposed to be with Meg?"

"Supposed to? For frackin' frickety'frock's sake, Ashley! Meg's 100 percent with Alex!" Melissa glanced down at her watch. "Shit. I gotta go." She looked Ashley in the eye and rushed her with a brief kiss on the cheek. "Remember to hide Brady's stuff!"

Ashley muscled the bags into the house and up the stairs. She encountered Devon in the hallway, and he, too, seemed to be in a hurry.

"Did a little shopping? Looks like you cleaned out the store!"

"It's Melissa's. For Brady's party. Where are you off to?"

"I'm late for school. My afternoon class. But I promised Chris I'd drop off his leather jacket, and I didn't realize how late it was. He might need it tonight. See you later!"

Ashley opened her bedroom door and tossed in the bags. Pausing only a moment, she turned and rushed down the stairs after Devon.

"I'll take it to him," she called. "I just need his address."

"Really? I mean, seriously? That would so save my ass." Devon pulled his wallet from his hip pocket and retrieved a business card from the bill section. "It's in Brentwood. Easy to find, not too easy to park. If you call him first, he'll meet you downstairs. Or not. Whatever."

"Okay. The jacket?"

"Oh, yeah," Devon said with an embarrassed smile. "It's in my car."

Ashley watched as Devon backed slowly down the driveway and into the street. She held the jacket against her chest. The rich leather smell wafted into her nose and she closed her eyes. She hadn't seen Christian in weeks.

What have I done? Am I ready to face him now?

But Melissa was right. It was time to jump into the pool.

Three weeks. Christian slammed hangers back and forth in his closet, seeking a dark gray shirt he might still own. But it didn't really matter, did it? What he wore to the club? Because no one there cared or noticed if he could still pay for drinks. But there it was, hanging forlornly, one sleeve almost slipping off the black, felt covered hanger.

Meg had bought them. They were designer and very upscale, she'd assured him. But they were impossible to use with his soft-fabric jackets, hoodies, and sweatshirts.

"Sweatshirts belong in drawers, not in closets," she'd scolded.

Right. Christian flung the hanger across the room and started pulling more of the offensive, fuzzy triangles from the closet, separating them from his garments which he tossed onto the bed. His closet was nearly empty when he calmed enough to stop himself. He stared at the heap of clothing on his bed and dangerous tangle of hangers at his feet. *Guess I'll be sleeping on the couch tonight.*

That didn't matter, either. Where he slept was of no consequence anymore because there was only one place he wanted to sleep: beside Ashley Pierce. And that wasn't about to happen, ever again. He'd blown it with her, killed any possibility of a future. He understood it, but still thought it was stupid. So, what if he had kept his memories of her a secret? It seemed like the right thing to do at the time. And how could he have known that she and Megan had such a ... a volatile history?

Ashley had made him feel guilty. Ashamed. Immoral. She couldn't possibly *get* his relationship with Megan because she didn't even know Megan. Just like Megan didn't know Ashley. Their stubborn polarity seemed inborn.

And ... it didn't matter. Tonight, like the night before and the one before that and any number of nights since his return from the Bayou, he would sink his pain into a bottle of good liquor. The girls would come around, like they always did, and he would buy them drinks. But after the first couple of attempts, he'd stopped going home with them. He was distracted, uninterested, drunk, depressed, whatever the Collins excuse-of-the-night might be for being unable to perform.

Christian pocketed his wallet and his keys, grabbed his phone off the bar and left the flat. Halfway down to the parking garage, he pressed the "Lobby" button in the elevator. He'd take a ride share or a cab tonight. From the elevator he crossed the building lobby and exited onto the street, noticing the chill in the air. Damn. Devon was supposed to bring his jacket by. As he waited for his ride, he called Devon and left a message. "If you don't mind, use your key and leave it for me. Thanks, buddy. I'll see you soon. Don't study too hard."

Thoughts of his young protégé put a smile on Christian's face. His smile remained as a cab pulled up to the curb right in front of him. "Lucky night," he muttered, just as the back door opened and Ashley stepped out onto the sidewalk. She looked as surprised as he felt.

"Need a cab, sir?" The cab driver called out.

"Uh, no, thanks." He stared at Ashley and all his senses heightened. In a short, silver, shimmery dress and high heels, she was dressed for a night on the town. Her hair fell in curls and waves, and she'd done something different — perhaps the spiky wisps of haphazard bangs brushing her forehead? She carried a Saks shopping bag, he finally noticed.

"Hi," she said, grasping the handles of the bag with both hands in front of her. "I brought your jacket."

"Oh. Um, thanks. I was just heading out. You didn't need to come all this way ... I thought Dev –"

"Devon has school tonight. I offered. He seemed to think you might need it. I guess he was right." She thrust the bag at him, and he couldn't help but take it from her. "So, have a nice night." She smiled, a sweet, sorrowful smile, and turned quickly. "Wait," she called to the cabbie, then got back into the car.

"Wait!' Christian also shouted, but the cab pulled away and back into West L.A. traffic. Shoving his hand into his hair, he looked around in frustration. A vehicle with an Uber sticker suddenly slid into the place vacated by the cab. Christian knocked on the window, and the driver nodded. "Christian?" His ride!

He got into the backseat. "See that cab? A hundred dollars if you can get me into that car."

"You got it," the driver replied, and she hit the accelerator the moment there was a narrow break. The chase was on. He'd have to be ready. He found two fifties in his wallet and set them on the seat, then pulled his jacket from the bag and put it on. He started to fold up the bag when he realized it wasn't empty. Inside was a small, sparkly silver clutch purse.

The cab headed into the steel, high-rise jungle of Century City. Christian's heart raced every time he lost sight of the cab or discovered the one he was following with his eyes turned down a side street.

"Did we lose them?"

"Nope. They're ahead at one o'clock." The driver chuckled and looked at him through the rear-view mirror. "Pretty special lady?"

"Pretty *and* special."

"Okay. Relax. This will pay for the ticket I got this morning so I *will* get you into that car."

It took three streets and several blocks to catch up, but eventually, the Uber vehicle pulled alongside the taxi at a red light. Christian shoved the bills across the center console and thanked the driver. He had only moments to move to the cab. He tried the backseat door on the driver's side but found it locked.

Ashley looked up in surprise. Christian held up the purse, and the driver unlocked the door. "This is most unusual," he said quickly.

"It's okay," Ashley said. "He's my assistant." She opened the clutch and pawed through it. "Just making sure you didn't steal anything."

"Right," Christian agreed, trying to disguise the fact that he was breathless. "Where are we going, boss?"

"That depends."

"On?"

Ashley didn't answer. Confused, Christian licked his lips. What did she want? Had she left the purse intentionally, hoping, no, forcing him to follow? He had to take a risk. It was now, or never.

He closed his eyes briefly and took a steadying breath. "Would you have dinner with me?"

"That also depends. Can we talk about what happened?"

"We can talk about anything you want," Christian said. "But I want us to have a proper date."

"Usually, a proper date begins with an invitation, not an ambush in a traffic jam."

"I'm asking you now. Consider this a proper invitation to go on a first date with me."

Ashley removed a lipstick from her still-open handbag. With a tiny mirror, she began touching up her lips, moving her head from side to side to get a look. "You were clearly already going somewhere other than to dinner with me."

Christian wasn't sure, but he thought he heard the cab driver chuckle. "It doesn't matter where I was going, which, by the way, was nowhere. Right now, where I'm going is anywhere you're going." Could he be any more transparent? That he wanted to be with her, no matter the time, the place, the circumstances?

Ashley put the lipstick away and seemed to be considering his words. He decided to go for broke. He took her hand, which she tried unsuccessfully to pull away. She turned her head to look out the window, but Christian gently took her chin and turned her back.

"Hi. I'm Christian. Christian Dupré Collins. I've noticed you around, we seem to have some mutual friends. In fact, your brother works for me on occasion. I'd, um, like to get to know you better, and I thought maybe we could grab dinner sometime?"

Ashley pinched her lips together, her attempt to hide a smile obvious.

Encouraged, Christian continued. "There's a little place not far from here. It's my favorite. I usually go there alone, but I think you'd like it. They have killer catfish and jambalaya."

"No! No jambalaya!" Ashley could no long keep a straight face. Giggles erupted out of her, rewarding Christian's intended joke. "And no freaking catfish. Ever. Again."

Christian leaned forward and gave the driver a new destination, to his actual favorite small steak house. Within minutes they were sitting across from each other with drinks in front of them.

"Thank you," he said quietly.

"For what?"

"For leaving your purse. For letting me into the cab. For not letting the past get in the way of coming with me tonight."

The purse. How mortifying. She hadn't meant to leave it. In truth, she was shocked to see Christian standing in the middle of Avenue of the Americas, surrounded by a thousand cars, waving her clutch in the air. He looked both charming and ridiculous, and her heart had fluttered wildly at the sight of him. And yes, a tiny part of her wanted to tell the driver to move on, to leave him there looking like a fool. He deserved it, on some level.

But now, observing him with a candle and two martinis between them, his hair awry from the chase, his hand covering hers on the table, she knew she could never willingly walk away from him again.

"I have so much to tell you. It's important stuff, too." He took a sip of his drink and smiled, but the smile conveyed anxiety instead of joy. "Not the kind of talk for a first date, but we can't have that first date until we put the old stuff away."

Ashley nodded. "Is this stuff going to make me want to get away? Because at this time of day, I should call for a ride in advance."

His smile softened into something more real. "No. And I wouldn't let you flee, anyway." They waited to order. He cleared his throat. "To quote an old song, I was actually born on the Bayou. Robbie and I, then Mari a few years later. Our parents were both from Nebraska and had ditched their conventional lives to follow the river people from Natchez. They apparently thought they were leaving behind all their troubles and stresses, but truth was, they were just trading them for new ones. A constant struggle to have enough to eat. To keep warm, or cool, to stay unbitten, to keep what was theirs, well, theirs."

"Sounds all too familiar."

"My father changed over time. I think he became bitter over his own choices. He became stubborn. Mom wanted to take us all back to Nebraska, but he refused. He probably didn't want to admit defeat to their families back there. Of course, we kids didn't know any better. Then, our mom got sick from some bad food. He expected her to get better. Hell – we were always getting sick from one thing or another – but she only got worse. It was salmonella, and it went to her brain. She died in my arms on the way back from the hospital where Dad had taken her, too late, obviously. Robbie didn't come with us, and he regretted it forever."

Ashley felt her throat tighten. Mari had never talked about their mother.

"That may have been the incident that pushed Robbie away from us. Dad was hard on him. They fought all the time. One of the women in our camp was an ex-teacher, and she taught us from time-to-time, just enough to whet my appetite for learning. As soon as I could, I left. I worked my way around, place to place, somehow managing to support myself through college. I even went to Europe, as you know. I lived in hostels and hung out with other ex-pats, kids like myself. I learned to be book smart and street smart. But sadly, I grew up and I knew I had to go home."

"Home, to the Bayou?"

"Yeah. It took me another year to get back to Louisiana. Things were bad when I got there. Dad was sick, and Robbie was a full-blown junkie. Mari had never been schooled past those few months when we were kids. The camp seemed smaller, dirtier, more rank than I remembered it. I left and went to Baton Rouge for a short time, but then I decided to move out here and I stopped in to see them once more. That was the night you and I ..."

"Oh. Yes."

"But there's a part you don't know." Christian took another swallow of his cocktail. "My dad and I were at odds. He was already sick, back then. He wouldn't go to a doctor, of course. I sensed that I was going to lose my only remaining family. Robbie and I argued that day. It was bad. I wanted him to straighten up and come to California with me. I offered him work. I offered him rehab. He was out of it and not in any condition to know what to do. When Mari approached me about you, I thought, what the hell? Why not? But I went to see Robbie one more time. We had words, and I said awful things to him. He was stoned out of his mind, and I lost my temper. I hit him. He fell back onto the cot."

Ashley uttered an involuntary gasp. "And later, you thought you'd killed him!"

"It crossed my mind. But no. I never believed it. He was alive when I left him. I regretted what I'd done, but I knew I hadn't killed him. He'd told me about the money he owed. There were drug dealers more than just little disappointed in him. So, I had a drink with some of the boys and then went to be with you. Later, Robbie turned up dead, or so we thought. I assumed it was the dealers, but no one had seen anything other than me coming and going. Mari wanted me to tell everyone I'd been with you the whole time, so I wouldn't be under suspicion. I couldn't do that, and I couldn't prove otherwise that I hadn't killed him, so I left. Martin thought that was best, and I couldn't argue with it. With Robbie dead, I thought his debts would die with him, and you all would be safe."

"You could have exonerated yourself by saying you'd been with me? And you didn't?"

"I couldn't do that," Christian repeated. "You didn't deserve to have your privacy breached. You were an innocent."

Ashley sunk back in her seat. He'd protected her, a stranger to him, albeit a naïve and silly one. He'd shown integrity and compassion when he could have broadcasted his innocence and left her vulnerable to judgment. She was speechless.

"You don't know how many times I thought about coming back for you."

"For me?"

"Yeah. For you. Mari and I kept in touch occasionally and she would fill me in on what was going on. She never mentioned you, and I couldn't ask. I felt like I wanted to rescue you from that life. There was just something ..."

"Why couldn't you ask?"

"There was that promise to never speak of you. I had to honor that with my sister."

"Whoa," Ashley said with a sigh. "I had no idea."

"No, you didn't. Even when she wrote me for money so she could fly to California, she mentioned a friend, but I couldn't be sure it was you."

The plane ticket. Ashley shook her head slowly.

"So, Dad lied, and he was the only one who knew – besides Robbie himself – that Robbie wasn't dead. He sent Robbie packing, told him to lose himself somewhere until things cooled off. But he told him to never come back to the camp. It all went fine until one of my clients spotted Robbie and thought it was me. That client had an ... associate ... who knew about Robbie's unpaid debts. It got all balled together. You know the rest."

It was Ashley's turn to take a gulp of her cocktail. "When you walked into our backyard that day, I felt something. It was weird. Probably because you looked like Robbie."

"Do you comprehend, now, why I couldn't rush up to you and ask how the hell you'd been? I was astonished, myself, when Megan told me who you were. Had she not mentioned your past, would I have eventually known? I can't say." Christian took a moment before continuing. "I wish I'd handled it differently. But once the day had passed, the further I got from telling you the truth. I feared your response. I worried that I would be unearthing bad memories and exposing truths you'd left behind."

Ashley nodded. "I get it."

"Can you forgive me? Give us a chance to start over?"

"Because?"

"Because that's what I want. To start over with you. Look, maybe it's the gypsy in me, that needs to go for it. The gypsy in *you* that keeps you looking my way. We're bonded, somehow, and it's time we acknowledge –"

Before she knew what she was doing, Ashley lifted herself enough to lean across the table and press her lips against his, cutting off his excuses. She didn't need his reasoning, not anymore. Because they *were* gypsies, and their futures were inexplicably entwined.

Slowly, Ashley lowered herself back into her seat. Christian's eyes bore into her, clearly trying to comprehend what had just happened. She didn't want to lose momentum; she grasped his hand and spoke with conviction. "Turns out, I'm not hungry."

"Neither am I." He motioned for the check.

THIRTY-THREE

Denouement

"Who does this? I mean, who in their right mind spends her wedding night in a tent in her parents' backyard?" Ashley made little attempt to whisper.

"Turn off the lantern," Christian whispered back. "Pretend we're back *there*."

"And why would I want to be back *there*?" she responded, but the fight in her waned. She killed the lamp and snuggled closer to Christian, the sheer fact that they were both naked within sight of the back windows arousing her.

"You know why." Christian said. "And besides, no one is home anyway. We wouldn't even need this tent if it weren't fifty-nine degrees outside."

"Gypsies don't care about the cold," she murmured as Christian kissed her ear, her neck, sending shivers throughout her body.

"Because we run hot."

"Oh, please. Don't be so cliché," Ashley managed, but she arched herself upward as he hovered above.

"And you're not?" Christian chuckled. As their kisses became more demanding, more desperate, Ashley lost focus of what she wanted to keep sight of: their first night as husband and wife. But what did it matter, she quickly reasoned? They'd been meant to be together from the start, and the ring on her finger was a simple formality.

The memory-foam mattress and the duck-down sleeping bag were a poor emulation for their first time, back in the dark, rough tent in the camp. But the lovemaking was the same, or better, especially with her recent realization that Christian did, in fact, love her. And when their bodies had quieted, their last orgasmic shudders had faded, they lay together with the sound of the pool waterfall tinkling in the background.

"Will Dane be pissed?"

"Probably. I was the daughter he was planning to walk down the aisle."

"Jessie won't mind?"

"No. She'll think it's all very romantic and fitting. She'll wish we were in a movie. Mimi will be relieved, and Dev will be scandalized."

"Megan will be mad, because Alex hasn't asked her yet."

"Yet?" Ashley looked up at Christian's face in the dark. "He's going to ask her?"

"He'd be crazy not to."

"Well. I'm relieved we were able to do it without any paparazzi. That little courthouse worked simply fine."

"We could still have a wedding."

Ashley thought about Christian's suggestion. "Or just a reception party. After enough time has passed."

"Because of my dad?"

"Yes. Out of respect for Martin's passing. We can wait."

Christian sat up. "Is the pool heated?"

"Twenty-four seven. My dad has to have a daily swim." Ashley uttered a gasp as Christian scooped her up, carried her out of the tent and jumped into the deep end of the pool. He came up laughing, she came up sputtering and cursing.

"It's too cold!" she shouted.

"Gypsies don't care about the cold."

They frolicked in the pool for some time, splashing and playing and arousing each other until suddenly, the backyard and pool lights came on. "Who's out there?" Dane's demand preceded him as he stepped outside, baseball bat in hand.

"Oh, shit." Ashley muttered. "It's just us, Daddy."

"Damnation." Dane turned his back for a moment while Ashley swam quickly for the side of the pool facing the house. Against the coping, her nakedness was hidden, but she knew her father had gotten a brief eyeful. She looked over her shoulder at Christian, treading water and smiling. The lights in the pool went off.

"Who is it, Dane?" Jessica said from somewhere behind him.

"You don't want to know," Dane grumbled, but Jessica squeezed past him and walked out to the pool.

"Well, aren't you two having fun? Aren't you freezing? Do you even have towels? I'll get you some," she said, smiling knowingly at her stepdaughter.

Within minutes, Christian and Ashley were both wrapped in thick, navy bathrobes and sipping brandy with the Pierces.

"You guys weren't supposed to be home," Ashley began, succumbing to a brief fit of giggles, which repeated every time she looked at Christian. Christian, too, thought the situation humorous.

"We decided to come home a day early. And it's a good thing we did! Look at the mischief you two are creating!" Jessica scolded, lifting her brandy snifter to her lips.

"It's more than simple mischief," Christian said. Leaning close to Ashley, he whispered –loudly enough for her parents to hear – in her ear. "Are you going to tell them, or should I? We never discussed this scenario."

"I know. It was supposed to be at a nice dinner somewhere."

Dane huffed. "Well, apparently we've ruined their plans. And unfortunately, we've already eaten."

Ashley could tell from Jessica's wide grin that her stepmom had her suspicion. Unable to wait another moment, she got up and thrust her left hand out in front of them. Dane glanced down, then up at Ashley's beaming face. "Engaged?"

"Married," Jessica corrected. "I see two rings."

"Married?!" Dane's eyes opened wide and then squinted. "You got married, and didn't tell us?"

"It was only eight hours ago. You weren't here," Ashley teased.

Jessica put down her glass and got to her feet, wrapping her arms tightly around Ashley and rocking her. "I am thrilled for you, darling. Oh, how I've hoped and prayed for this, for you. And Christian," she gushed, now turning to the young man who'd stood up beside Ashley, "you are so welcome to the family." She gave him a hug as well.

Dane rubbed at his chin and then smiled. "This is a good thing. After what I witnessed a few minutes ago, I was about to get out the shotgun." He stood and shook Christian's hand. "Congratulations, son. And like my truly better half so eloquently said, welcome."

They toasted and sat back down.

"Why the rush?" Dane asked, peering intently at Christian.

"If you're wondering if I'm pregnant, I'm not," Ashley said.

"I had the ring for a long time. I was just planning to ask when my father died. Then, the trip to Arizona, the funeral, helping my brother to get his business established ... I didn't want anything to dim the moment. But –"

"But we couldn't wait. Christmas is coming, and there just didn't seem like a good time to plan. I'm sorry if you guys were hoping for a big white wedding," Ashley said.

"What we were hoping for was only your happiness, sweet pea. And you can still have the big white wedding if you want one."

"Thank you, Daddy. Um, where is Jilly?"

"She's still with Mimi and Brady. We thought we'd pick her up tomorrow, give ourselves a little time to recoup from the trip to New York. Mimi is still getting re-settled in the house. The remodel after the fire is phenomenal. You should go by and see it," Dane answered.

"It was nice of you to give her the house."

"It was your mother's house. I'd already given it to Rita years ago. The insurance paid for most of the fire damage and rebuilding."

"Most?" Ashley asked.

"Well, there may have been a little help. Now, with you moving out, it's going to be a lot quieter around here with just Dev and Jilly."

"Will you move into Christian's condo?" Jessica asked.

"Uh, no." Christian took Ashley's hand and squeezed it. "We've put a deposit down on a modest house in Agoura. It closes in a few days."

"Wait 'til you see it! It's so cute. It needs some work, but –"

"But I'm on board with doing it." Christian smiled at his bride. "Three plus two. And there's a garage, a yard, a fireplace and a home office."

A commotion at the front door got everyone's attention. "Now, what?" Dane muttered. "We're in here," he called out. "Might as well join us, whoever you are."

"Oh, we didn't know anyone was here. Thought you were coming home tomorrow," Alex said, holding Megan's hand as the pair entered the family room. "Sorry to interrupt."

"I'll get more glasses," Jessica said, getting up. "You two sit down. Brandy?"

"Sure," Alex said, leading Megan to the adjacent couch. "You want some?"

"Please," Megan said, taking off her coat. "Sure we're not interrupting something?"

"Glad you're here. Your sister has news." Dane said.

After the "news" had been shared and congratulations given, easy conversation continued around the room. "So why did you come by if you thought we weren't home?" Dane asked.

"No particular reason. Well, we possibly thought we'd get in a nighttime swim."

Warmed by the brandy and tickled by her brother's comment, Ashley burst into laughter. While everyone had expected Alex to quit his job when his screenplay was bought by a rival studio, he'd surprised them all by re-upping at the L.A.P.D. for another year. Now all that remained was the expected marriage proposal. But Megan, Ashley knew, wouldn't be one to jump quickly. It was her prerogative. Her life had made her wary of relationships, and Alex would need to prove himself worthy for the long haul.

As Ashley began to drowse off, she heard her father tell Christian to leave the "sin palace" in the backyard until tomorrow. He'd turn off the sprinklers, he assured, but Christian needed to get his bride upstairs to bed. The next thing she remembered was waking with her cheek against his bare chest, her legs entangled with his, and the soft rhythm of his breathing.

"If I hadn't walked into Megan's gallery showing, would we have ever found each other again?" he asked.

"Yes. I'm sure of it. It was part of a plan. Something else would have happened ... like Dad renting a limo from you."

"I would have been in the wrong place. With the wrong person. My life would have been meaningless."

"Mine, too."

"Instead, I get to fall in love with you every single day," he said softly. "Happy Wedding Day, my love."

"Do you think we made a baby tonight?"

"I hope so."

Dane looked around the house. Lights off, doors locked, alarm set. Sprinklers off, he thought with a smile. He climbed the stairs, noting that Ashley's and Devon's lights were off, then continued to the double doors leading to the massive owner's suite.

In the bedroom, Jessica sat up in bed, reading glasses perched on her nose. She closed her book and placed it and her glasses on the nightstand. "Everything buttoned up?"

"Yup." Dane shut off the light and took off his clothes. "Glad I showered earlier. You know it's two a.m. in New York."

"I know. I'm tired, too."

He climbed into bed beside her and turned on his side to face her. He took her hand and gently cradled it in his. "The talk tonight, downstairs, brought up a lot of feelings for me."

"Men aren't supposed to have feelings, are they?" Jessica said.

"No, I guess I'm just flawed."

"It was all good, wasn't it?"

"Very good." Dane let go of Jessica's hand and stroked her hair away from her cheek, then leaned in close and kissed her. "I was drowning when you found me, you know. More than once." He felt rather than saw her lips smile against his. "If it wasn't for you, picking up the pieces of my life, and by default, hers, this – tonight – would never have happened."

"Don't be silly. You've been a good father. To all of them."

"Only because of you. And, if I'm honest, Mac. He was a great father. There have been times over the years when I've been forced to ask myself how he would have handled things."

"He would be happy about Megs and Alex."

"Yeah. You're right." He paused and then uttered a little laugh. "Tonight, them out there swimming in the buff ... reminded me of us, twenty years ago."

"Me, too." Jessica snaked her arms around his neck and pressed her body against his. "Twenty years or twenty minutes. It's all the same. I still feel the same." She kissed him this time, a sensual, wet kiss that expelled his fatigue and replaced it with passion. He slipped his arm around her waist and tightened his grasp. Their kisses grew more urgent until he stopped for a breath and pulled his lips away.

"You really want this, right?"

"Still do. Always will."

Dear Reader...

Thank you for reading THE GYPSY IN ME, Book 3 of the StarCrossed Romance saga!

If you enjoyed this book, now would be a great time to post a review. Many thanks!

Ready for more? Watch for

TO LOVE A VAGABOND:
Devon's Journey
StarCrossed Romance Book 4
Coming in 2023!

About the Series

StarCrossed Hearts – Book One

Silver screen heroes Dane Pierce and Cory "Mac" MacKendall are as different as cognac and Perrier, and newcomer Jessica Taylor loves them both. Despite his tantalizing green eyes and raw sexuality, Dane is not the man she thinks she needs. It is the solid and devoted - if hot-headed - Mac who wins her hand and heart, and who must endure a lifelong challenge to keep that heart safe from Dane's unending pursuit. From Hollywood soundstage to the Grenadine Islands, StarCrossed Hearts makes a journey around the world and through the lives of some very real characters you will not soon forget.

A Hero's Promise – Book Two

If you read **StarCrossed Hearts**, you know that heart-breaking, womanizing Dane Pierce will not find it easy to walk away from the one woman that sets his soul on fire. Promise or no promise, Dane will do everything he can to win back Jessica's love. Now, the heart-stopping sequel you've been waiting for: **A Hero's Promise**, a story of pain and redemption, and a love that survives the very worst of life's challenges.

The Gypsy in Me – Book Three

Their children have grown. Some are his, some are hers; some are half-siblings, others step-brothers and sisters. Growing up the offspring of Hollywood's brightest stars, Jessie, Dane and Mac's kids are each special, each a little neurotic, and each seeking love. The MacKendall and Pierce daughters square off in this next installment to the **StarCrossed series**; who would have thought that history would repeat itself?

To Love a Vagabond:
Devon's Journey – Book Four

He's the son of not two, but three Hollywood megastars. The legacy he's inherited feels more like a ball and chain than a fairytale. Devon MacKendall's life has never been easy, or simple, and when the worst possible tragedy befalls him, he heads for the road in this heart-wrenching installment of the StarCrossed saga. Meeting the elusive Brandy Owens is the last thing he wants, but she just might be the salvation he needs. *Coming 2023!*

Meet Anne Carter

Creating fiction gives one the power to design other lives, filled with romance and adventure, intrigue and passion. My own writing career began in middle school creative writing class, inspiring me to later major in literature. All it took was one teacher' encouragement and I was on my way.

I'm the author of nine published novels, including mystery, romance, paranormal, alternative romance and even a middle grade reader. As for the personal stuff, I'm a Virgo, a procrastinator, like warm better than cold and drink neither Coke nor Pepsi. I was born in the Midwest but migrated to California as a child. My hobbies include doll collecting, photo restoration and writing, of course. My favorite sport is ice hockey, my favorite TV shows include mysteries, romance (Duh!), cooking shows (Great British Baking Show!) and crime series that make you think and not count bodies. I am married to my hero of 40+ years and have 3 great kids and two--wait, THREE--delightful grands. Visit me and find purchase links at Beacon Street Books.

Also By Anne Carter

THE STARCROSSED SERIES

StarCrossed Hearts – Book 1

A Hero's Promise – Book 2

The Gypsy in Me – Book 3

To Love a Vagabond – Book 4 (2023)

THE BEACON POINT ROMANCES

Ever & Always

Point Surrender

Cape Seduction

Angel's Gate

Amaroso Pass (2023)

PAULIE & KATE

Unmasking Paulie Bingham

For the Love of Katrina Bingham